Origamy

Origamy

Rachel Armstrong

NewCon Press
England

First published in 2018 by NewCon Press,
41 Wheatsheaf Road, Alconbury Weston, Cambs, PE28 4LF

NCP153 (limited edition hardback)
NCP154 (softback)

10 9 8 7 6 5 4 3 2 1

ISBN:

978-1-910935-77-4 (hardback)
978-1-910935-78-1 (softback)

Cover by Ian Whates

Text edited by Ian Whates
Book interior layout by Storm Constantine

For Rolf Hughes

Prologue

A dry sweetness softens the air. Everything is semipermeable. I can see through doors, faces, instruments, lights and the latex gloves that fold down my fingers and painlessly introduce cannulae into my veins.

I stare disdainfully into my innards and then up past the anaesthetist's mask, through the cloud-laced stratosphere, past the spinning crusts of space junk and on into the cosmos. Matter, time and space possess an odd elasticity.

I am trying to condense from the ether filling my vessels, releasing its volatile gases into my blood and allying my tissues with vapour. It's harder to stay focussed than you might imagine, as I cannot coordinate my thoughts sufficiently to access a specific memory or purpose for myself.

Instead, I choose to think forwards, upwards and outwards into the inky cosmos through my mind's eye, in search of happy ever afters that resist the idea that we must die.

I want to speak of the revolutionary potential within the unruly substances that make up this realm and the worlds beyond it, to provide a counterpoint to narratives that describe reality as violent and feral. Indeed, if I can retain a healthy distance from the myriad difficulties that encumber me right now, I may become oblivious to the inevitability of my demise, transcend the pain of this existence and perhaps become immortal.

As instructed, I begin to count down backwards from ten, while pungent volatiles carry my thoughts. I am full of purpose – but it's not my own.

Did I reach ten? Let me try again.

My lipless voice shouts for a second chance but nobody seems to hear me. Another chance – help me someone, I can't drift now. I'm dissipating, but not at all ready to leave this place.

This world.

I choose to believe in happily ever afters, as they bring a kind of peace that persists long after this particular existence has gone.

PART I

The Child

"Chase me," she says.

The light that folds around her coal stare seems to recede into other universes.

"Why?"

"Because I'm about to disappear."

Where Am I Now?

I am still trying to condense, which is harder than you might imagine as I cannot coordinate my thoughts sufficiently to access a memory or purpose for myself.

Perhaps, if I can foreground my existence with a particular context – rather than making generalisations about the nature of existence in an endless cosmos – my embodied existence may begin to precipitate around a meaningful form and identity.

I hear my parents, Shelley and Newton, singing of their love for me. I am happy that I know their names, although I still do not know what kind of people they are. Their indelible passion channels my being into 'this' form that becomes contaminated with the seeds of my existence. Yet my conception is sweaty and ugly. While I am not especially grateful for them starting the processes that bring this body to life, the sequence of events that is shaping my genesis fascinates me. Perhaps, at some stage, I will understand the miracle of existence sufficiently to alter my present circumstances – even now.

I attempt to decentre my parents from being the authors of my life and shut out their songs. I hope to establish a purer relationship with the substances from which I am forged. In this manner, I can inhabit this body 'my way' – not the way of my parents.

I am made up of inconstant forms that arise from twisting, pulsating, undifferentiated landscapes, which the union of gametes have set in motion and are beginning to consolidate through some kind of enfleshing process.

I am witnessing my own embryogenesis – the rolling, pleating, folding and twisting of organic building blocks, marinated in plasma and grown inside a capillary rich bed of tissue that allows my roots to spread like soil – I am becoming alive. I'm made up of excitable fields that spew lively materials and serpentine metabolic networks into a tangle of matter that becomes my flesh.

This vexing condition of existential uncertainty may be choreographed through pulse-like fields, which continually separate and re-condense into structural arrangements that are rich with many potential states of existence. I need to make decisions about who and what I want to be, so that I may shape these constantly contested boundaries – particularly those that operate in the realms between life and death. There is as much metabolism in a decomposing corpse as in a living body – but the qualities of exchanges in the dead are more diverse. The dead diffuse, while the living condense. Yet the distinctions between these states create the platforms for those acts that constitute the art of living, where for example, in forming fingers and toes, certain cartilage cells must agree to die. This is no simple matter. Life is its own paradox.

Now my body fluids seep sideways and upwards as ionic liquids permeate my tissues. In uterine weightlessness they mingle in provocative new ways with their neighbours and begin to reshape my expanding fields of biochemical interaction in concert with the molecular repertoire of my genes. Exploring the conventions of object-boundedness and relative permanence, I begin to establish a particular relationship between 'this' body and 'my' surroundings.

Despite the odds against my existence, I blossom and breathe in a piercing cry – a song of my own. I see my chocolate-red flesh, coated with a cheesy layer of dead cells, for the first time.

Today the world is messy and noisy. The vegetation rustles and shakes in the thin winds. The sod bleeds water. Nacreous algae form oily puddles on the ground and the stones resonate like bells from their bombardment by restless atoms. It is not a day for dying, but a time for incarnation and discovering something new about the cosmos.

But I must hurry if I am to (re)invent myself. These windows of opportunity do not last forever, so I will no longer deliberate and decide where the story of this life – 'my life' – is going.

Sleep

Instinctively I know that I'm not a novice origamer but my father Newton, who is a giant, tells me that I must learn my art again. I unquestioningly accept his verdict, as I cannot recall what this actually means.

I feel that I've been away for a long time. Certainly today I've been returned to the world of half-familiar persons. Or perhaps it's reality that's not quite right.

I tried asking Newton if he'd noticed anything strange about me. He says that it's probably travel amnesia. Sometimes coming back from ambitious origamy expeditions can leave weavers with memory loss, gaps in their knowledge, or a profound sense of unreality.

"Was I gone for long?" I wonder.

Newton shrugs unhelpfully "You'll never know. Nothing's simple when you manipulate spacetime."

Then he makes things worse by asking if I'm worried about something. Apparently, extraordinary feelings of unreality are common among people who suffer from anxiety. Now I'm anxious. Anxious about being anxious. This is most unhelpful, I don't want to be anxious.

"Blowing into a brown paper bag, is good for anxiety attacks, it slows down your breathing," observes Newton.

"I'm not crazy. I'm tired."

"Then you should sleep."

"I can't. It's not as simple as that. You've upset me."

We sit uncomfortably in silence.

I start to observe how incredibly dark my father is. I don't mean pigmented skin, of course he's pigmented. We're all pigmented. I mean, he's remarkably nonluminous. Light seems to avoid him. I decide that perhaps he just doesn't want to be seen.

After a while Newton assures me, yawning, that all creatures need sleep, even bees; that all living things are magic wells, which – through sleep – continue to replenish when their water is drawn from them. If this filling system is interrupted, it produces unpleasant effects.

"When bees are sleep deprived they're sloppy. Their legs start to wobble and they stagger around as if drunk, dragging their heads along the floor. Finally, their antennae stop moving."

I protest that I'm not intoxicated but instead want to know more about sleepy bees.

"Bees dream," he says.

"Of what?"

"Colour, smell, heat, ultraviolet light. They sense the world in a very different way. Perhaps we could think of the images they construct in their sleep as alternative maps of reality."

I don't know whether to believe him. Besides, he seems to be making a buzzing sound, so I can't take him seriously. Maybe he's just got blocked airways, or is making this all up to help me feel better.

"Of course, all of this is very logical. Bees talk to other bees by dancing in a waggly way that encodes important navigational information. If they're too tired they forget the right movements and lead the others astray. If too many bees make mistakes in their dancing, the whole colony suffers."

I decide he's telling the truth and wonder if I'm simply a wobbly bee. Maybe if I practiced a few acrobatic moves, I'd quickly confirm that I'm just exhausted. It might stop me worrying about whether I'm going mad – I mean anxious. All this sleep talk is making me tired and I need to lie down. I excuse myself as my father waves me off with a final observation as he hugs his feet.

"The oddest thing about sleeping bees is that they hold each other's knees."

Origamy

Origamy (noun). The circus art of spacetime travel.

It's something that emerged from among the folded spaces between linen sheets. Or maybe it's just about how thoughts move around my head. Whatever it is, it results in the compulsion to relentlessly explore and push at the limits of existence, by creatively transcending the conventions of spacetime.

Origamy (verb). The artful and athletic practice of weaving spacetime fabrics to discover outlandish places and events.

Threads are harvested from the Implicate Order, the interconnected matrix of the cosmos, using a copper condenser from spacetime dew. They may also be individually plucked from the ether using special chopsticks that can be wielded by practitioners with subatomic precision. However it may be harvested, spacetime liquid is spun into fibres, which are then woven into geometrically shaped trajectories using a variety of weaving technologies that include looms and knitting practices.

Spacetime fibres can be cast out into the universe by origamers as a transportation network, which is akin to artfully launching fishing nets into the sky. Origamers apply art, science, music, acrobatics and the synthesis of folds to orchestrate life's processes within the many niches that comprise the universe. Wielding knotted spacetime threads, acrobatically gifted weavers and explorers draw distant sections of the cosmos into folded pleats, generating chains of multiple wormholes. Origamers travel to other worlds and parallel realities to experience alien landscapes, different timeframes and alternative forms of existence that are not bound by terrestrial conventions of space and time but are frequently far stranger, diverse and contrary.

Semantically, origamy is a condensation of three ideas.

Orig(ins). This root refers to the origins of life. It is concerned with the art and science of making life, the transitions between inert and living matter, as well as the craft of 'living'.

(G)amy. This stem indicates the game-like qualities of spacetime fabric folding. Conway's Game of Life is invoked, not merely as a form of pattern making, but the tactical exchange and sheer enjoyment that arises from the relations, materials and exchanges within the ebb and flow of 'being'.

(Gamy) also refers to the 'gametes', the seeds of life whose fusion gives rise to new and varied bodies.

Origamer (noun). One who explores various dimensions of existence and encounters different life forms by applying a range of practices to travel through spacetime. Players are required to continually adapt to ever changing circumstances, experience breathtaking spectacles and to bring back stories from throughout the cosmos.

Knitting Peace

There she is. Atop a cloud of dark matter, floating with no visible support. Legs crossed. Knitting peace.

"Hey!" I shout at her, but the void transmits no sound waves. She is engrossed in plucking vibrating strings out of spacetime dew and spinning them into yarn. Entangled and bent by strange gravitational forces, they coalesce into translucent veils. This time I try waving to get her attention, but she doesn't see me.

Intrigued by the fibre that seems to be appearing from nowhere, I watch the fabric form and hitch a ride upon photon streams, where it drifts like cherry blossom. But there is something wrong with the threads she's casting. The photon membranes start to wane and char around the edges, disintegrating before they ever reach their target gravitational wells.

Shelley

She's at it again, juggling.

For a midget, it's some achievement.

Of course, I'm biased – she's my mother. I love her.

Shelley is her name, she has beautiful chocolate red skin and she's always singing. Sprouting from the top of her head is a plait, which she uses as an extra limb, a whip, a climbing rope and even the scaffold for aerial trapeze. I'm pretty sure she inhabits parallel worlds although she never says much about them. Simply, she doesn't have the time to be idle.

Listen, my mother can keep a dozen younglings in the air. They duck and soar like shuttles on a loom while she simultaneously carries out all kinds of activities – humming, washing, quantum physics, astronomy, writing poetry, cleaning, Loom repairs, banjo practice, calculus, correcting spellings, supramolecular chemistry, accountancy, interpretative dance, molecular gastronomy, sewing, material philosophy, project management, medicine, brokering diplomatic exchanges, art of rhetoric, social strategy, plus let's not neglect the all-important keeping the peace and cleaning stuff up.

She is, as you might therefore expect, no stranger to laughter.

For those who meet her for the first time, Shelley never appears still. But look up, rather than down, and you will notice that she effortlessly navigates two worlds simultaneously – the macroscale and a diminutive version of it.

She does not resolve these contradictions but inhabits all realms equally through her spinning, turning, doing somersaults and defying the classical laws of physics. And once you notice her, somehow you're up there too, free from all the cares in the world, cocooned in a plane of delight.

Don't ask me how it all works. Rational explanations don't really mean anything around here. At two hundred and sixty three, she says she has just learned to accept the strangeness of existence.

Tag

"You're it!" she says, touches my shoulder and vanishes before I can ask her name.

I look over at my mother, who is seemingly oblivious to – and yet in complete control of – her circulating cloud of younglings. I try counting my tiny kin to see if they're hiding the child but give up. There are too many of them and they move around too quickly.

"Over here!" she whispers.

I think I see her somewhere in the youngling cloud but it's impossible to clearly separate one cherub from the next, as they're so high in the air.

"Mother, who's the child?" I wonder, hoping that she can work her magic on this enigma.

Singing, she whips me up in her long plait, catapulting me high into the air so that I soar momentarily, like the arc of a whip. Then I drop as surely as Newton's apple but before I shatter on the floor like rotten fruit the tip of her plait tips my body into a spin, so that I roll to the floor unharmed.

"Did you find who you were looking for?"

"No, Mother."

"You really should get yourself into shape. That was a clumsy landing. Something's up with you." She trills.

Loom Garden

I feel as if I've only just walked into my life, that I am an outsider among my kin. Determined to orient myself, I seek Shelley's advice.

"Who are our people?"

She studies my face quizzically without ceasing her singing, nods assertively and begins the tale of our kin as if she was reciting a nursery rhyme to a small child. Younglings hover, preparing for a story.

"Our ancestors are cosmic messengers that can be traced back to the time of the Jacquard loom, its flower-and-leaf algebraic patterns and the Analytical Engine and entwined these crafts with the physicality and spectacle of circus."

"So, we're a circus troupe?"

"Not exactly. We are first and foremost a culture of spacetime weavers. Purveyors between worlds. Over the ages we have developed a whole range of technologies and traditions that allow us to travel through space and time to gather stories and share knowledge. But to use these apparatuses and travel through the most challenging realms of the universe, we've embraced the circus arts, which help us to inhabit spaces way beyond the Earth. These skills allow us to stay physically connected to our expanding cosmic reality. By working through the body and its capacity for deception, paradox and error, we are able to keep on thinking and responding to a changing universe using our time travel systems, and so promote new persistence strategies that can be shared with the broader community of life."

"And how exactly do we manage that?"

"We are centred on the technology of the Loom, a spacetime weaving apparatus that is situated in the Garden. It detects, translates and displays information from the cosmos and offers access to the incomprehensible vastness of space. Unseen events are transformed into decipherable patterns, which are at the heart of our storytelling culture. It's not a substitute for science. Indeed, we deeply rely on scientific knowledge to inform our interpretations of the tapestry."

"What does the tapestry tell us that science doesn't?"

"The Loom is real time. The events did not happen aeons ago –

which is what mechanical space probes capture. It produces a spacetime tapestry that is composed of individual spacetime fibres, forming both a map and manifold storybook that can be read at many scales. Depending on what viewpoint you take, different interpretations of events can be made. We read them according to the character of their warp and weft. Indeed, those who encounter the tapestry for the first time remark that the fabric looks remarkably like reality itself. This is not surprising as it affords molecular details of real-time cosmic events. It can also pinpoint the locations of constellations, stars, planets, moons and asteroid belts. While science can do all this, it continues to obey the laws of classical physics. This means that scientific instruments are crippled by time delay because of the massive distances that digital information has to travel. However, since the Loom is a time travel apparatus, it employs quantum phenomena like tunnelling and entanglement to close the gap between celestial bodies. What we read, is what is happening right now!"

"That's impossible."

"Not when you learn to view reality from many different perspectives. Our unique art is weaving 'embodied' knowledge, ideas that we can see, smell, touch and explore. You see, the Loom also does not 'represent' the cosmos, it is a manifold of cosmos. We can physically dive into the information it records in the tapestry to experience galaxies, stars, solar systems, planets and moons as they're being born – and as they perish. But we can also go closer still, to witness the particulars of forests, rivers and oceans on any given celestial body. Trained observers, for example, may notice how a terrain pulses under the ebb and flow of gravitational, or magnetic tides. Some can even plunge into the chemical make up of soils and rocks."

"It's an incredible visualisation system."

"Not visualisation. The Loom is more than a surveillance system. It's a parallel reality – one that entangles with this current one. Think of it as a hyper dimensional apparatus, with more planes of possibility than the four dimensional world that we're habituated to."

"You mean volumetric space and time?"

"Yes, now go beyond those conventions. Once you learn how to invent your own impossible knots and weaves, you'll have access to a garden of cosmic creativity that retains the capacity for change. The Loom draws together these vibrations emanating from spacetime and creates impressions with them that allow us to explore how reality might be – if we wove it in different ways. The Loom is therefore an instrument of conversation, synthesis, poetry, possibility and wonder – it's not simply a source of facts. Nor do the Loom's outputs bear a simple relationship to time, or any sense of cause and effect. Indeed, its final interpretation is always open to the individual viewer and, of course, the consensus of our community. Therefore the Loom is fundamentally an instrument of trust."

"We want to weave!" plead some of the younglings.

"Not yet, darlings," reassures Shelley. "You have many years to practice before you can begin."

"But if the tapestry is only woven by the Loom, how do they learn?" I wonder.

Shelley whips her hair into a lasso, tugging the youngling cloud into a tight formation and wipes a few noses.

"Actually, spacetime fibres can be plucked from the cosmic dew by hand. So, the Loom is not the only way of making spacetime tapestry, it is an apparatus that draws bodies, skills, matter and time together. Our skills are first learned by observing time and space so that we can grab leptons, hadrons and muons using our fingertips. Younglings quickly get the hang of finger knitting complex polymers, forming threads of different textures and making lengths of ropey yarn with them. Later in their repertoire they learn how to produce fabrics using biological programs and spacetime fibres. Rather than producing simulations and sounds of leaves and flowers, they start making these very things anew."

"But doesn't that require a lot of thread? How do we keep up with the demand?"

Shelley is being very patient with me.

"We can gather spacetime threads on a colossal scale using a series of giant copper condensers, which are tuned to collect spacetime dew. Portable versions of this apparatus exist that can be transported by weavers to different locations around the cosmos. Of course, the smaller systems make less fibre than their titanic counterparts but are still much more efficient at producing material than working by hand. Generally, if we've had a good night's harvest the condensate will appear as a reflectionless, sticky pool of molasses. The liquid is then drawn out into threads that may be used to make cloth, or repair breaches in spacetime. These rips are generally caused by universal wear and tear and so mending is an artisan practice that's integral to our circus traditions.

Charged with the process of universal connection, we become an immune surveillance system for breaches in reality, producing manifolds of meaning through our physical and material interactions so they are infused with meaning."

"We want to travel to stars!" squeal the younglings.

"When do they get to do that?" I wonder.

Shelley entertains the children with her plait, which turns somersaults of knots before rising like a giant snake that plunges to tickle their tummies.

"It takes a long time to turn a spacetime weaving practice into origamy, which requires artists to become conjoined with their threads and cast themselves into the cosmos. The first training begins as soon as the younglings demonstrate they've mastered the mental and physical agility required to become Loom shuttles. Rather than obeying the information condensed from the cosmos, younglings begin to interpret the patterns. Increasingly, they become bolder and carry the spacetime threads in more ambitious ways, until they travel further afield into the reaches of spacetime itself.

"But those are incredible distances to be traversed."

"Of course, but by casting spacetime bridges using knotted origamy folds at time-sensitive opportunities, we can make wormholes. These allow us to travel instantaneously between spaces, dimensions and worlds. By pleating spacetime, more experienced origamers can move huge distances with a high degree of specificity, while less expert weavers may need to throw their thread a number of time before they reach their destination."

"Isn't that dangerous?"

"Certainly. Everything about origamy is dangerous. It takes a very long time before an apprentice is ready to leave Earth's gravity-well. The danger is even greater because these manoeuvres are time sensitive and the fibres are retractile. While these properties mean that we don't have to make exact calculations in producing the fabric, as there is a lot of give in the system, it does mean the degree of flexibility cannot be easily predicted. It's vital, therefore, that while we make repairs we stay vigilant to changes in our environment. Sometimes shrinking of spacetime happens much faster than expected, resulting in navigational errors.

"What happens when we make errors?"

"Mistakes are bad news with deadly consequences. They produce glitches in spacetime which can leave weavers stranded in the remotest parts of the universe, with no means of returning. But if we remain vigilant, glitches can be recognised early by their oddness and repaired before they generate untoward events. It is critical that we recognise the first signs of contraction and either quickly cast our threads again, or follow the recoiling fibres back to their origin. While most of these irregularities are caused by our own limitations, the nature of cosmic matter, and erosion – occasionally they are the result of sabotage. In fact, our biggest threat comes from fanatical creatures that inhabit the dark universes which do not share our ethics. In fact, it is our moral duty to resist these destructive intentions and incursions on our cosmic reality to maintain its wholeness."

"What creatures?"

"The worst of all we call spiders. They seek to destroy all the luminous matter in the universe, to make their own terrifyingly dark realm."

"It sounds so complicated and frankly, frightening."

"It is. It takes more than a lifetime to become a weaver. In fact, there is so much to understand about working with spacetime fibres that we actually live multiple lifetimes longer than most people. We could not take on our current responsibilities if, along with mastering our art, we had not evolved this particular fitness. Yet, despite our great age and agility, we follow cardinal rules for safe conduct: we cast good knots, stay connected to our threads and bring nothing back with them."

"Why do I not remember all of this mother? Why?"

Shelley laughs musically as she produces a ledger. She opens it with a snap and I try to peer over her shoulder, which seems an easy feat given that she is so small, but it's impossible to see what she's writing as she angles herself so that the pages are always observed from my view. She lifts her face and stares at me with coal eyes.

"Look, the best way to become acquainted with origamy is not to talk about it, or even think about it, but to become immersed in its practices and the worlds it provides access to."

I shake my head defensively and want to voice my dissent since I am convinced there is no way I can origamy.

As I begin to speak, I realise that Shelley has vanished along with her parallel stack of tasks.

Disappearing

"Scaredy cat!" taunts the child.

"That's not fair," I protest.

She conjures a set of aluminium chopsticks from the aether and slides them telescopically to an infeasible length.

"It's so easy when you know how," she smiles. Then she casts incredible lengths of yarn, I want to think of her as a spider but her appearance is more like a lace-winged fly, whose veins project their intricate patterns into the sky. I can't fathom out how she's producing the threads. I can't even see anything. She's buzzing around me like a pest, the clicking noise from the chopsticks is irritating, mosquito-like.

She's enchanting.

Just as I remember I don't know her name, the child casts a throw that soars upwards to infinity. But as she waves at me, soaring like an atmospheric helium balloon, I notice a black sooty patch on her left cheek, as if she's weeping charcoal.

Visible Invisible

Shelley appears from nowhere, singing happily with a cloud of children circulating around her, like bees that are high on pollen.

Using her plait as an extra limb, she produces a set of weaving instruments, including a set of aluminium chopsticks that have apparently been with me since childhood. I am struck by their similarity to the child's, so I assume they're standard issue.

"You'll be needing these." She says.

I wonder how she knows about these things, such as counselling me about origamy. Does she already know about the child?

"Mother's instinct."

I say nothing but worry that she can read my thoughts. Can she? Or are her comments mere coincidences. Is there even such a thing in 'this' place, which suddenly feels unfamiliar again?

Shelley conjures an iridescent elastic garment like a second skin and a pair of goggles with incredibly thick lenses fit for the portal of a deep-sea helmet. I reluctantly put them on and a few younglings tighten them.

"You look like a giant insect," they tease.

Shelley also shows me how to apply a mask with tubes that must be threaded into my nose, mouth and ears. Just as I think I'm finished, she brings me a set of underpants that look like intestines but are worn on the outside.

"These 'space knickers' are full of purifying bacteria that will maintain your nutritional and hydration states in extreme environments," she hums.

Then, crooning under the bemused gaze of what seems like a thousand giggling children, she shows me how to thread the garments hose-like systems, yes – into my nether regions, just so I don't leak in the vacuum of space – as only a mother can.

There is absolutely no privacy around here.

The Dare

"Dare you to find me."

I can't see the child but I recognise her voice. Sweet, like chocolate serenaded to the high pitch of a violin.

It's not the taunt that goads me, but the irrepressible feeling that something is amiss. Why are her cheeks stained with charcoal. She's in danger.

"Where are you?"

"Behind you."

But she's not. Did I miss her? I being to realise this is a game whose clues reside in the quantum realms. A reality that I am woefully ill equipped for. But if I am to reach her I must origamy.

Starting Again

I pick up the aluminium chopsticks. They're light, like air. Instinctively, I know to use them like lobster claws. Or perhaps, they know how to exploit me.

The chopsticks enable me to see events taking place at the nanoscale, so that I can grab hold of subatomic particles traveling at the speed of light. All I have to do is to remember how to observe the telltale signs of drifting spacetime fibres. At first I grab blindly at the air. Soon I notice strange shadows that lurk alongside objects, which appear as cracks around window frames and spill unexpectedly from interfaces between vibrating molecular fields. To skill up, I start searching for the weirdest black spaces and practice catching drops of spacetime dew within them.

I lose myself in coordinating my gaze with the chopsticks and my threadcasting abilities – or, lack of them. As I start to get the hang of things, I see reality in a completely different way, or perhaps it is a parallel future. It is impossible to tell. Bizarrely, all matter is made up from a variety of stabilised black holes, which look like dust that are particularly drawn to water and reflective surfaces.

I take advantage of the sudden appearance of my father, who looks particularly lightless today.

"Newton, what are these specks?"

He examines the air with an unfocused stare and gestures at "nothing" with his inky claws.

"Matter," he affirms.

"Matter?" I squint, unsure that the tiny voids are of anything at all.

"At the sub quantum scale. All matter is made out of black holes."

"Is that where I've been focussed? Beyond the strings and fields that make up the physical realm?"

Newton snorts.

"Pay attention to detail and don't seek to confirm your preconceptions about reality. Nothing is as it seems, if you observe it closely enough. Indeed, we used to think that black holes like these were smooth and bald like a mountain. Now we know that they're hairy on the inside. Back then, of course, we were ignorant. Rubber gloved by machines that we hailed 'intelligent', where everything was virtual, colourised and texture mapped, we sought logical explanations for the material realm. Yet it is matter that is illusory. What exists is the void. But there are different kinds of void – some are just more luminous than others. However, once we learned the art of time travel we started to knit, pleat and fold the very fabric of the universe according to our dreams and desires. Feeling, tasting and inhaling the material realm, we found hairy black holes everywhere. Tiny ones formed in the kitchen sink along with the dirty crockery, which we turned over like stones; delighted and revolted by the molecular creepy crawlies we unearthed. Sometimes these hirsute realms appeared as shadows in cities that lengthened strangely and swallowed the geometry of alleyways, or sad spaces."

"Is this science?"

"It's the truth."

"Your version of the truth?"

"No, the actuality of shared experience. You see, once we began to perceive the tiny black specks, they followed us everywhere. They were most dogged in occupying the gaps between each other, where they cried inconsolably behind hardened hearts and minds. Finding no solace, as they simply could not escape the rot of disillusionment, we tried to help them by knitting strange terrains from fine spacetime threads, and littered the emptiness with soft and silky copses. At other times we cast scrubby expanses that were coarse, like pig bristles for them to shelter in. On happy days we knotted our threads to make succulent mangroves, which were rich with strange scents – rotting, yet floral. Here, in all the varied in-between worlds and spandrels, we invited the tiny black hairy holes to celebrate with us in in Chthulean joy – the ecstasy of multiples – rolling and tumbling as hordes of proteans, chimeras, and shape-shifters together, stubbornly refusing to conform."

"They're not dangerous then?"

"Everything's dangerous. But be particularly careful of their anomalous character. The way to get around the tiny hairy black holes is to keep very still. Then they'll start to cluster around you the way that iron filings accumulate around the subtlest magnetic fields."

"Why do I want to do that?"

"You'll become weightless. It's much easier to origamy when you weigh nothing at all."

"Is that what you and Shelley do?"

Annoyingly he's gone. I don't know why but I'm disappointed. So much of this world is mysterious, dark and there is a lingering dread in all the uncertainty. I try to conjure elaborate molecular landscapes to cheer the intermolecular gloom, but the sad feeling refuses to go away.

I can't origamy when I'm gloomy, so I construct an attractor for these fuzzy dusts by pouring water on to a dark surface. Now I have a better chance of finding them so that I can entertain them with atomic cheer. Instantly, many shades of black split and shiver over the quivering surface, spilling out into fractals of absent luminosity, even on this overcast day.

The conditions are far from ideal but soon I can read the many shades of darkness that ebb and flow from this interface: jetblack, midnight blue, cold grey, sloeblack, creeping black, ebony, taupe, Davy's grey, saturated black, lightlessness, pitch, outer space darkness, café noir, warm black, black bean, slow black, licorice, designer black, charcoal black, inky black, eyeblack, tar black, pure black, bible black, rich black, black olive, phthalo green, CMYK black, RGB black, Bombazine black, standard black, black leather jacket, crowblack, vacuum black, cool black, star black, Charleston green, eerie black, onyx black, deathly black, absolute black and pitiless black holes.

There's one!

I grab at a twisted and rather granular shadow, with details like a miniature impressionist painting. The abyssal black spacetime thread shivers within the tips of my chopsticks, then, stays still. But it's not the pressure of the sticks that stabilises the filament, the aluminium points of my tools are channelling primal intermolecular forces that hold the fine thread in an invisible pincer grip. I quell my breath, so that the metabolic oscillations that feed my cells do not accidently push the precious fibre free from the sticks, but I can't hold this condition of airlessness for long.

I must make my move.

I already know that the first origamy throw will be the most tentative. I cast my thread in the direction of the child's voice.

Cannibal Planet

This origamy throw is poorly conceived and ill coordinated. There is no sign of the child here.

I am traveling in the wrong direction towards a parallel universe, at a time around four billion years ago known as The Great Splat, when young planets had not yet learned to moderate their appetites for each other and the Earth weathered a series of massive collisions with a number of Mars-sized planets. During this carnivorous time, our planet swallowed its sibling Theia deep into its fiery core. The scars of this tragic union remain a guilty secret within the molten circulation of our planet's cruel iron heart.

This is a deadly place and so very far from where I want to be heading.

I must origamy again and decide much more precisely where I intend to go.

Newton

My father doesn't agree with anything, or anyone. Even himself.

At two hundred and eighty nine, he enjoys paradoxes and alternatives and has a habit of speaking in riddles and breaking rules. Especially his own. Frequently he has me thinking in knots. One moment he likes to deal with logic offering a straightforward view of the cosmos. Minutes later, he's lecturing on the art of magic, or quoting from passages in the Bible, with insights that are so challenging and unconventional that he's impossible to follow.

I have learned to consider everything that he says at face value and concentrate not on the details of his conversation but on what he does. For in his actions he tends to betray the big picture perspective that he's sharing. It can take me days to recover from a conversation with him and sometimes I can't figure out what he's telling me at all.

His sole ambition in life is to adore my mother. Despite scores of children, their passion and interest in each other has not waned.

However, this has not extended as far as finding each of us names. They gave up trying to do that long ago. Instead, we are each given coordinates. The figures are decided by the position of the Loom in the vastness of spacetime when we were delivered into the world. Officially, I am (024, 375, 669) which, apparently, is somewhere in the Centauri system but since twenty-seven of us cannot all be named "Centauri" – unofficially, I am "Mobius."

Now, all of this may sound confusing to those who have grown up with the expectations of logic-based conversations, 'nuclear' family units and conventional modes of existence, like exchanging labour for money. I've learned that our kin really don't indulge any of those customs. Differences aside, we really are just like any other family group of spacetime weavers. Just bigger.

Much bigger.

Ladders

"Spacetime weavers travel as much by ladders as they do knots and stitches," says Newton.

I hadn't thought of casting my throws as ladders but it makes sense – after all, the rungs may be thought of as a series of ornate knots.

"Sure, they're less flexible but great for specificity, particularly over short distances."

"Okay, so what kind of knot might make a ladder? Reef, slip, sheet bend, clove hitch, square, rolling hitch, taut line, Prusik, the figure eight, overhand, halyard, half-hitch, bowline, sheep shank …"

"You know, the book of Genesis describes Jacob's ladder, as a pathway for angels that could move between heaven and earth."

"That's great, Newton. What kinds of knots was it made of? Help me out here."

He's irritating me now. I have no patience with this religious nonsense.

"You need poetry, Mobius, not facts. There are no facts."

"Don't mock me, Father. I can't listen to you when you talk down to me."

Then Newton stands up and spreads his gargantuan dark wings above me, which seem to be carrying the cosmos like the canopy of the night sky. He grunts and starts singing, which is such a deep sound, like tiny explosions erupting deep within his flesh, that I wonder if it's borborygmi.

I've had enough of his showing off.

"You're ridiculous, Newton, we're circus – of sorts - not angels."

Hairy Ground

I have decided to study the Loom without my parents' interference, before I make my next throw. Perhaps it will help me unlock my hidden art, so that I can better prepare myself for encounters that seem, frankly, absurd.

I make my way to the Loom Garden, where everyone gathers to share stories about their travels and exchange tips about their circus skills. It's a reorienting experience.

Several characters that I assume are kith if not kin, raise their chopsticks as I approach the dark fabric that is spewed from the apparatus, which suddenly squirms and glitters like a living landscape – a section of cosmic bowel.

"Are you all right?" asks Shelley lyrically.

"I'm not sure," I say.

"Go on, explore the tapestry," she seems to be speaking from within the chubby cloud of flesh that is bobbing around me. It's impossible to be alone in this place.

"But how?"

"Treat it as a form of meditation. The whole garden is a contemplative space – where it's possible to view reality differently through various lenses. It's like taking a walk in an endless garden that may equally provoke delight, or anxiety. How and what you encounter there depends on its material moods It doesn't solve anything. The point of the Loom is simply to experience reality in different ways."

My kith or kin depart, nodding in my direction. I suspect they find the back-to-basics lessons irritating. But I am no longer self-conscious and gradually start to see the blurry outlines of younglings in training, shuttling their spacetime threads across the tapestry's weft, too focused and busy to acknowledge me.

I think about the child that I know so little about, and wonder if the Loom's manifolds can help me search for her.

"Where shall I start, Mother?"

"Use your chopsticks to open up the manifolds," she sings while pointing at the nearby Centauri constellation.

Does she read minds? I must ask her.

However, the Loom has its own ideas about what I need to see. I'm taken aback by the sudden appearance of a newly emerged, five legged black carpet beetle, which clambers to the top of a hair shaft that is woven deep into an earthen landscape. Having spent several weeks in four successive larval forms, the insect is desperate to dry its crumpled wings. It tries to reach the apex of the strand several times. Off-balance and also unable to get proper traction on the tissue, it tries again, swinging around the tip. Still it can't find its footing. It feels steady enough to spread an improbable pair of wings once more. A gust of wind draws it off balance. It slips down, starting to tire. It tries again, attempting to launch from the structure. It plummets. Up it rises, doggedly, its stump-leg moving according to its biological program, mandibles grinding furiously with the effort. It drops again. But now it kicks its five legs upwards trying to flip over. Unable to escape the viscous stomach juices, the creature's vigour gradually diminishes, as it dehydrates in the warm winds and constant light of the synthetic terrain.

Clumps of hair slowly sip the beetle's dissolving mummified remains from the inside out. These transplants, which are hand-stitched into the nutrient medium by the environmental growth surgeons that made up the founding settlers of this once sterile terrain, are nourished by a rhizomatic, pitcher plant-like highway. The fifty-seven hairpin bends of this thin path of caustic puddles meander through the shaggy, flat terrain in a parallel reality.

The fascination for the number fifty-seven in this city relates back to an old terrestrial organisation, the H.J. Heinz Company. By 1892 it had grown from a small company that sold horseradish condiments in clear glass jars to one that sold more than sixty products that were promoted as "57 Varieties." Henry Heinz had decided that fifty seven seemed lucky, poetic and approximately reflected on the number of choices that were actually available to his customers on a journey to New York when his carriage passed an advertisement for a footwear company selling twenty-one varieties of shoes. The H.J. Heinz' company eventually produced over five thousand seven hundred products.

For a long time the number fifty-seven was little more than Heinz's marketing ploy and certainly not of any relevance to biotechnological engineering. During the twentieth and early twenty-first centuries, science routinely made claims based on empirical methods and data gathering. During the second Cambrian Explosion of biotechnology, around the mid twenty-first century, an incredible number of new substances were revealed. Data and life forms were simultaneously produced – so much so, that the digital computing systems used to evaluate such findings could not amass the data produced. Methods of numeration based on natural numbers fell into disorder. With rapidly revitalising ecosystems that spawned from an unfathomable variety, complexity and contingency of presence, alternative ways of assessing proliferation and vitality were needed to settle the barren land on which the city was proposed. However, the aesthetics of the old forms of counting were still dear to the hearts of the empiricists. And so, fifty-seven became a token, a symbol of times when things were simpler. Its history was woven into a new future for an expressionist science – one that promoted feelings, hypercomplexity and wonder through the experience of its discoveries rather than through their impartial measurement.

Today, fifty-seven is still just a lucky number.

The pitcher plant stomach highway is not the only predator in the dense follicular ecology.

Hair transplants are clipped upon by fifty-seven varieties of hair bunting. Their scissor-beaks trim the ends of the growths to build ornate nests like wigs, which they adorn with all kinds of trinkets. Each species of hair bunting has a particular dressing style. The Moss Mountain bunting, for example, only builds towers with fluffy green curls, while the Rafflesia Bunting plaits stinking red flower buds into giant tapestries, where hundreds of birds of many species come to roost in murmurations of joy and rear their young.

The most voracious predators of the follicular transplant fields are the fifty-seven species of woolly bear caterpillars, which feast exclusively on keratin. While other insects such as silverfish, crickets, and cockroaches damage these proteins by chewing them into a sticky pulp, only the young of carpet beetles and clothes moths can actually handle an exclusive diet of hair.

Yet the true apex predators of these hirsute lands are the fifty-seven types of round-bellied transgenic goats. It takes a year of intensive rearing to raise an ecological beast that does not destroy the crops from the root but trims them back like a shaver. Leaving the regenerating growth follicle in the ground, transgenics rummage in the infested border, for hair, beetles, bears and all. Their toothless, nimble upper lips pluck the shaft, cleaving it with their sideways swinging, sharp bottom teeth and tongue, and then roll it into a bean-sized pellet.

Down it goes in a swallow through the oesophagus.

Hair plants decompose into fifty-seven different varieties that include amino acids, albumins, globulins, gliadins, fibrous protein, hormones, growth factors, DNA-binding proteins, immune system proteins, chaperone proteins, enzymes, artificially produced proteins, glycoproteins, lipoproteins and complexes with multiple components like nucleosomes.

This takes place within the four chambers of the stomach – rumen, reticulum, omasum and abomasum – a juggler's intestine that choreographs metabolic process, infestation, matter and opportunity within a manifold landscape of innards that hosts an impossibly expansive ecology.

The rumen is the first space to receive the hair bean. It's a barrel-sized microbial factory that is teaming with bacteria, fungi, archaea, viruses and protozoa.

Transgenic rumens also become infested with multicelluar life forms that have survived the grinding of lip against razor teeth.

Shoals of hundreds of microsquid, around a centimetre in length, swim alongside the surviving wooly bears, beetles and moths. They are all hungry for hair, but infestations of squid can be particularly problematic.

Reputedly aggressive, these microsquid are particularly volatile at feeding time and may even turn cannibal. They are said to have the intelligence of dogs, being able to flashlight communicate with each other using tiny organs in their skin that are colonised by symbiotic, bioluminescent *Vibrio fischeri*. Sometimes shoals get trapped when swimming against the digestion currents. This renders the building organ of Scylla, which protrudes into the rumen and secretes a strong salt solution that emulsifies fats, vulnerable to serious lacerations by the microsquid sharp 'teeth', which are on the underside of two long feeding tentacles and a parrot-like beak that can tunnel into muscle. Fortunately squid beaks lack the strength to crack heavy bone.

Some natural historians that specialise in transgenic pathology, protest that miscrosquid are actually very peaceful and only behave badly when they are being observed, or threatened.

Periodically the ruminants cough up an already partly digested knot of hair from the rumen, called a 'bean curd' and chew on it delightedly, before swallowing it again. Always chomping, bloating, phonating, and bleating, the most affectionate goats even generously regurgitate their food for others to share as rancid pellets of spit. The digestive process produces a huge amount of gas. Indeed, transgenics offer the kind of company you might expect to keep with a brass band suffering from dysentery. At some point the goats decide not to vomit again but pass the 'bean curd' onwards to the next chamber, the reticulum.

This is a smaller chamber with an incredibly powerful fermentation system. It has the capacity to break down fifty seven non-food substances like glass, metal, plastic, pebbles, concrete, electronic circuitry, cavity wall insulation, masonry, explosives and gold ingots. Although these may take a lifetime to process, transgenics can handle all kinds of trash by keeping the most resilient materials, like diamonds, in this part of the stomach. Their capacity to transform materials means that the transgenics are routinely autopsied at the end of their lives as part of their burial ritual and their reticulum inspected for 'bean pearls'. Some indigestible objects are coated with iridescent fibres – and are extremely collectible.

After it is sorted from trash, the chemically melted 'bean curd' moves onto the omasum.

Here, the curd is physically ground into sludge. Transgenics have often been seen swallowing beads, cutlery, gravel, swords, jewellery, broken glass, ceramics, bathroom tiles and scrap metal to assist this process. Soapy fats form scum here, which is quickly absorbed through tiny, blood-rich, finger-like extensions and provide much needed energy.

Finally the bean paste enters the abomasum, the true stomach and last chamber in this intestinal landscape. This bloated viscera is thin like a drum and weeps powerful hydrochloric acid and enzymes. Anything that remains of the bean curd is liquefied here before it flows into thirty metres of undulating intestines with tyre-like surfaces where the heat produced by metabolism starts to intensify.

At the point of entry into the upper intestine, the bean paste is generally around forty degrees Celsius. The hot, humid intestinal treads drain the bean slurry of its minerals, small organic compounds and water. Gaseous emissions pass freely through these endless spaces. Occasionally, transgenics throw flames from their hindgut. This is not well studied because it's episodic and thought to be caused by the production of highly combustible organic gases like methane and ethylene spontaneously combusting under the incredible high temperatures within the colon.

After nearly a week the waste is expelled as rabbity droppings with many intricate structural patterns such as spiral or annular markings. These material details express the intestinal processes and structures with an equivalent resolution to a top of the range 3D printer. Transgenic droppings are waxy, flammable, jet-black, complex materials that contain many hundreds of microsquid beaks. Dedicated collectors harvest these excrements for the production of perfumes, dyes, aphrodisiacs, airborne disease-deterrents, epilepsy treatments, hair loss treatments and musk.

Although the lights dim to dusk in the city, its physiology does not go to sleep.

Another clumsy insect rises to the top of a hair fibre under the evening rainbow of lights and plops into the toxic liquids that flow in the pitcher plant stream. As night falls, meandering fluids whisper metabolic recipes to the transplanted hair roots through secretory epithelia. Transgenic goats shut their long lashed eyelids yet never tire of chewing the curd. With deep breaths they belch sweet organic vapours from their nostrils, while fire bursts from their backsides. It is impossible to think of them as being asleep. Under the cover of darkness, digestion continues. Nothing is spared – the chitin in the insect integument is split open, squid and bird beaks are softened and ground into paste, even the minerals that nurture the ground – all eventually fall prey to the transplanted hair follicles.

Indeed, the follicular lands are the regenerating organs that encircle the land. Through them, all living things will one-day pass. Without them, there would be no living city and without these, there are no thriving planets.

Shelley puts her hand on my wrist.

"I think that's enough for now," she trills, "you're letting yourself get sucked in."

Dazzled by the unfolding world, I have no idea where I have been. The strangeness of the place took me by surprise.

"I forgot to search for the child," I turn to Shelley, "I've got to go back."

"Not today. You need more practice. More poetry. But you'll get there."

The cloud of giggles moves away and I know there is no point asking more questions. After having been immersed in the Loom's details, memories are stirring of the extraordinary realms that I once knew. They may even start to feel familiar.

Oracle

"Mother, are any children missing?"

"Of course not." She sings.

"But I can't find her. The child."

"Then you're looking in the wrong place."

On days like these my mother is even more confusing than my father.

"Aren't you even a bit concerned?"

"No dear. It is simply impossible for spacetime weavers to be lost. We are woven into the Implicate Order, which connects all known space and parallel worlds. Everyone has to exist somewhere, and if you read the Loom in the right way, you'll find what you're looking for."

Drool

Newton is asleep and sprawled over the Loom. A cluster of novice shuttle-younglings are trying to navigate the cosmic coordinates condensing in the apparatus, while also figuring out how to avoid my father's talons.

He's drooling. A glutinous web of saliva drips from his mouth, trapping ebullient dust as it rises upon convection currents and terminating the flight small careless flies. Snorting intermittently, his brow wrinkles from the effort of heavy breathing and swallows his prey but although he heaves fermenting breath into the air – sulphurous oxide, methane and putricine – he never quite breaks into a snore.

Holding my breath so that I won't breathe the same fetid air that he exhales, I shake his shoulder in an attempt to wake him.

"What do you want?" he bellows, drunk with sleep and lashing suddenly at me with his claws.

"I need to read the Loom and find the child."

"How dare you! You that cast me out, now seek my counsel."

Enraged, he's absolutely terrifying. Towering above me, he clenches his fist in a pre-emptive hammer strike. But his gaze is unfocussed and his eyes darting around some other world, playing out an imaginary scene, or reliving memories. In any case, it's clear that although fully animate, he's not awake. But he's dangerous.

"Father, you're not making sense."

The vapour in his breath turns to billowing clouds of rising steam.

"How often have I told you? Stop theorising and get out there. If you don't practice your origami, you'll lose it entirely."

Stunned, I wonder what kind of semi-lucid state he's in. His wing muscles are tense and there's a story unfolding behind his eyes.

Suddenly he slumps and he's sprawled out again on top of the weaving machine. Since I cannot risk asking him to let me have access to the tapestry, I may as well try to find the child using origamy – without guidance.

Knotting

Knit one, travel one. Knit one, travel two. I'm pretty sure I can do this origamy throw, *but* I'm casting too many threads and am frustrated that I am not better at my art. The only way to gain mastery is to practice and fail and learn from each gesture. Every twitch of my body is extended down into the molecular scale through the chopstick tips and out into the cosmic scale through knotted trails of spacetime fibres.

In fact, the knot-making principles of origamy stretch back into ancient times.

I've been practicing making knots, which are symbolic counting systems, or computers if you prefer, able to make a record of repetitions like incantations. But since they are also embodied, they are more than symbolic abstractions like geometry, capable of building structures like basket weaving, making fabrics, designing labyrinths, or assembling cities. Additionally, knots are channels and vessels that can prolong the passage of media through a space, they may also be spatially organized in ways that store and release vitalising flows. In other words, the tying and untying of knots changes movement within spaces, not just their mathematics. Knots therefore act as spatial puzzles and labyrinths that cause obstructions and temporal delays in the system. The duration of this impediment depends on the types of knots that are encountered – from simple braiding, to nautical knots and even the impossible Gordian knot, which was given to Alexander of Macedonia when he led his army into Persia. Some knots propose to block the flow of energy; some to trap channelled forces into endless geometries and others are cast in such a way that they condense the potency of matter.

These knots are also my body. I thoughtfully take my bearings, visualise an encounter with the child in my mind's eye, and cast my imperfectly knitted fibre out into the cosmos.

Temporary Moon

This is another poor throw. I was much more ambitious for this spacetime knot. I will not give in to frustration.

I've landed in rather a peculiar place where I'm spinning like a dance partner around Earth's orbit and I've been joined by asteroid 2016 HO3. This forty metre quasi satellite has been practicing these dance steps for more than a century. Slowly, it twists back and forth in a giddy trajectory. Together, we never wander farther away than a hundred times the distance of the Moon from the Earth, or indeed come any closer than about thirty-eight times that same distance.

Remarkably we are not Earth's first consorts. For a short while over ten years ago, asteroid 2003 YN107 performed a similar orbital ballet but ultimately excused itself from the stage of Earth's masterful command, as it was not bound by gravitational decree.

As much as these strange orbital realms intrigue me, my spacetime thread is short and I can't stay much longer. I reach for the wobbling asteroid and brace my legs against it to stop my tumbling. Then I kick out with all my might and simultaneously cast a less tentative spacetime knot. These knots are much more secure.

Klein

If I could cast my origamy threads like anyone in the cosmos, I'd make them as Klein does.

I've never met Klein but I've seen traces of her in the Loom's tapestry where she produces the most magnificent spacetime weaving configurations.

"She doesn't actually exist," growls Newton. "Her manifolds are tapestries that are actually made by a secret consortium of hyperbolic spacetime weavers."

I don't care for these rumours. It's Newton nonsense. She's more than real for me. I've collected fabric details of her, cut my hair like her, dressed like her and even tried to act out some of her adventures.

Klein represents the genius that I can never achieve. Her manifolds are beautiful geometric spacetime structures that possess a life of their own. I want to believe in her extraordinary creativity and capacity to excel against the odds. I need the magic of the universe to be tangible for me too.

"She certainty does," I retort. "She's an extremophile. An Australian. Six foot, or thereabouts. She has short, blonde cropped hair and never wears make up, except for a lick of mascara. She's an acrobat who soars with underwater wings. She has scaled the Martian Olympus Mons with little more than with a silver spandex suit and a face-bar oxygen cylinder. She once fought a tiger shark with her bare hands, holding on to its gills with her fingertips until it submitted to her will. She walks with rewilded megafauna, like mammoths and woolly rhinoceros, and has way more than nine lives."

Newton snorts.

"And just in case you're not yet impressed enough," I add defensively, "Klein has also woven some of the greatest contemporary spacetime architectures. Structures that would just blow your heart-valves out. I'm specifically thinking of God's Pagoda, the Panta Rhei Tunnel and of course, the Globular Bridge."

"Mere tangles," he yawns with sulphurous breath that stinks like it's been spewed second hand from a geyser.

"God's Pagoda, is over two million light-years from Earth and offers the most extreme panoramic view of the Andromeda galaxy. Its pancake-like pleats are masterstrokes. Each fold is made from a billion granular stitches, whose algorithms are pressed together like grains of rice. These scintillating material fragments can support the weight of a quasar."

"Nothing to boast about."

"Okay then, the Panta Rhei tunnel is where 'everything flows'. It is a construction of unsurpassed virtuosity, a constantly moving structure that is brilliantly held together by living stitches. Shelley once told me in a song that self-observation in the structure enables the sutures to adapt to environmental change. I said that I still didn't get how it works but she trilled that was the point. Only those with no knowledge of quantum physics will pretend they understand it."

"Quantum physics, where's the poetry?"

"The Globular Bridge is the biggest enigma of all. It's the most well-travelled structure around the constellation of Sagittarius. Located close to the Galactic Bulge, it reaches out into the dense mass of stars at the centre of the Milky Way. Composed of extraordinary circular pleats that nobody has yet been able to reproduce, it is said that they're identical to the oldest structures in the universe, which came into being over ten billion years ago. Frankly, they're superb. You'll also notice that light from the stars in the central cluster in the view from the Globular Bridge, is not as bright as it should be. It is dimmed by dust and gas that are leftovers from the early universe." My eyes are moist; Newton can't dismiss Klein's subtlety and poetry.

But my father's stony darkness sinks my enthusiasm.

"Klein is awesome. Whatever you, or anyone else says about her. Whether she really exists or not, she's one of the wonders of the universe."

"You're star-struck," sniffs my father, who grimaces like the end of a blood sausage. He has developed an unpleasant field of acne upon his brow, which start winking at me like tiny constellations. He revolts me.

I slam the door and leave the Loom Garden in a huff.

Philae Lander

I rehearse my casting manoeuvres several times, imagining I am weaving a great Klein-like opus. Perhaps I will find the child through the virtuosity of my craft. It's a well-cast throw, which catapults me into blackness.

My goggles, fogged with sweat, now shed their tears and I watch the Philae II lander smash into the surface of its target comet only moments before I do. I leap instantly to my feet, impressed with myself, and begin to slow-bounce over the surface of the frictionless rolling comet. I'm closely followed by the awkward robot, whose airbags instantly inflate, throwing a ripple of frozen dust over the comet's smooth terrain.

My origamy throws are getting better, and my confusion is settling, but I'm still not clearing the spacetime distances that I am hoping for. Although this location is certainly progress, I am terribly out of practice.

The robot and I frolic in the frictionless environment for a kilometre or so, before the lander's artificial intelligence modules take control of the situation and bring the giddy machine to a complex stop in a dark ditch. I take advantage of the sudden halt, using one of its base legs to brake and regain my orientation. Several minutes later the vehicle's digital sensors are reoriented and a fist of solar panels is thrust into the surroundings, where it rotates on many wrists to establish maximum orientation towards the sun.

Content with its calculations, it cries.

Its orbiting mother, the delivery vessel that released the robot, seems to pay no attention to its distress. Instead, the vessel proudly relays endless images of the new arrival back to a terrestrial observatory, where expressions of embodied impotence, as selfies and data, are presumably squirted into the Stardust@home network.

After a while, Philae II settles into a new way of living, making the comet its home. It tirelessly chews on the rock's surface. Its stone-crunching stomach establishes that these minerals are born in fire and do not arise from ice. This celestial body is therefore unusual, arising from a location close to the Sun and not in the distant recesses of the solar system.

Sniffing out traces of organic matter and hunting for water and other signs of life, the lander makes unlikely friends with chemical aluminium rust worms that dig pits in its feet. Exchanging shivers of pleasure for use of its metals, Philae II's flawless skin is turned into salt crystals, hydrochloric acid and hydrogen. Yet the lander appears to revel in its exquisite dissolution, wearing the evolving corrosive tubes and chimneys as scars of delight. Stretches of time begin to fold as I feel my origamy thread start to contract, speeding up the course of natural events. Soon the robot's legs are digested and the structurally compromised lander sits on its belly and pokes its solar hand higher, waving at the sun. Or perhaps it is drawing attention to its material crisis.

But while the lander has many observers, none of them can intervene in its fate. Although I am moved, I can't help the lander as spacetime weavers cant' bring anything back.

Time continues to accelerate. Extremophiles on the robot's pitted surface that have also journeyed through the Earth's dirty atmosphere are activated despite tough sterilisation protocols before its launch. The opportunistic organisms that have secured traction on the robot's body rapidly respond to the extreme new environmental conditions on the asteroid and establish fruitful connections with the buzzing motherboards. Although these negotiations are initially primitive, where machine and bugs barter electrons, a new complex relationship emerges, whereby the seeds of an alien mind gain an extended sensory system. In return, the growing biofilm offers a rich flow of energy and more landers to follow as 'meat' for the living rock.

But time is jerking forwards without continuity.

I move to snatch at the suddenly receding spacetime threads with my chopsticks and vow to cast better knots before I attempt to travel beyond this solar system.

Witches Ladder

Back in the Loom Garden, I'm trying to locate the child. She's disturbingly quiet and I am ill at ease. As a shuttling youngling bounces across the weft, I'm drawn to an odd but compelling tapestry detail because of the power it's carrying.

It's weird. I dive down through the tapestry to discover that it's little more than a dangling rope fashioned by three cords strung together, braided with tatty goose feathers and looped at one end. This magical object is the very first witches' ladder, hidden in a room that can only be accessed by the roof but not directly entered from the interior. Outwardly it is forged from ordinary objects that have deteriorated with age and, while this is not a handsome structure, it is captivating in the way its constituent charms have been woven together. For such a simple structure it is full of contradictions and appears to condense a huge amount of energy – perhaps something equivalent to an industrial power plant.

Conceived as a dangerous spell-casting instrument, I can feel its power. It tells me that it is able to quickly form a bridge that can carry travellers from above, to below, and deep into the dark worlds. I am reminded of Jacob's Ladder, then dismiss this thought as my father's – not my own.

The simplicity and ambition of this apparatus intrigues me. Perhaps, in a parallel universe we origamers are angels casting witches' ladders, not origamy stitches.

Again

There she is, a sooty face, her right eye now almost eaten by dark dust.

"What's your name?" I ask at a distance, for she has her arms extended towards me.

But she doesn't hear me, as the rot has claimed her ears and part of her skull. Her right leg is charred and although her expression suggests laughter, it slips into a countenance of horror as she rapidly recedes backwards-facing, into the future.

Tapestry

The peristalses of the Loom are tirelessly splitting spacetime fabric asunder. I vow not to lose focus in search of the child again, but struggle to concentrate as I notice a tormented landscape whose terrains are flattened by bleak dusts and emptied by sticky contagion that is enacted through the metabolic excesses of decay.

Instantly distracted, I gaze down into the intricate details of this realm and find myself upon the surface of an exoplanet where thin, toxic, vapours once lingered over its life-bearing sands. When this world was flourishing, islands of organic matter thickened the seas like soup. Dragnets were clogged with fish. During those times, they said there was 'too much' life when the air hummed with mosquitoes and swallows fell from the air like plumb lines. Back then; they coveted clear skies so they could get a clearer view of the sun.

Then the tectonic plates tore the ground asunder and fractal scars glared through angry fissures, which clawed the blackening terrain. They said it was 'warming' when hellish molten bodies spilled to the surface and brought the world to the boil. Then, when the ocean's bounty stewed in a series of runaway heat waves, they gorged on steamed seafood. Fighting for survival, phytoplankton stole the oxygen it had once produced on a global scale, causing countless creatures to suffocate. Yet even when they picked the bones of their cities for something to eat, they stooped to hoard the detritus of excess.

"Technology will save us," they said.

To escape the runaway climate that stole the rain, survivors dug deep holes in the ground with fine instruments. Like locusts they consumed all remaining vegetable matter, razing the remaining plant systems that might offer a chance of survival. They believed their existence was merely a matter of attitude and so they re-purposed all they owned. They used stones as furniture, and built tiny new water cycles in apparatuses that reused their tears and urine many times over. Reeking from planetary malodors and ecological sweat, they discovered new uses for their dead. Still, their world baked and drove the atmosphere from the land until nothing rotted.

Then they pledged to build gargantuan launch pads to make the craft that would take them to other worlds.

I can see them now. A handful of them sitting together in a sulk upon a platform, fashioned from the remains of an oilrig. They appear barely as speckules upon the surface of their exoplanet in the Loom's weave: the embodiment of insignificance. They do not make polite conversation with each other, but wait bickering like fishwives for skyhooks to rescue them, which just won't come.

I sigh with relief and remember the child. There is no sign that she has ended up in this forsaken place.

Approval

Newton remains remarkably hidden for a giant.

"It's a non-question," he asserts, darkly. "You're confusing your role of observer with the uncertainty principle. Or you've misunderstood how the quantum wave function is measured."

I'm nearly always surprised when the Loom speaks with my father's voice. I assume that because of his stature I will always immediately notice when he's present. But I do not. He has a shocking ability to remain invisible – that is, until he's contrary. Then he's imposingly present – you can't blot him out, or get rid of him.

"But everything is entangled in the Implicate Order," I protest, alarmed that I may be unconsciously broadcasting thoughts – or perhaps he's reading my mind. "Everything affects everything else. Including our observation of reality."

Newton shakes his head. "Mobius, you're in danger of losing your art. You are starting to simply encounter things as they are. Find ways of conjuring how reality 'might' be instead."

"Stop talking in riddles. Why do you overcomplicate everything?"

My father remains calm at my growing frustrations and picks up a pile of spacetime thread, which he begins to fingerknit into a strange tentacle garment. I can't work out what anatomical detail it might relate to. Perhaps the bowel? He says it's the mesentery. Pedant. But that's just like him. Weaving a fabric for something that belongs on the inside.

"Clarity is not the only instrument we have access to. Follow the shadows that arise from the primordial interfaces which hover at the tips of your senses before they ever become thought. Those places where the pathways of becoming are not already determined. Feel how pregnant these overlapping fields are, giving birth to powerful dissipative structures that eventually lose so much energy they become the stable objects and systems which you've become so attached and accustomed to."

"What he's saying," sings Shelley under a forest of fat little legs, "is that you've become an explainer. Stop telling us how things are, and show us what they could be. Try something new. Experiment."

Nothing is really making sense. I hate that my parents can appear seemingly from inside my head to mess with facts. My father is distorting the logic of reality and my mother is making things worse with her constant singing. I came here to the Garden to gather my thoughts and align my bearings but my parents have just made that impossible. The Loom starts to produce odd forms that squirm in the manner that Newton described as sensory shadows, and although I have some sense of what they're getting at, I shake my head. I still don't understand it and I certainly don't like it.

"You don't need to understand, Mobius. Sometimes too much rationalisation gets in the way. Makes you neurotic. Anxious. Just make space for the unexpected and irrational. Much more space than you think you can." Says Newton as his intestinal garment grows.

I wait for my mother's interjection but all I can see is a fading mouth stretch itself soundlessly around someone's teeth. Both of my parents have disappeared from view.

I wish they wouldn't do that.

Circus and Life

Although I'll never admit it publicly, I am taking my parents' advice.

I have not found any sign of the child within the Loom, so I've been honing my rudimentary origamy skills and am determined to use my increasing abilities not only to explore realms, but also to observe 'life', or modes of its expression, where it has never been seen before. In this way I hope to be able to search and travel at the same time. This is certainly taking me out of my comfort zone and challenging every expectation I may have harboured about my existence, or identity.

Surprisingly, I don't feel as insecure as perhaps I should. Shelley's invitation to conduct experiments and set aside my preconceptions of reality has taken the pressure of having to know how everything will end before I even begin to explore. In the process, I hope to find out much more about myself.

Crocheting Law

Concerned that she's making me another infernally intrusive vestment, I ask Shelley if she's inventing a new pair of space knickers – with sleeves.

"Oh no, dear," she croons, "I'm knitting a model of the law."

I concede this is probably why it's so difficult to establish any kind of recognisable anatomy.

"Would you like to try it on?"

I can't decide whether the circulating clouds of giggling children are actually laughing at me or are simply intoxicated by fun, but I decide to indulge my mother's invitation simply because it seems the right thing to do.

"It's a Maxwell system, designed to take away the pain of everyday living while we continue to carry out all our basic functions," she tunefully adds.

As I try to make head, tail and middle of the stretchy fibre, which hugs me like a drowning man, she begins humming a melody that I half recognise, but can't think where it's from.

Mire

I cast my spacetime thread into a caustic void. It's a shocking space, a world before thought, where feelings quickly die. As my breath freezes and the plugs in my suit contract in the bitter vacuum, I can hear the faint echo of a child singing.

I pull firmly on my spacetime yarn and accelerate through this mire.

Learning

Recasting my throw, this time I focus on terrains that no longer harbour familiar life forms. These parallel worlds are rich with empathetic resonance and uncanny encounters. While I regard myself as a spacetime weaver, my art must also embrace a kind of natural philosophy that applies to observations of life, so that things I've never encountered, or considered before, do not confuse me.

This, of course, is not what most people would associate with the circus traditions. Indeed, in the exotic display of biological oddities, the strangeness of the world has often been regarded as mere spectacle. Outlandish trophies re-presented with little compassion or critical depth. Think of the times where exotic creatures such as lions, or giraffes were exhibited in the coliseum. Or perhaps recall the curiosities of the European circus where people with 'lobster' hands, crippling 'camel-like' spinal deformities and various statures, were paraded in a manner that struck ambiguous relationships between human and beast. Indeed, these transgressive scenarios were even acted out through dangerous circus acts, such as a trainer finding a means of subduing a fierce animal into the controlled environment so they would experience no harm. Circus is familiar with alternative life forms.

Of course, my interest is not in cruelty but in ethics by which I can appreciate alternative notions of identity, through which all life forms – including myself – may be observed at the margins of existence. In this manner, I may become receptive to new ways of being. Given the chaotic way things have been going, I want to expand my capacity for encounters with the living realm and, ultimately, be prepared for anything.

Orange Negation

There is something extremely strange about this region of space. As if it's not a woven piece of fabric at all, more a blockage in a drain. Perhaps its sewer is sick.

Moving through something analogous to an asteroid belt, nasty fragments of life are being vomited into contested territories. Not diced carrots. Orange Nazis. They're trapped in a bouffant hair plug with their enemies and other losers, caked in rot of their own making, swimming around angrily, threatening to make orange walls which they insist are terracotta. They are not. They're orange. They begin to fight among themselves. The vacuum thickens with tiny, tumbling beads of blood. Everything now is terracotta. As the mayhem settles, there are far fewer of them than I last remember. I notice how sharp and pointed their teeth are, sprouting at odd angles, like outgrowths of skin. I wonder if they're piranha but establish they're just diseased goldfish. They must be removed from this cosmic swamp. I swing at them with my chopsticks but I can't reach them. They're too slippery. They continue to fight among themselves, unable to remember exactly why they tore each other asunder only a few moments ago, and they deny doing it anyway. Around and around they go, in the claret cloud until a terracotta wall suddenly rises and they're gone. I reach into the filth of this indolent barrier and tug on the matted blockage, until the icy shrapnel slurps back its sickness.

But I know this contrary matter will be back. The temporary containment will leak and these creatures will doubtless return with a bad smell about them. Belligerent stuff always does.

Dark Kudzu

Despite coming across material configurations that appear to be inhabited in ways that don't make any sense, I continue on through this void. I want to see beyond the present condition of these spaces and encounter landscapes the way they used to be, and contemplate what they may become.

I am fearful.

Within another cluster of vagrant rocks I notice a village with sickened streets. In dark alleyways devoid of hope, dreamers' sighs that once spoke of shared visions, rich ecosystems, community, fairness and tolerance between all living things, are vaporising. Now fear, conspiracy, skulduggery, rot and troll bile bleat within these labyrinths and scrape their invisible fingernails down the walls.

It's an environment of suppressed hatred, but no sudden material revolution has happened here, it's dense; a quiet sense of ongoing decay. Grey stone enclosures turn their backs on the comings and goings of common people, who dart under shelters moulded in brute concrete. Nothing in this public space is maintained. Even tarry surfaces crumble into dark fragments around their edges, which are etched with tenacious weeds like greedy fingers that are rasped by lichenoid teeth. An oppressive malevolence stalks the city's streets like an atmospheric condition. But there's no natural air here. The dwellers rot down the carcasses of the deceased to produce gases, which they pump through the settlement, so people can breathe.

When I listen to the hollows in the place, the stagnant gases whisper that dark kudzu is coming.

Luminous kudzu is a plant with a voracious appetite for land. Once its creeping vegetation gets a stranglehold on a site no other lifeform can coexist. Everything withers under its barrier as it tears down power lines, swallows homes and stifles all prospects of future growth. Dark kudzu is just as common as its visible counterpart, but it cannot be easily detected by conventional instruments and therefore its presence must be deduced through the transmission of heat. Its capacity to squeeze its organic matter right down into seemingly, nothingness, characterises its darkness.

Eventually, dark kudzu becomes a strangulating metallic sheet of matter that crushes the life out of things.

One of the biggest unknowns of dark kudzu is just how it will behave in new places. The settlement has therefore become fearful and taken precautions against its anticipated invasion by reducing the diversity of species that are encouraged to flourish here.

Now the rooftops, gardens, parks and open air spaces are colonised by a narrow range of plant species that are considered authentic natives, descended from the settlers' original seeder strains. Believing that this narrow gene pool will protect the purity of the city, authorities exert control over dark 'foreign' leaves that are said to spread contagion. They are blamed for choking birds' nests with tenacious overgrowth, turning brilliant walkways into tombs and rendering popular public spaces as unfamiliar spandrels, where artificial street lighting is installed that attracts clouds of vicious mosquitoes. Colonists are resigned to the idea that nature is already wrecked. Terrified by the notion that dark kudzu will alter the fundamental character of city life, citizens uphold vicious agendas that are no longer limited to evidence of alien invasion. But nobody can point to any signs of dark kudzu within the city limits. The suggestion that boundaries may be transgressed is enough to provoke precautionary measures. Alleyways are guarded by suspicious looks, and citizens walk with soft footsteps rejecting sudden acts of kindness for fear of the dark plague. Plants seem blacker than before. Those with obvious deviancies, inky spots, hyper pigmentation, or unusual patterns, are considered harbingers of dark kudzu invasion and are uprooted as a precaution. Tarnished with the trappings of bad luck, they are burned in park pyres but dark kudzu is not here and I am sickened at the injustices of this terrain.

"You need more sleep," says Newton, but he is not here.

Yet he seems to look at me with hypnotically, lightless eyes – his pupils offer no solace. I get the feeling my father sees souls.

I don't believe in that stuff – but he does.

Synthetic Space

I begin to wonder whether origamy induces a trance-like state. Although I am seeking encounters I do not understand, my experiences are exceeding expectations.

From the surface of a tiny moon, a brownish-red horizon catches my attention.

It's an unusual detail and on further inspection appears to belong to an artificial world, – most likely a worldship interior, where etiolated creepers climb upwards from spongy soils, towards a diffuse light source. The total habitat mass of the vessel is around three hundred and fifty billon tons, with an ocean weighing one and a half billion tons. With each step the plant life edges towards the invisible sun. Yet it only gets so far before it slips back down again to turn around the grey sky, which is pregnant with water vapour. In this realm rain does not fall of its own accord but has to be milked from the sky. Around a million tons of water clings to weightlessness and lurks in the atmosphere refusing to tumble.

Rotation is supposed to shake the vapour down from its aerial location, forcing the fluid to a fixed point at ground level five kilometres away from its axis. Each revolution takes three hundred and fourteen seconds so that Earth's gravitational force may be replicated in the way that all artificial worlds do. It only does so, however, at the ground level. Gradually, the land grows more humid as water becomes aerosol and inches skyward without breaking as rainfall. Slowly the oceans are sucked upwards into microgravity where steam congeals in crystal balls and splits like giant amoeba along the worldship's axis of rotation. Although the colony is supposed to live along the worldship perimeter, the climbers amongst them ascend skywards to milk the clouds for their reluctant fluid.

To reach this place they weave rope from the tall grasses, which sprout like thinning hair from its plains. The founding guide ropes are several centuries old, with threads that span the entire worldship interior. Now, these have become a spider-like web of knots and aerial pathways that enable climbers to relentlessly pursue vagrant water globules, which are collected in plastic bags, like insects on nectar. A moisture relay of climbers herds the escaped ocean back to where it belongs and sinks their container contents into the thirsty soils.

The moisture-rich yet brittle earths surrender their water too easily. Burrowers toil alongside the climbers, evenly distributing the colony's bacterially soaked waste into the soil. Sometimes these slowly decomposing islands hold on to the water long enough to facilitate islands of fertility from which the grasses spring. The finger pulps of the climbers tear from plucking and threading the grasses, their drops of blood add nutrients to the ground from which more skywards threads may spring. Yet the climbers do not wear protective gloves, which interferes with their delicate sense of touch, since without a sufficiently tight weave the ropes become waterlogged and traction is lost at the higher altitudes. But falling is not a concern in the upper realms where climbers move in slow motion acrobatics amongst the clouds. Even so, great care is taken in the dense mists among the lowest kilometre of fibres, where slips and falls can be fatal.

Up they go. Scampering like beetles on reeds, leaping sideways from one stem to another in keeping with the way the world falls. The higher they climb the bolder they become in devoting life and limb to making the rain because – despite the grand intentions in the original worldship designs – the escaped water simply won't fall on its own.

Bernaldians

My origamy technique remains patchy. Darn all these uncertainties!

I am alongside a starship that is traveling around one percent of the speed of light. I swing into its slipstream, allow my threads to get caught over its dust shield and somersault around its shell until I come to a relative halt. I make a short origamy knot to take me inside. The perfect refuge while I gather my strength and bearings again.

"An artificial world will never possess the stability of a real planet," grumbles the Astrogeology Director. "Active maintenance will be constantly needed to maintain the optimum environmental conditions."

"It doesn't have to be perfect," asserts the Director of Space Engineering. "We could cheat by packing just a tenth of Earth's mass – say, seven-hundred quintillion tons – into a sphere the size of the Moon."

More discussion follows, as communications are missed, meetings postponed and tannin-stained teeth are lubricated by an overabundance of over-boiled coffee and tea. Everyone is snacking on packets of tasteless biscuits.

"Maybe we could use a bottom-up process of construction to acquire core material? You know, like growing a star."

It's a compelling idea. Newly forming stars grow by nuclear fusion, aggregating hydrogen atoms that condense into elements and over millions of years have the potential to develop into a world.

"It's been done before. That's why we're here," says the Director of Space Engineering. "Potentially, super-fusion technology could speed this process up by using magnetic fields to artificially accelerate the evolution of matter. All we need is a spectacular fusion technology."

"I like the idea of using a mega structure to make a mega structure," observes the Chief Systems Engineer, "One that actually obeys the classical laws of physics."

"Ingots of these materials could be launched piecemeal to the construction site of the artificial planet," continues the physicist. "The building process itself will generate significant heat, somewhere in the region of the surface temperature of the Sun."

Several astrobiologists attempt to interject but are waved down by the Committee Chair.

"We could layer crustal elements, such as silicon, magnesium, over the dense core. This would only take about ten thousand years, before we could introduce water and begin the first steps of a life-making process."

"Unless something happens that you didn't expect," insist the irked astrobiologists, "making your own planet appears is no quicker, or easier than colonising a new one."

They agree that colonists should live in the hollow of an inflated metal structure that slowly leaks breathable air, like an old balloon. Dubbed Planet Bernal, the proposed structure is not an artificial world but an engineered construction. Residents will not remember any other kind of existence other than what they encounter on the artificial world. Any unanticipated technological glitches and gravitational inconsistencies will simply be assimilated as everyday experiences. Bernaldians will talk of days under soft yellow sunlight, which makes them sleepy, red eyed and even bleary on some occasions and skies that bulge vein-like into a varicose atmosphere before they slam tightly shut as night falls.

My strength recovered, I wonder whether citizens that have only experienced an artificial world find the unruly realm that we think of as 'natural' alien and strange.

The sooty malignancy at the forefront of my thoughts, I am growing anxious for advice and preferably for companionship in a superhero like Klein. Once again, I spin my origamy threads back in the direction of Earth's solar system.

Calling

"Beware," calls a black particle cloud.

Its voice is so fragmented that I cannot tell whom it belongs to. I pull tightly on my origamy thread, my heart in pain at the thought of the child, perhaps now in great distress, vowing to speed up my progress.

Carbon

While slingshotting around planetary orbits to gather momentum, I try to align with a vagrant comet entering our solar system. Angling my chopsticks, I throw a complex but loose knot, so that it curves under the influence of the local gravitational fields.

Already I can see that the comet's surface is scarred by sooty fractures that plunge deep into its core. I'm reluctant to land. Although these marks could be the result of wear and tear – given the punishing speed it's traveling – they appear to have a distinctly organic character. If this is so, then the matter cannot be from this solar system, as no such substance exists here.

I have seen something like this before in the Loom tapestry, produced by a rare class of star that creates planets and are almost entirely made up of graphite, carbides, and diamond. Such anaemic carbon-enhanced metal-poor stars contain only one hundred-thousandth as much iron as our Sun. They are very old celestial bodies that formed before interstellar space had been widely seeded with heavy elements. However, given their primordial character and their relative abundance, these stars contain far more carbon than expected.

The nature of this substance bothers me, as I cannot characterise it and hope it's a material aberration of spacetime travel.

Light

I am becoming part of an aurora, its brushstrokes are pulling me skywards.

We know much about the spectrum of wavelengths, which make up the electromagnetic spectrum, but light remains a truly mysterious phenomenon that breaks the established laws of physics. Although its laws are incompletely understood, the quantum character of light can be experimentally demonstrated. While most experiments have been conducted in cold laboratories under highly controlled conditions, quantum effects can also be shown to be active in living things. While people don't directly turn solar energy into food as plants do, we consume plant pigments and assimilate their quantum technologies into our flesh. Ultimately, we are not simply creatures forged from clay or other brute matter, but are spun out of far, far more peculiar stuff, which is paradoxically woven into our existence in ways that we simply cannot see.

Until moments like these, when I realise that I am at least partly made of light.

Hollow

"Can you hear me?"

I begin to wonder whether I've left the planetary surface at all. Will I ever reach the child?

I'm disoriented and unsure whether I'm actually exploring the tapestry, or the actual cosmos.

"Why does it matter?" asks Newton. "The Loom and the cosmos are entangled."

Falling Woman

The trouble with inhabiting a cosmos where it is possible to cast origamy threads into parallel worlds is that linear causalities between events do not exist. Time is uncoupled from notions of logical progression. Storytelling is fractured. Observations are never universal truths, they exist only in the here and now. Reality is mosaic. We therefore rely on the Loom to make its tapestries and produce the kind of circus spectacle that has us guessing time and time again.

This establishing knot is disappointing. It casts a lens in space and time, bending events through it but not reaching escape velocity from this world. I appear to be traveling but 'actually' going nowhere.

A woman rises up through the stratosphere in a space capsule. I am secretly hoping that it's Klein. Our trajectories appear to pass but our parallel paths do not connect, although the membrane between our worlds is so close and clear that we might as well be in the same space.

She looks like she's in trouble and I am reminded that even in origamy, we can still fall.

"Sky, off with your hat," she says. "I'm coming to see you!"

Although she has the nonchalance that I associate with my idol, she's dark haired and much shorter than I imagine Klein to be.

The hollowed out cannon ball Vostok 6, atop a stocky R-7 booster rocket developed on the back of technology ordered by Stalin during the Cold War, opens its door for who I now recognise as twenty six year old Dr. Valentina Tereshkova, a textiles worker with a passion for skydiving. She's been chosen from 400 applicants and certified fit to become the first civilian in space for the launch from Baikonur Cosmodrome.

As her capsule ascends, she's speaking live with Premier Nikita Khrushchev over the radio. He decrees with fatherly pride: "Under no circumstances should an American become the first woman in space. This would be an insult to Soviet women."

She's traveling at thirty three thousand kilometres per hour. Even at such proximity to the world, space and time are distorted. Each day in orbit lasts ninety minutes. In total, she circles the Earth forty eight times, setting new records. She photographs the environment, capturing the layers that make up the Earth's atmosphere and takes pictures of the Moon. From this distance, the sky bends around the Earth, splitting the membranes of life into flimsy rainbows at its horizon. Constantly she monitors the effects of spaceflight on her body capturing everything with an accountant's eye for detail – what does she feel and see?

At two hundred and thirty two kilometres from the Earth's surface she discovers that her toothbrush is missing. Being resourceful, she uses her hand and water to remove the bitter grit of plaque and rubs her teeth finger clean to refresh her minty smile. Yet this is nothing compared with a control program error that begins the spacecraft's aberrant ascent. Now she is set to go continually upwards instead of back to the ground.

Caught between two faces of death, she chooses falling.

"I reported back to ground control and they corrected it."

A new algorithm is composed on the fly so her drop through Earth's atmosphere can begin. The fiery comet, traveling at twenty-seven thousand kilometres an hour, burns as a blue halo of welders' light into the blackness. As the capsule singes, her perspiration congeals on the inside, seemingly shedding tears.

From the ground, Vostok 6 is just a scintillating spot in freefall. From the sky, Lake Vostok's ancient ice sheet that formed fifteen million years ago documents her situation in deep time. It captures the world's events in odd materiality where gases are enclosed in an icy cage of clathrate structures, which look like packed snow. Sealed in a network of subglacial rivers and tides, the frozen liquid under extreme pressure is a unique habitat for hardy ancient bacteria whose gene pools have been isolated for half a million years and counting.

Her quickening breath and deafening heartbeat, begin the countdown to her impending impact. Hastening beneath her, the Ice Age landscapes of the Altay region approach the spinning Kazakhstan-Mongolia-China border where kaleidoscopic landscape mosaics of mountains, coniferous forests, steppe, alpine meadows and wetlands shelter horses and reindeer, persisting in the present through ancient forms. Indeed, except for a few extinct species like mammoths and woolly rhinoceros, there are few differences between the current ecosystems and their lumbering, ancient counterparts.

Tense and silent, the world watches the fate of the capsule. As it reaches four miles from Earth, a great cheer goes up when suddenly they see the parachute blossom. There is still time to draw together the splayed spacetime fibres of multiple pasts, with many possible futures. But she does not know origamy and I cannot intervene.

Below her on one side, the colossal cotton factories occupied by immense machines that enslaved her mother seem little more significant than toys. As she hastens towards the ground another view brings into focus the diesel tractors that her father drove, which scatter ant-like over the surrounding dandelion wool-laced arable land.

The present does not wait for her.

Mountains and scrub earth jerk relentlessly closer and swell beneath her feet. She must urgently find a landing site. A big lake yawns beneath her but the big heavy parachute, which must be opened at two miles above the ground, cannot be steered. She's out of control, but there's still time to live. She tugs on the reluctant threads of possibility and lands with a 'boom' in the water.

Miraculously, she even avoids drowning.

Falling women aren't supposed to have any say in their descent. They're meant to titillate in slow motion aerial striptease and tragically shatter into meaningless pieces on impact. But Valentina concedes no such spectacle. As she's helped out of her spacesuit by locals, she's just a sweat-soaked woman in her ejector seat tangled in parachute silk and guide ropes. Her bitter yet minty breath trembles as she accepts the invitations for dinner. With only a bruise upon her cheek, her dignity and integrity are intact, while thousands of jubilant women gather in her honour in Red Square, Moscow.

At a time when government employees cannot be seen making mistakes in the Space Race she is reprimanded for breaking protocol and accepting hospitalities without undergoing medical tests first. But Valentina understands such rituals and even spares the spaceship designer Sergey Korolev -- the man who made the error that put her life in peril – from punishment. She will keep that secret for thirty years.

Her burnt out capsule goes on display at the Science Museum in London, alongside a dog ejector seat, space toilet, shower, fridge and a gold mannequin of Yuri Gagarin that was flown around the Moon to test the effects of space radiation.

"We are thrilled to bring together such an outstanding collection of Russian space artefacts,' say the museum officials.

Unbroken still, the old woman declares that she will go to Mars if the opportunity arises.

"We know the human limits and for us this remains a dream. Most likely the flight will be one way. But I am ready."

Our paths diverge again. She's not Klein but I am happy our worlds aligned. She's shown me how to fall.

Falling

Pushing my origamy limits, I'm trying out a new series of knots. Just when I think they've completely secure, they unravel again.

This spacetime distillate zone that I'm entering is not behaving according to my expectations. Using spacetime threads to conjure and replay different sequences of events after the Big Bang, I am attempting to envision other kinds of matter, bodies, worlds and voids that may help me navigate strange spaces better.

Here I go.

At 10^{43} to 10^{11} seconds — our physical laws as we currently know them do not exist. Between 10^{43} and 10^{36} seconds the universe is evenly packed with energy and inflates exponentially. At 10^{37} seconds temperatures are so high that the random motions of particles produce fundamental particles, with matter being more abundant than antimatter.

Things are still as I expect them to be, I'm willing this series of events to take place at an accelerated rate.

Nucleosynthesis begins to form the universe's first chemistry only a few minutes after the Big Bang as neutrons and protons combine to form deuterium. I tug on the spacetime fibres to observe that within 379,000 years these primitive building blocks of matter have begun to combine with electrons to form hydrogen atoms. Let's go faster, faster! Now radiation decouples from matter and expands in all directions into space forming the Cosmic Microwave Background — the oldest light in the universe.

Despite my haste, everything still remains as I thought it would.

Forward through another few billion years and a condensation of matter shaped by gravity gives rise to bodies that are recognisable as the modern universe. Separated by enormous gulfs, bodies fall towards each other, growing denser, with gas clouds, stars, planets, galaxies, galaxy clusters, and super clusters.

Wait! Something's happening! My threads are getting tangled up in a sticky impasse. The more control I try to exert over them, the more they resist me.

A sooty residue sticks to my chopsticks and spacetime thread, like dark clusters of grapes. It's everywhere. I can't tell where it's coming from. My chopsticks are starting to get tangled in this knot, as the malignant dust rapidly organises into crystalline bridges that encase everything. I've never seen anything like this before. Perhaps the subatomic particles left over from the Big Bang have become cancerous – a hydatid mole, an embryological malignancy that produces all kinds of weird forms and, worryingly, is fatal to its host.

If this is true, then I need to stop imagining alternatives and change this trajectory – fast.

I cast an extremely ambitious spacetime knot right through this malignant treacle and hope it will take me back to the Loom Garden.

End of the World

"The Loom always existed as a fully formed and functional apparatus since the beginning of time," warbles Shelley. "It will continue to produce spacetime fabric for as long as the cosmos exists."

Right now, I am trying to figure out exactly where the sooty substance is coming from – but can't help but wonder where the river of tapestry material woven by the Loom ends up.

I'm rather shocked this is the first time I've really thought about this, so I step back from studying stitches and take some time to examine the Loom's set up. At first it seems like any other weaving machine. It's width is finite, spanning around ten metres, but carries a warp that appears to be infinite. Younglings traverse the weft of this undulating network, diving in from the framework, launching themselves like swimmers as they transport shuttles that carry spacetime threads through a series of tiny black hairy holes. Effectively, they become part of the apparatus. Their acrobatic manoeuvres are so fast that they're impossible to see in real time and can only be observed using molecular vision. Manifold tapestry landscapes are produced by this frenzied motion, which are never cut, or severed from the Loom's material origin.

But no one has ever seen what might be described as the start of the fabric, or knows who was responsible for its first initiating throws.

"There is little point in imagining what happened 'before' the Loom, as it is of no relevance to us. Our beliefs are a question of trust, which is a founding principle of circus kith and kin," observes Shelley in an unnervingly timely manner.

I nod and look for the end of the spacetime tapestry as it elongates and wriggle across the Loom Garden. Its glimmering constellations squirm under a mirrored walkway and I decide to follow the pleated folds for several hundred metres. Here, the spacetime fabric is diverted across a muddy lane cluttered with stinging nettles. I follow as it advances over a series of rather shabby wooden planks and tumbles over the end of the walkway, and spreads out like oil across the surface of a lake reaching out to the horizon.

"The End of the World," says Newton, "a place without shadows."

Rachel Armstrong

I notice that his acne has calmed down but he's cultivating a boil on the right side of his forehead. Just where you might expect a horn bud to be.

I turn away. He's disgusting to look at. But just as I realise that his comment needs further clarification, he's gone again.

Rancid

I can't speak to my father today. No, really. I'm not being mean. He smells awful.

It's more than a powerful natural body odour produced by the actions of skin flora like Corynebacterium, Staphylococcus hominis, or epidermidis, that make small, volatile sweat-based molecules such as butyric, propionic and acetic acids – but rather, he's gone out of his way to foster a rancid odour that is unmistakably produced by fetid organic matter. It's more evil to the senses than the worst kinds of malodorous cheeses, reeking in putrescine, agmatine, spermine and cadaverine.

"Biogenic amines are common food flavourings. We love this stuff," he says.

"You stink."

I can't decide whether the stench or his erupting boil is more revolting. In combination, they're socially obscene. I can only deal with one of these horrors at a time.

Newton looks at me like he has no idea what I'm talking about.

"You cultivate your hum, like some kind of perverse couture. I've caught you at it – rubbing orange peel, butter, balsamic vinegar, bay rum and even potato peelings into your scalp."

Newton smirks darkly.

"You even rot the stuff down under your armpits, as if you're making an anti-(anti)deodorant."

He continues to stare through me, as though I'm talking nonsense – rolling my eyes and holding my breath.

"Look, I understand perfectly that natural essences, including earthy potato peel, are a really interesting idea for nuanced bouquets that could be blended with original body odours with some art. But compost is not 'in fact actual perfume', which – for your information – requires a complex blend of carefully extracted organic fractions that are released gracefully into the air using a system of carrier agents, like oil and alcohol solvents."

But, as usual, Newton is not interested in facts, or opinions, as he's enjoying the experiment too much – like a hound rolling in nastiness.

He waves me away, as if I'm inconveniencing his practice, and continues to smell worse than a garbage patch.

I can't waste any more time on Newton's hygiene issues. I have so much work to do on my origamy.

Nowhere

I'm concerned. Nothing. Not even a breath. The sounds of falling soot are ripping the universal fabric stitch by stitch.

Wounds

I cast my yarn and notice that deep sooty scars are starting to patchily appear throughout the solar system. They're not simple fractures but possess foamy rolled edges that could be symptomatic of deep space infestation. Not my specialty of course, but I've heard stories about such things in conversations overheard in the Loom Garden, although I've never considered them to be true. So far, these lesions have not shown up on the Loom's tapestry, which does not reassure me. In fact, it's making me anxious.

Perhaps I'm worrying too much. Taking a rational view of these blemishes, it is possible they are debris left over from massive impacts that occur between carbon rich cosmic bodies known as interstellar 'splatter'. These formations occurs during 'star blossoms' when gargantuan bursts of nebulae form rivers of massive stars from interstellar dust and gas clouds, reminding us that 'birth is 'messy'. It's astonishing that the cosmos is full of unseen and undocumented events, even when they take place in full sight in massive spawning grounds. Indeed, the fundamental processes from which this universe springs remain mysterious as they are hidden deep within the densest regions of dark and cold molecular clouds.

I try to imagine what Klein might do in my position. Perhaps she'd have brought a portable copper condenser and milked for spacetime dew so effectively that she'd have the whole place patched up by now. But all I have are my chopsticks and I can only make limited spacetime repairs.

Whatever these malevolent patches are, they're more than material manifestations. They exude bad feelings and I am concerned they indicate a malignancy forming within the cosmos somewhere.

But I have no way of verifying this. It's just intuition.

Oort Cloud

The spacetime fibre that carries me wobbles as it passes through this asteroid beach.

I'm passing the Oort Cloud, a vast assemblage of cometary nuclei that have washed up at the outermost limits of the solar system at around two thousand Astronomical Units from our Sun. The Cloud is composed of around two trillion objects, which originate from a protoplanetary disc that now contains ices that are variably composed of ammonia, methane and water, and used to be much closer to our young Sun. As the gas giant Jupiter coalesced, its gravitational ripples banished these icy objects from interplanetary space and pushed them to the limits of our solar system, where they sprawl out into interstellar space almost a quarter of the way towards the nearest star, Proxima Centauri.

Today's Oort Cloud is a trembling, particulate membrane that can be disrupted by cosmic events such as the passage of a star, birth of a nebula, or ripples in the galactic tide. These perturbations may dislodge Oort bodies, which plummet like stones towards the gravitational pull of the Sun, where they may finally combust in its fiery orbit. As they dive, their primordial matter sizzles across vacuums and wanes in the friction of atmospheres. Sometimes, their ancient icy nuclei skip over planetary orbits and scour the skies with brilliant trails and plumes.

We call these falling bodies 'comets'.

Right now, I am troubled by their capacity to serve as carriers of the strange dark dust throughout the solar system.

I hope that as they come to their end through collision with other celestial bodies they scream a cosmic prayer of planetary protection.

Metastases

Black carbon soot trails stain the solar system like drips from a bleeding nose. They are leaving small but ugly tears that appear to lead right across spacetime fabric. Since I have no copper vessel to draw down a significant volume of spacetime dew and make a proper repair patch, I try to make the best of my darning skills with scant thread and a coarse weave of loose fibres. I'll have to make sure the stitches are well anchored if my repairs are going to hold, but there is almost nothing interesting around to work with. It's an upsettingly barren environment with very little spacetime integrity. Everything is the same shade of charcoal that swallows so much light there are never even any shadows. I look around for inspiration, to find a detail or an intriguing narrative lurking somewhere, perhaps behind rocks or under stones, but this place is equally bleak in all directions.

The only thing that seems to alter is my visual focus, which has already adapted astonishingly quickly to the featurelessness of space. However, I find it impossible to discriminate between one thing and another. In fact, I am suffering from so much sensory deprivation that at one point I realise that most of the time I'm only seeing cosmic bodies by virtue of their shadow patterns, which are viewed through the spontaneous discharges at the back of my eye. After a while, though, delicate dark threads appear. All of them resemble spacetime fibre shadows, but they can't be. They're highly clustered and disorganised like a malignancy. They're also not at all quiet and are producing significant gravitational wobbles that ripple right out into interstellar space.

I'm convinced these scars are malevolent. Seeking out the vicious seeds of darkness in this place, I make a whole series of repairs. Each time I change the technique I'm using to cast my threads, because this diffuse body has the capacity to learn. I am sure it's anticipating and resisting my technique. The whole experience is taking me further and further from any kind of comfort zone.

I'm upset by these persistent findings and need to discuss what I've discovered with my parents. I can make do with these ad hoc responses any more. Although I really do not wish to be lectured by Newton, I need

84

formal instruction. Maybe my parents have already come across this kind of thing before. I cast an ambitious origamy knot in Earth's direction but – especially with my imperfect technique and impaired concentration – there is still a long way to go.

And I must find the child.

Unknowns

There's nothing that can be called vegetation here.

Biofilm blooms explode over the surface of loose rocks. They're nothing remarkable, little more than dusky blotches that form upon old walls, their diameters expanding with the regularity of analogue clocks.

Nonchalantly, I kick at one of these stones and it explodes into dust. Myriad creatures glitter in surprise at their sudden exposure to harsh dryness of the ground – but none of these slimy beasts are as shocked at their sudden exposure as I am. My viscera writhe sympathetically in distress.

I notice a transparent worm-like creature moving uncomfortably on the surface of an exploded rock. It has recently ingested a woodlouse. Although the worm's meal is fully enveloped within its simple gut, the ingested crustacean's shell has protected it from digestion. The worm is now at risk of being split open by the woodlouse, which kicks out against the soft but suffocating space. Perhaps an unlikely truce can be struck between them.

While the louse continues to struggle in its transparent organic bag, a gelatinous swarm of cells surrounds the coupled bodies – anticipating that one of these battling systems will fail. The amorphous mass pulses as tiny particles moving through its very simple spaces, or veins. Its approach is marked by a trail of translucent slime that exteriorises and records its primitive thinking and I watch it climb atop the wormlouse. In its own manner and at its own speed, the formless blob attempts to swallow the conjoined creatures whole.

Gathering my composure, I draw closer to watch the last of the critters seek shelter elsewhere in fissures and under rocks.

Although unexpected, the 'under stone' vanishing creatures seem familiar, suggesting their metabolic landscapes demonstrate that all life forms – earthworms, slugs, snails, centipedes, harvestmen, spiders, pseudoscorpians, woodlice, millipedes, centipedes, beetles, springtails, grasshoppers, ants and their larvae – share more similarities than differences, even within extremely hostile environments.

However, the initiating events are bundled together; lively events seem to happen in clusters and are not isolated from one another. We tend to prefer unifying theories to account for events that generate great diversity – the Big Bang, the Last Universal Common Ancestor, biogenesis. In the bigger scheme of things, a whole range of tactics are likely to have enabled these platforms to generate their idiosyncratic portfolios. Indeed, the story of life is not rational. For example: during Earth's deep history, the story of evolution can be accounted for in part by incomplete digestions. Born from bellyache, these anatomical couplings are possibly even more important than sexual reproduction in producing diversity – as back in primordial time, body plans were likely to have been more plastic, looser and less differentiated than modern life forms

Even today, single-celled life forms and creatures with simple anatomies such as worms, corals, jellyfish and sponges, frequently attempt to eat each other. Perhaps these forms of organic siege allow organisms to couple together in ways where mutual survival is possible in these gluttonous systems. Indeed, they may have enabled the emergence of complex cells, hybrid bodies, diverse colonies and rich biofilms. At some point, in their couplings cooperatives may have merged and fused, to produce descendants that were more resilient and complex than their parental forms.

How far these strategies pervade the totality of our cosmic fabric is uncertain. Indeed, the story of Earth and Theia exemplifies partial digestions within an inanimate realm. Even when we assume there are no living processes at work at the planetary scale we only have to look towards the complex material transformations that occur, for example, in the belly of stars. These transmutations from simple matter to heavy metals such as gold, may be much more prevalent within the materiality of the cosmos that we have previously assumed. Such strangeness invites a range of storytelling narratives that move away from the kinds of accounts typical of classical object forming, or mechanical systems, and move us towards the stranger orchestrations of the living realm.

I notice the ground is getting smutty. I must press on and cast another origamy throw.

Celestial Body

When I am traveling, my body is no longer unitary. Instead, it becomes part of a group of bodies that are loosely coupled – an ecosystem of human and nonhuman things. Indeed, what I am experiencing may be a typical feature of hyper dimenional existence, but I don't remember hearing about or witnessing it so clearly before.

Simply put, as I travel through spacetime I am aware that I am no longer just 'me'.

From a distance, however, my body is framed by the usual conventions of human anatomy. My chocolate-red skin appears to be folded into hands, eyes, legs, head and torso that connect in the usual way. But as I venture further into the cosmos, and glance at where my features should be, I see no sharp boundaries, no border that I might call skin. In fact, I no longer possess a recognisable exterior to conceal my innards. My face is swollen by tissue plasma, making it almost impossible to recognise my own reflection in the surfaces of things, and the relationships between the different layers that make up my flesh, no longer possess a discrete form. I begin to think of myself as a series of overlapping fields that are in continual flux.

I wobble continually. To others I am no more than a blur.

As I travel even further afield I start gaining mass, by absorbing and condensing matter around me. Although this increase is so tiny it does not decentre me, I wonder what people with powerful telescopes see when my spacetime fibres stretch across the sky.

Further still and light passes through me, as if I were made of glass.

My tissues are mixtures of formerly unrelated things that cannot be simply described in terms of their relationship to specific organs or anatomical structures. My legs – a condensation of human tissue, bacteria, light, spacedust and circus fabrics. My eyes – screens where space radiation collides with plastic lens implants and vitamin-A enriched nerve cells. This is weird, because I can still 'see' even when I shut my eyes. Even my flesh – is extruded into its environment where it seeks affinity with odd materials and fundamental particles that are yet to be named.

More than human, I am a cosmic hyperbeing, wormholing through space, where I am assimilated into many systems and porous to invasion by a host of 'other' agents such as bacterial biomes, tissue-cultures, trees, carbon-fibre implants and electronic gadgets. Some of these relationships are already compulsory as part of being human, like the primordial energy-producing networks of mitochondria and bacteria that enable me to produce energy and digest food. Other interactions are associative, like my spacesuit, goggles and cosmic watch that adorn, augment and even extend my capabilities.

Although I seek to continually expand the limits of my abilities, I do not invest in reckless metamorphoses. Rather, while traveling, I joyfully participate in the editing processes implicit in origamy where I have the chance to meet other bodies, materialities and fields of experience and mingle with them. This creates the conditions for a radical explosion in my own identity.

Perhaps stargazers don't even see me as a blur or twist of light as I traverse the sky like a specific moving entity – but as a streak of darkness, like a tiny caravan of black hairy holes.

Boglands

At first I assume that the tree roots are yelping. They do that when short of water. But it isn't the tendrils. The sobbing is much more plaintive and pitiful than is typical of a stressed root system.

I dip my chopsticks into the rippling surface water. The grey tissue under the floating island monitors, evaluates, and records this action. From the surface display I can see that the glades are getting plenty of oxygen and the floating vegetation is healthily saturated with water. Sometimes, the light convection currents desiccate the upper soils, but today the peat is moist to the touch. Even the effluent appears well behaved, lapping gently at the thirsty mangroves whose eager roots continually strain towards dry land. They sip on the salts and organic matter while detritus blackens the tips of their foliage, which stirs the endless bay. This sodden place wants to walk in the air.

Spanning thousands of square kilometres, the shallow ocean is littered with many swampy settlements. It's hard to imagine the scale of this open expanse. Water is never more than a few meters deep and it is possible to wade indefinitely. While most settlers travel by canoe, creatures cluster around hoop-shaped islands that bob and gurgle under foot. Beneath the island flotsam – a knitted hybrid of silicon and carbon earth interfaces with trembling biofilms – make spongy new land. A group of structural knitters wearing snowshoe-splayed stilts weave strands of vegetation into islands, roads, bridges, nets, and homes.

The awful shrieking continues. It's not loud, but pervasive. I try to tune it out but like an infant's cry it is impossible to ignore. Where is it coming from?

Two small birds spiral out of a shrub. In a stranglehold they flutter voicelessly. I shoo them so they will separate but they ignore me. I swipe again and temporarily break up the affray before they recommence their violence only several meters away.

Anything without a backbone flourishes in this primordial ecology. Soft-bodied creatures meld with unlike bodies and mate with each other, arranging themselves around radial and bilateral axes of symmetry. Through contamination practices they continually invent new species. It is impossible to categorise every creature living in the glades. The air and waterways buzz with the mating calls of soft hermaphrodites, clones, chimeras, and budding cell colonies.

The sobbing quells. I dip my chopsticks in the black water again – probing the smart earths for more information. They detect nothing untoward. So I look for the spacetime tear. Leaping across the soft soil, I search for the sooty scar among the scant glades where dissolved gases rise to the surface like black champagne. It stands out from the mud like charcoal as if someone had razed an entire village to the ground. My aluminium chopsticks only just draw enough distillate from the aether to seal the gash with deep stiches, so I brace them with a mesh. I weave a second more superficial row to restore the natural appearance of the land. Water begins to move into the space and the whimpering returns. A tiny sooty black leech is attached to my leg veins. Its outer skin starts to swell like expandable foam – a malignant entity feeding on me. Our fluids mingle, but I cannot let this creature become part of me, we must take nothing back during origamy – not even parasites.

I rip the tenacious invertebrate from my flesh, so that we are no longer coupled and with a gaping hole in my shin, I origamy.

Worms

I've landed again on a sweltering planet, where every bead of moisture beyond the shoreline has been driven out of the land. It's a steaming day. Airless. Yet this helps me feel less tense. Trails of salt crust creep toward the shore. Succulents hiding between the rocks are flaccid. Everything is evaporating. Even the tide appears to be boiling.

Having walked a short section of the shoreline and beachcombed an impressive pile of plastic pieces, I'm parched but happy. Rope knots, faded carrier bags, packing tape, fishing line sections, clingfilm sheets, split garbage bags, clothes pegs, net bags for oranges, microbead agglomerations, lumps of toilet paper that masquerade as plastic, melted polystyrene and fragile squeaky bath toys. I sort them according to their colours and grade them into a spectrum of sizes. I'm short of red materials, so I skip along the water's edge looking for this treasure but it's a bit thin in this part of the beach, so I roll out a few cartwheels and a backflip to pass the time. The sand is scorching, so I finish off the rest of my routine in the sea. I am happy, recalling childhood memories of the beach when I used to collect things and bring them home in jam jars – shells, sand sample, pebbles, dead creatures, water, seaweed and worms. It's also possible that I'm excited, because I am about to conduct an experiment.

When I've collected enough red plastics, I break them into smaller pieces using a simple knife fashioned from a loose flat pebble and a sharp fragment from a tin can. It's more effective than I expect and as I apply pressure, some fragments shoot off into the rock pool. Oh! I quickly retrieve them before the floating pieces are split by the waves.

I pause for a moment, catching sight of my playmates. There! See those funny little fronds there? That's them! Sabellariid worms.

A few of them are already vigorously passing a plastic fragment around like water polo players. I quickly snatch it off them with my chopsticks. They must wait!

These sand worms make their own reef. Each creature is about a metre long with an intriguing fan-like set of tentacles, which work as 'sniffing hands' that feel and taste their environment. The worms pluck minerals, diatom frustules, sponge spicules, and other small fragments from the water and deposit them around their bodies in a tubular layer of snot. These grainy bogies are packed back-to-back and can stretch out for as far as the eye can see. In fact, the whole of this shoreline is made up of worm casts.

I limber up again, stretching into a back bend. Then I flop the other way to put my elbows on the ground. I straighten my legs and sit on my heels and repeat this movement several times. Now, I'm ready to begin the Sabellariid tapestry experiment.

It's mostly an exercise in improvisation. I develop an algorithm that I want at the heart of my design. I've picked these programming techniques by eye from all those times I have been watching the Loom. I'm inspired by a particular calligraphy produced by the waning moon on black mirror surfaces, which seems similar to Korean. I find a way of altering several variables in the spatial code using a few punch card style moves. I'm going to try them out as a first run of the worm tapestry.

I'm hoping to produce a section of beach made from coloured plastics that are cemented into place by the worms. Delighting at the idea of a worm Loom, I hope we'll produce something as magnificent as the Gaudi mosaics in Barcelona, where fragments of ceramics produce blooming organic forms at the scale of a cathedral.

Now that all pieces are in place and the worms are keen to begin play, I flick the coloured plastic fragments on the surface of the water using my chopsticks. They bounce on the water tension and rise again on a fine gust of air, just over the polychaetes. There's a sudden bubbling and slapping as a dozen worm hands snatch at the plastic. The water churns to milk and as the tiny bubbles settle sniffing polychaete fans shuffle and poke their treasures into a layer of newly produced mucus that rapidly cements the coloured particles.

The creatures are even more excited than I am. They're making so much foam it's really hard to see what's happening, but I continue feeding the wriggling bodies with plastic fragments. All the while I keep the algorithm in my mind's eye, so the movements I'm making feed the plastic pieces to the worms in a continual flow. We work swiftly and seamlessly together, beginning to anticipate and respond to each other's moves. My chopstick, eye, hand coordination is at a stretch as we dance in an intuitive exchange between material flow and synthesis of a reef tapestry. I'm not the expert here. Challenged by the inexactness of executing the algorithm through my body movements it's a great exercise in mental and physical dexterity.

When all the plastic fragments are gone I'm exhausted. I stand back to wriggle the blood back into my fingers and let the gurgling waters settle.

As the surface stills, the sniffing hands stop moving and the reflections settle. Now we admire our work together. Amazing tapestries are emerging from the plastic fragments. At first they look like an underwater Persian carpet with a script that seems similar to Aramaic. Then, from another angle, they have the appearance of lacework, like Reticella. Contained within these patterns are symbols that are more like Sanskrit. As I study the details of the weave, an expanding, parametric bridge-like structure rises that is etched by a kind of hieroglyphics that I do not recognise. It seems to want to extrude a garden between the abyss and the sky. The sniffing hands slam suddenly under tightly snapped protective hoods, as jointed legs fracture their reef and pincers raised high. Vandalism! What are these invaders?

Skeleton crabs made entirely of chewed bones trample the worm colonies. Each horrid creature has two eyeless sockets on its shell, which are sunken islands of opportunistic algae. There are suddenly so many. They're multiplying and there are way too many of them!

The spectral crustaceans continue to advance. I throw rocks at their brazen white carapaces to stave them off but I realise the missiles are simply bouncing off and making holes in the plastic tapestry. The voracious raiders drag the sniffing hands from their snot-secured shelters tearing them into pieces. I think I can hear them screaming. But the rock pool is opaque to events, thick with foam, bubbles, air, plastic particles and something else like ink. I can't tell. It is impossible to see.

Our tapestry is undone. Are there any survivors? What remains of our strange Macramé?

The violent skulls advance towards me. Horribly, they're running up my legs and lacerating my flesh. How did I let them get so near? Without so much as a backwards check, I turn a series of somersaults, spraying a fountain of fist-sized skulls into the air.

Dripping with blood, I snatch up my chopsticks and instantly origamy.

Hollow

I can't hear her. Can't feel her. Can't sense her, but I know she's 'there'. Perhaps she's just too good at hiding, covering herself in cosmic coal dust.

I tilt my head to one side listening for a break in the hollow stillness but only find the roar of seashells inside my skull.

I wish for my own portable Loom to help guide my search but am left instead with naked instinct that insists within my bones that all is not well.

Flies

This was a mistake. An origamy folding error.

It's already too late. Intensified under the glare of two suns a sooty shadow spread outwards with shrub-encrusted edges. Sooty crusts of earth display the typical hallmarks of malignancy with rolled edges and gaping wounds. Am I too late to conduct repairs here? The fractures are toxic and fray as I attempt to darn the breaches. The ground starts seeping, oozing, shifting and sliding treacherously around me.

Trees fold in on the landscape like flowers at dusk.

I try to find my footing on the liquefying earth but my steps ripple backwards and forwards over the ground making my gait unstable. Staggering over a giant charred waterbed. It's hard to make any progress. Impossible to stay upright.

Twisted shrub roots are uncovered by the violent shaking. They reach out for spreading sods of earth, trying to coax their return in vain. Desperate tendrils snap, their heartstrings breaking in slow motion.

I feel seasick.

Sandboils appear as groundwater rises. A rash of lavaless volcanoes continually split and heal, scarring the earth. Nothing is still. Water oozes out around my spreading feet as they're swallowed by the landscape. I wonder if this is how the dinosaurs made their exit in their last fossil footsteps.

A cloud of midges dogs me. I don't know where they came from. They're in my face.

I am sure that some just went up my nose.

I try to snort them out but the undulating terrain steals my balance. I'm on my knees. Hopelessly upset by the idea of tiny insects inside my head, I try blowing my sinuses clear through pinched fingertips.

I snort again. I'm looking for evidence of mucus stippled with midges so that I know they're gone but none comes. Perhaps they are inside my brain.

I think of all the spaces in my head. I wonder what pathway a snuff of flies could have taken. Tiny holes between my nose and brain might provide them access to my olfactory lobes. Cribriform plates, like salt and pepper pots. The files are small enough to go through. Perhaps, if I am forceful enough, I can flush them out before they get stuck there.

I resist the thought that I might be getting a headache. Are the flies really invading my head? I feel sick. I wish the ground would stop moving.

I imagine my own death. Drowned in plague amber.

Will my fossilised bones read like runes at some future time? Perhaps they will be arranged on a wire frame, numbered with little hand-written stickers as an exploded topology. A forensically organised accident that speaks of the sad fate of some space-faring human that died miserably from the treacherous conduct of sliding mud. Tragically, all of this was caused by a mere origamy misfolding, an accidental snag in a knot.

Nature appears to be boiling. I must find a thread of spacetime fabric again but I'm so nauseous I can't think how to do it. I remember the midges. I try to clear my nose again. I have no idea what happens to insects during spacetime travel.

Where the hell did they go?

Everything is moving. More trees fold in on the ground.

There! By the edge of that loosened clump of earth, I can see a telltale shadow under the harsh sunlight.

I snatch at it with my chopsticks but I'm knee deep in quicksand. If only I can reach it.

The sliding mud of time is creeping in on me. It's paralysing.

I snort one final blow, but only cast a streak of gelatinous blood on to the ground. I am wasting time. The flies evaporate from my thoughts as a steady drip of metallic fluid runs back into my postnasal space. I sniff and roll, instinctively lying on my back to stem the blood flow. My eyes are bulging with the pressure that I'm trying to build up in my head.

Through an unfocused gaze a strand of spacetime thread appears that may now be just within reach. Stretching myself out like a looping leech, I grab the fibre and reel it in with my aluminium chopsticks.

The great weight of folded gravity begins to push down into my lap. My body begins to sink into the dissipating earth.

I remember the insects. Perhaps the blood has congealed them into a harmless scab. Not even a flesh wound for legends like Klein, but, I have no way of telling what the effects will be – I have already started making my knot, and I'm out of here.

Water

I'm orbiting a quasar, which is powered by an enormous black hole that is twenty billion times more massive than the sun and produces as much energy as a thousand trillion suns. It is steadily consuming a surrounding disk of gas and dust.

I am repairing small but deep lacerations that run like claw marks down a condensing cloud system of asteroids. These scars are twisting slowly around a colossal mass of water vapour that is at least 140 trillion times that of all water in the world's oceans combined, and 100,000 times more massive than the sun. This oasis originates from the early universe, when it was just 1.6 billion years old, and implies that the gas in this star system is unusually warm and dense by astronomical standards. Just like life, water is pervasive throughout the universe and I'm concerned that whatever is producing these lacerations is spreading around the cosmos as effusively as life itself.

Increasingly, I am convinced that some kind of dark alternative reality is breaking through into this cosmos. I can't think what to do to combat the problem. It doesn't respond easily to my attempts at temporary repair. I'm unable to draw down enough thread for starters and, worryingly, I'm soaked in damp sooty and potentially malignant matter.

I will need help in tracking the source of these spacetime wounds. I could really do with some back up from someone awesome like Klein, but I'm more likely to have to consult my parents. Still, I'm a long way from home and it will take me numerous castings of threads to even get close.

Magic Beans

I'm looking to cast a slipknot so that I can hook myself a slingshot into a better orbital trajectory than my current one, which seems a little too unstable. I cannot fix the spacetime malignancy on my own and must return home without having found the child. I'm oscillating, in danger, and it's making me feel sick. If only I could steady myself by purchasing traction on a projectile traveling in my direction and at a similar speed I might be able to dampen the movement and gain some control over this pathway.

I manage to hook on a twist of space junk that seems to have collected at a Lagrange point between two small moons and find myself traveling alongside what seems like a vessel, or asteroid, covered with grey dust.

I cast a length of thread so I can double it up. I aim to lasso the object but the fibres simply bounce off the surface. After dozens of attempts, I finally cast a reef knot around its girth and take the slack up around my waist, slowly hauling myself towards the slowly spinning body. I pull on one side then the other, like a seasoned sailor, steadying my sail in the wind.

I yank more spacetime fibre length from out of the aether and since the wobble is taking a while to dampen, I fashion a safety harness with some finger knitting.

As I reach the surface, I squat right down to lower my centre of gravity and notice some rivets in the surface of the projectile. Scraping my foot over the studs, a series of panels appears. It's some sort of interplanetary vessel. I try to rouse a sign of activity from inside with a series of foot stamps.

There is, of course, no transmitted sound, the the insulation is probably too thick to be heard, or there is nobody home.

Then I notice the sand twitch.

Yes, there it goes again. I'm not mistaken. It's jumping – like tiny Mexican beans. Perhaps these are just cam-like irregularly weathered dusts. Maybe it's judder-waves from the wobble, but there they go again. Off-centre.

Rachel Armstrong

I reach down with my chopsticks using a fine spacetime filament to magnify these erratic grains. The ground is composed of innumerable water bears and space monkeys. Like an overturned stone, but the creepy crawlies are on the outside of this space can.

Most of them are in some form of hibernation, or antibiotic state. Physiologically desiccated by ice they are awaiting reanimation. Those around the bolts appear to be drawing sustenance from escaping moisture, the vessel slowly leaking its precious air and water into the ravenous vacuum. A water bear turns over, shooting its retractile pistol styles at me from the barrel of its nostrils. Its tank-like body extends eight claws in my direction. I have no way of telling whether this is an aggressive or welcoming gesture. I sweep my arms and legs of dust as the powdery creatures appear attracted to me. I move the spacetime lens over a small sample area to assess the relative ratio between bears and space monkeys – around 3:1. The monkeys were invented in the 1950s as a cult sensation – magical "beans" of life – an artificial breed of brine shrimp, which springs to "instant life" the moment their magical grains come in contact with water. There's already one on my glove. Gripping me with a tail that remotely resembles that of a monkey's prehensile grip, the translucent living dust chases the light, which promotes the growth of the vegetable matter they feed on. Except there are no vegetables here and I am the most water-rich system in the locale.

The dust continues to thicken and I pat myself down. The sand is jumping towards me. Darn! In their thirst for water they're going to find a way into my suit. Perhaps like those that once lived inside this can, if I stay here long enough, they'll drain me of my body fluids too.

Vampire sands.

Except I will not be the living dead, but a mummified shell, just like the living dusts that now choke my threads, and vision. Fighting to rise above their sticky sandstorm, I draw down the most tenuous spacetime threads I can grab hold of, and origamy.

Error Storm

I'm off balance, disoriented and trapped within an error storm.

I don't need Newton to tell me that I'm in trouble but his voice travels with me anyway.

"Stay focussed and bring nothing back."

I snort into my mask, convinced that the flies are still up my nose.

Maggots

The ground is getting stickier with every step, like setting porridge.

I'm on the surface skin between the edge of a swamp and a great sea that is formed by an over-grazed portion of wetland. To my left, a handful of thin pine trees cling to the imprints of shallow channels, which are scars from a dried-up stream. These features border a great stinking and rottenness. The ground starts giving way and I break into a slow run.

My speed doesn't keep the overwhelming sweetness in the air at bay. I think of cooking, oast houses, fermentation, blood, kitchens, distilleries, biological laboratories and compost. The skin I'm standing on is trembling and I know that if I stay still for one moment I will be swallowed by softness.

An orbless blackened skull shivers as I pass and turns its sockets up at me. Disgusted, I flip it over to hurl in some other location.

The oatmeal skin splits and a multitude of black soldier fly maggots spill on the ground and churn up the earth around the remains of the hide and bones that presumably, once accompanied the skull. I am unnerved by their formlessness.

A sheet of larvae race over the ground piling up inch by inch in breaking waves over what might be old cow tracks, or some other cloven-footed herd. Carrion beetles and their grubs surf upon the migrating swarm, hitching a lift. From between their ranks a few prematurely metamorphosed flies rise and hordes of predatory fire ants drag their nutritious maggot-prey back into the split in the ground. Each larva contains up to forty-two per cent protein, which is double the amount in the average chicken breast.

Millions of maggots spill into the stretch of dried stream. Intoxicated by gravity they race to burrow into the ground for protection. Pressing, harder and increasingly urgently on the soft surface they twist like corkscrews, desperate to escape from the sun's reflected glare on the waves.

I feel a strange pressure growing in my head.

It is time to origamy.

Everywhere

Shelley's singing.

Although I search, she's nowhere to be found in this series of wormholes. Momentarily, I think her plait brushes against my dissolving skin.

I'm unsure whether to find her strange accompaniment intrusive, or reassuring.

But it's not much of a dilemma as she's already gone.

Perhaps I was imagining things.

Nostalgia

My spacetime distillate is too syrupy. I don't have enough control over the fibres I'm casting. The error storm is hard going and I need to land but can't rest here, as there is a malignant tear in this watery planet.

As I slingshot around it, I'm struck by the oddness of the place, which is occupied by pioneering explorers called Newmans.

Having come down from their artificial moon, they are joined in their terraforming activities by Oddlings who are not quite Newman – they have a sprightlier stride and a quicker eye for new signs of life. The Newmans have travelled across the centuries to establish themselves on the planet Gliese 581g. This was rather a mouthful, so they renamed it Nostalgia. Their first terraforming move was to sprinkle the precious dirt from their homeland into the planet's atmosphere, which carried living seeds from their laboratory experiments. After decades, these creeping chemistries went 'native' with interesting results. Now slithering scoundrels flop, gaping out of the silt and flap tirelessly on the beach in an evolutionary race to gain a colonising foothold on the hallowed dry land. While the sentinels, who have only just evolved their magnificent tri-legs, raise their skinny bodies out of the puddles, scream 'no room!' and pick off the scoundrels in droves as they flail helplessly, in the effort to dry-dirt upgrade.

But these frantic events make the planet sound as if it's teaming with life, when it's not. Despite the sentinels' protests, there is plenty of room. Yet the ecosystem is fragile and if it were not for the Newmans it might have been a few billion more years before the carbon rich silt yielded any life forms at all. However, once loosed, their laboratory cultures have made a very good job of metabolising the dirt, and have literally succeeded in eating themselves into existence. Every evening in the thirty-hour diurnal cycle, which is precision marked by the geyser clock, the Newmans stroll down to the brimstone lake and dip their bread with a giant spoon into the simmering waters, so they can feast upon the protein-rich pinworms that devour the succulent bait. The pinworms have only one collective neurone that glows prettily when they swarm. But as lovely as their thin thoughts may be, they can weave no memory of the previous night's feast. So the pinworms learn nothing about their fate and continue to devour the bread – made by the Newmans from flour that is carefully ground from the leftovers of pinworm feasts. Yes, it's a strange place – but no stranger than the planet from which they hailed – a former blue, watery planet where the ice caps had long melted and the only remaining evidence there were ever oceans was a steam-clogged atmosphere that never stopped spewing torrential rain.

The evolutionary ancestors of the Newmans built their worldship from space debris and fled their planet, which was in shockingly poor condition. The ship ripped itself from the world's orbit as the nuclear fusion engines were started and the already nostalgia-struck explorers rubbernecked for one last fleeting view of their home. They were expecting a memorable spectacle and were disappointed. The massive communications holofields gave them no farewell view of the pale blue dot of legend, but soiled their memories with a dirty, greyish mass – which was scarred by the creeping cracks of vast gullies and poisoned by leaking piles of toxic plastic. Indeed, these inhospitable conditions would drive the Humans that remained to seek shelter as their world collapsed in an eyeless, subterranean existence.

And now, the Oddlings look up to the sky under the green reflected light of their artificial moon – simply called Newman. Sometimes they can see the stars twinkling between the cracks in its regolith and asteroid shell. At other times they wonder how things might change when the other Newmans come down to settle Nostalgia's surface. But each night, little changes. The pinworms continue to swim brainlessly in the brimstone, the scoundrels flounder and the sentinels wrap their long necks around their tri-legs, as they settle down for ten long hours sleep before the dawn breaks – and all the metabolic slithering starts again.

Strange shadows appear like cracks around the first rays of light as my velocity suddenly increases again. It's time to origamy.

Song Space

Something is singing here. Nothing material. Just the songs.

I start to wonder what exactly is vibrating and how the sound is getting into my head. After all, space is a vacuum.

The noises, I suppose, must be coming from within me.

Perhaps this is a symptom of my strangely dissolving anatomy. But I'm still surprised. Experiments in soundless environments such as the anechoic chamber are said to produce chaotic sounds, like the hiss of white noise, which expresses the sum music of the body. But the singing is very different. The reedy tunes resonate within me, stirring my bones and I recognise them, profoundly. They invigorate and even sustain me. I wonder whether I am listening to the sound of some kind of anatomical oscillations that bring coherence against the odds of this being possible – a kind of quantum coherence at a perceptible scale.

I am convinced I can smell Newton's putrid breath.

I wonder if he's able to communicate through media other than sound. Darn his interfering ways! He's inescapable. And now he's got me wondering whether my ephemeral embodiment could be consistent with a soul.

This is so ridiculous. I am a material pragmatist and don't believe in such things.

Black Hairy Holes

For all the things it shouldn't be, gravity is instrumental in producing the familiar constellations of our cosmic landscapes but although it is universal it remains strange and not entirely known. Gravity is a spacetime weaver's friend and foe, as its effects simply cannot be taken for granted.

Gravity makes stars, which are formed from enormous hydrogen clouds that collapse under their own mass into a central core. Here, they are fused into increasingly denser nuclei like helium, carbon, silicon and oxygen – a process that releases a colossal amount of energy as radiation. As long as there is fusion in the core, the radiation pushes outwards against gravity and the system remains stable. Yet for those stars that are much more massive than Earth's sun, heavier elements begin to fuse under the extreme heat and pressure at the core, expanding its elemental portfolio until it reaches iron. This fusion reaction does not produce energy and therefore the metal builds up until it reaches a critical state. At this moment the heaviest elements of the universe are produced under massive gravitational forces, as the star dies in a supernova explosion. Strong gravitational forces then feed even more mass into the core, so everything that passes the event horizon falls without hope of resistance – including elemental particles and even light. This incredible process may produce a neutron star. But if the star is massive enough, the entire core collapses to form a black hole – some of the strangest things in existence and natural gateways to alternative universes.

Black holes are infinitely dense and drastically curve spacetime. They can continue to grow by absorbing mass from their surroundings. At this point they become supermassive structures that are thought to lurk at the centre of most galaxies.

Black holes are not, however, the eternal prisons they were once thought. They are transformers. Once it was believed that anything, which falls into a black hole, would be destroyed and lost forever but if we look at the structure of black holes more carefully they actually appear furry. These fine structures are 'soft' translation hairs that record what has been lost inside the black hole. They are made up of exquisite matter formed by soft gravitons and light particles that are located on the horizon. This hirsute halo – like a monk's tonsure – stores the information for the things that were consumed on a holographic plate at the future boundary of the horizon as evaporation products. These are actually a different kind of soft hair but are in all other ways, identical to the sensors. Therefore, unlike humans, the older a black hole gets, or the most structures they consume, the hairier it becomes.

With the advent of structure and process within the former void that black holes were thought to be, they are now no longer no-go areas. Instead we may think of them as hirsuite, monumental, outwardly-facing soft precipices from which we origamers may begin to fall – or soar – into the deep, dark unknown.

Island of Cheese

I'm convinced that I only have to make another few origamy stitches to make it safely home. The error storm seems to be subsiding and it will be easier to cast longer and more accurate threads so that I don't have to deal with so many diversions.

Famished, I find myself sitting across from a chisel-featured woman, with the countenance of a doll and hair like an old brush. Between us are an old wooden table, a couple of drained bottles of Ceres mead and a colony of gelatinous snails. Unsure how I've arrived here, I assume I'm suffering from spacetime amnesia and, since I'm tired, simply go with the flow of events.

Evening is drawing in. The sky phases its rainbow palette, fading from one brilliant hue to the next. Right now, the infrared warmth of the day is still with us and everything seems radiant under a healthy shade of deepening pink.

She's an architect, talking about her work in cultivating impossibly large landmasses. Her latest project is the Island of Cheese. It's an island-sized deposit of Gruyère made from congealed kitchen waste and samples of underarm skin bacteria, which discusses sclerotic tumours that are growing in sewage systems everywhere.

We are all suffering from systemic atherosclerosis. We're dying of toxic residues building up in our flesh and environment. Not just inside, but contaminating the environment too as a new kind of reality. Once these substances – plastics, fats and microbeads – were something we consumed, but now their manufacture is detrimental to our wellbeing. All of them are completely divorced from their original contexts – plastics as flexible packaging, fat as high calorie nutrition and microbeads as tiny grinding instruments. Yet now they are contributing to a profound disturbance in the flow of materials that shape our lives because they resist decay in our bodies and the environment.

I usually think of these plastics and fats as attractive materials with slimy, jewel-like luminosity. The doll takes a small cheese from her pocket and drops it into her glass of mead, which is contaminated with tiny worms. They quickly swim to the surface and start to nibble at the sticky detritus from the cheese unevenly restructuring the mass so that it begins to rotate erratically, like a Mexican jumping bean.

Her eyes are strikingly blue and I know I've seen them somewhere before. But I'm developing a headache and it's hard to concentrate on what she's saying. Have I had too much to drink?

&^^%$£!!£$^%£$^%scrape_)&^$%101010rustle)(*&&^&^£!@ %$hiss(*&*^*&^%%^%$%$@£^^&***(*&^&thisisnotnormal*&(&& ^^&%£@!)))*&^^&$*$ignoreme101011011100011100101010101010101 01000101010101010101010101010010101001101001101001101010100 101011

The world is now obsessed more with dumping mounds of fats and tiny plastics than it is with feeding the hungry. Her hands spin around the cheese and, despite the worms, I start to feel hungry. How much bread would be needed to turn her island of cheese into a sandwich that could feed everyone? I want to nibble on its voluptuous body. Just to see what it tastes like.

She tries to draw attention to a fold of skin around her middle to demonstrate her obesity and plastics argument but she's painfully thin. She barely pleats her flesh into an inch of body spread yet insists that she's embodying the idea of corporeal excesses. I'm swayed by her conviction – not her evidence.

The snails are misbehaving under the yellowing light. Their conduct is distractingly odd. Firstly they're traveling way too fast for their kind and, secondly, they're producing phenomenal quantities of slime. It looks like melted cheese. I wait for their trails to congeal like molten plastic. One snail in particular is sitting atop the empty bottle lip just in front of me and is milking itself of mollusc snot into the container.

Drip, drip, drip.

Copious amounts of fluid bleed from its body. Surely the snail is producing more of this stuff than its entire volume. Where is it all coming from? Is it sucking something directly out of the air?

I look over at the doll whose coarse mop is framed beautifully by the soft evening light. Today her bone structure adopts an algorithmic perfection. On other days, when the light's not so kind, I suspect that her features may be more truncated and at odds with one another. Right now, though, she's a mannequin a framed by snails, cheese, plastic, mead, empty bottles and slime.

I can taste metal at the back of my throat and my head hurts again.

Could one of those bottles of Ceres mead have been mine? I don't even like alcohol and I would never drink and origamy.

The sky looks very strange when it's green. The doll's eyes seem plucked from the sea and we start blowing underwater blowing bubbles of conversation at each other as if in a shuttle game.

The snails are now part of the worm-infested cheese island and continue oozing excessive amounts of slimy matter, which runs across the table and hangs on the edges like rock formations. My formerly empty bottle is a container for these copious snail secretions.

Now the sky glows a brilliant shade of blue. The doll's gaze is laser shrill. She looks through me into a distant, watery sunset as she explains the architectural details of making an island-sized cheese, which is all the while undermined by the worms – doesn't she notice them?

More snails slide onto the table. The darkening indigo sky etches odd optical illusions on them. One moment a saw-toothed patterned snail is heading for the bottle and the next it appears to be returning from the end of the table. Inanimate things are also moving when they really shouldn't, but I'm losing track of these absurd comings and goings now and I stop trying to control them.

The swarming snails begin humming, then scratching as if they're trying to light a match, then buzzing.

This isn't right! What kind of noise does a snail make? Surely they rip and crunch vegetable matter as they grind their horned rows of teeth together.

The snails plummet from the table and continue to secrete vast amounts of viscous fluid, which could be slime, fat, cheese, plastic, mead or candle wax. Maybe it's all of them. Whatever it is, it's translucent and spewing folds that produce a crushing pressure behind my eyes.

I must origamy.

Interference

There is something wrong with my thoughts.

&*&^&^%^scratch$%%£$@%@$%$%^scratching(&*^*&*(_&()
)rustle(^VBOYVO^^whitenoiseP&^%^&I&%$&whisper1010100010111101101010010100101011.

Maybe I'm just tired and hungry, but I must shut them down for now.

Strange Attire

Newton opens a door to me.

I want to tell you it's a spacetime portal but I'm convinced it's the front door to our home.

He is wearing nothing but an old string vest, baggy cotton pants whose elastic seems too loose to defy gravity. The pants are sufficiently grey to be at least a week without a wash. He is holding a peacock's feather that he has sellotaped on to a pencil. His boil is pointed and green. He does not seem to have been interrupted mid flow of writing something, but rather channelling sound.

"We shall not all sleep, but we shall all be changed, in a moment, in the twinkling of an eye, at the last trumpet. For the trumpet will sound, and the dead will be raised imperishable, and we shall be changed. For this perishable body must put on the imperishable, and this mortal body must put on immortality." [1]

Through held breath, I tell him to get properly dressed and that I am not interested in biblical citations, and then I slam the door.

---

[1] *1 Corinthians 15:51-55 KJV*

Hidden

"Just a few more throws," I tell myself.

I'm tangled up in something in the outskirts of our solar system that theoretically, shouldn't be there.

I tug on it and it's massive, "Planet Nine," the remnants of a huge world – the first exoplanet discovered inside our sun's orbit. It's about ten times the mass of Earth and was stolen by our sun when it was just a young celestial body in a cluster of newly born stars. Most likely Planet Nine had already been 'shoved' out to the farthest regions of the forming solar systems by other planets and wobbled into an incredibly wide orbit. This instability and tenuous attachment to its original sun allowed ours to steal it from its original host without much persuasion and it repositioned itself around the outer orbital margins of our solar system.

Planet Nine remains all the more mysterious as there are no images of it – not even a point of light. Its existence is deduced through its gravitational influence on a group of trans-Neptunian objects. It is said to be similar in material composition to Neptune, or Uranus, forged from iron and ice.

I pull again on the spacetime thread and it instantly jerks free.

Was I simply pulling on a stubborn knot in my origamy thread? Perhaps there was nothing there after all.

I quickly cast another origamy knot.

Stomach

I've had to land again owing to the pain in my head and I'm overwhelmed by gurgling sounds that remind me of the last splutters of bathwater disappearing down a plug.

By the time I establish that this is a real landscape and not caused by my physical symptoms, the liquid has already gone. I'm crunching wet crystals under my feet. There's an acidic taste in the air, which makes me want to cough. Moisture lingers and starts to sting my skin. I feel itchy. Unclean. I draw the edges of repair to a gaping spacetime tear with my chopsticks, taking some time to embroider a structure that reconnects the reality breach with the landscape.

I'm inside what appears to be some kind of dwelling. A bathroom. Thin fingers of sunlight lazily reach down towards me. The building could be more than four stories high. It's impossible to tell from here. The light is hazy. Perhaps it's the lingering moisture in the air.

The walls are encrusted with fist-sized diamond-shaped blue crystals. Manmade fittings protrude uncomfortably into the room. An exploded light bulb has become a chunk of sculpted azure. A bathtub rudely exposes white enamel walls where the mineral crusts have been unable to gain traction. I scratch at a granular green layer of crystal fog that tries to smother a silvered mirror surface. Although I can break some of the coating away, I can't find a reflection. There is sharpness on my tongue and I'm starting to feel something like heartburn. Sulphuric acid. I want to cough again. I can't stay here.

Cautiously, I leave the bathroom and make my way along a dark narrow corridor. I run my fingertips over the surface of both walls with my arms completely outstretched, as it's too dark to see. It will be impossible to catch a spacetime fibre here.

I quickly make my way towards a bioluminescent blue door that glows invitingly at the end of the walkway. Noting that it's the right kind of place for a wayward colony of extremophile bacteria.

Inside, a giant many-headed candelabrum towers at the head of a banqueting table. The heat from the flames is fuelling a river of dripping wax. There is an over-abundance of meat on the table. No places are set for dinner.

A large dark slab of offal suffocates the far end of the table. A haggis-like organ protrudes from under this giant lip of liver but it's hard to tell exactly what it is. In fact, it's hard to see anything at all because of the volume of sausages. Braunschweiger, or liver sausage, slithers from side to side across the entire table, while Andouille, a coarse-grained smoked sausage composed of intestines and stomach, knots itself through a smorgasbord of bacon rashers, black pudding, tongue, summer sausages, which are semi-dry, smoked meats, bangers, Boterhamworst, a Dutch sausage, Bratwurst, Chorizo, Frankfurters, Frizzes, Goetta, or breakfast sausage, Kielbasa, Knackwurst with extra garlic, Longanzia, which is uncooked like sushi, Lolita, Pepperoni, Mortadella, Salami, Weisswurst and Wiener.

The dripping wax melts even faster. It starts to trickle over the raw liver, around the domed haggis and down through the spaces between the sausages. Everything starts to fry and gurgle. There's an overwhelming odour of cooking meat. Acid scratches at the back of my throat again.

The door slams. Perhaps it's a sudden gust of wind from the rising candle heat. A torrent of wax is spilling sideways now, down from the table and onto the floor. The meats are sizzling, spitting and gurgling.

My feet are wet. I look down. The fluid is cool. It's not wax pooling around me.

I watch spellbound as sticky blue secretions exude through the Persian rug. The sides of my shoes are softening.

Suddenly, I know what's happening. I try the door. It's locked.

I'm in deep trouble.

Blue amber is rising all around me. I've seen this on the Loom. I'm inside the belly a giant blue pitcher plant whose digestive juices literally set flesh on fire. Just my luck.

I'm now desperately looking for an escape route. It's impossible to get near the candlelight because of the intense heat. I am in the midst of a metabolic fry-up and can smell the ends of my hair singeing.

I scramble on to the table to avoid getting trapped in the spiralling islands of fat that are forming at the gurgling confluence between blue amber and candle wax. It's way too hot and I am developing a headache. I can't find any tell-tale shadows.

Although instinctively I know I should stay with the light, the acidic vapour is erasing all traces of shadows, so counter intuitively I head for darkness, hurling myself into the pile of well-seasoned intestines, making a desperate lunge at the liver. Using its great girth as a fire-retarding blanket, I wrap the organ around me and reach for my chopsticks. Fishing blindly in the direction of the candelabra for a spacetime fibre, I hope that I'll get lucky.

Somehow, I origamy.

Scratching

SSsss&^(&*&sssssssssscratching^&%$^$£(((^)*fffffilthy&%whispering1
01010001110101101010100010101001

These are not songs. This is not white noise. It's the sound of friction, one thing rubbing against another, as if someone is trying to make fire.

I glace at my translucent self to see whether anything is loose. But it's not. It feels more like someone is popping bubble wrap. I try to ignore this intrusion but it's impossible. I am going to have to distract myself until it dies down, or preferably, quells entirely.

Newton's trying to get in the way of these sounds, I'm sure of it. Interfering as usual.

Poetry. I'll try poetry.

But I can't think of any. Nothing but my father's voice quoting from the Bible.

"If I have told you earthly things and you do not believe, how can you believe if I tell you heavenly things?" [2]

---

[2] *Footnote: John 3:16-17 ESV*

Troubles

I'm exhausted from having cast so many origamy knots and concerned that I won't make it home if I don't stop awhile and gather my strength and resolve.

I'm resting on a small moon that gives me a view of a civilisation that is trapped by the stasis of its own political systems, social structures and cultural outlets. I can't tell if I am witnessing the passage of seconds or aeons.

I inhale chimneystack stench, industrial fumes, belching methane from brownsites and sickly volatiles escaping from piles of refuse. Meanwhile bakeries ooze lard into sewers, pizza parlours feed swarms of flies and coffee shops pile paper cups into binliners that become home for rats. Three teenage boys dare each other to run across friction-shined railway lines, as road rage swells at the level crossing and a lollipop lady clucks at the traffic while she gathers giddy schoolchildren around her at the school gates. Passengers wipe condensation from the windows as airline carriers etch moisture in the sky and narrowly avoid sucking seagulls into their jets. Clouds of parachuting bacteria carried by the weather get washed back to earth again by the rain and await reactivation in the urban environment, as the nutrients usually produced by rotting matter are absent. In fact, matter decomposes so slowly here that it is already fossilised at the time of manufacture.

It's an affluent society full of contradictions. People are comfortable but not happy. They only measure the weather according to degrees of cold. There is no heat. They are wealthy but not rich, and well-read with narrow horizons. They take no collective responsibility. It is always someone else's job to balance inequalities of power, remind youths to respect their elders, combat the strangling hold of the super wealthy on inner city property prices, keep dirty feet off the seats on public transport, prompt dog walkers to clean up their pets' mess, or bring wayward politicians to task.

This place is constructed from a dizzying array of numbers that bud by default from the information infrastructure like vermin. These data spawn demand to be mined, visualised, analysed and interpreted by whatever mood they infect. They herald a culture of sentiment analysis

Rachel Armstrong

where stable, factual representations of the world are superseded by unprecedented new abilities to sense the general vibe. Mood monitors shape the financial markets, indicating the whims of investors. Economics no longer becomes an indicator of actual events but a hall of mood tracking mirrors. Data spawn is turned back on itself, depicting cultural sentiment, worlds away from the business of truth telling.

Consumers persuade each other to 'eat data' and inject silicon chips in their heads so they can be funnier, sexier and smarter. To have better moods. Inefficiencies in societal performance are discussed in satisfaction surveys that are viewed on countless hand-held screens. Those tasks that cannot be monetised are left to rot in corners and refuse tips. Here they mature into something most unpleasant. Unchecked, these dregs mingle with the creeping social malaise that springs from cultural blind spots and community inaction. From the distillate of neglect, malevolent fields emerge. A very dark atmosphere engulfs the city and stifles the flourishing of equity.

This malicious matter is smog that slips through the city under doors, around window frames, through sewers and down vents. The plague particles that it carries feed upon societal non-decisions and breaks out into epidemics of absurdity, whereby irresponsible leaders are elected into positions of influence although nobody actually agrees with them. Corporations publicly commit crimes for which they cannot be held to account; no one supports their conduct. Banks receive bonuses for destroying national economic frameworks and human rights abuses are entrenched in the fabric of society without defenders.

Seemingly, nobody and everybody make these decisions. At first everyone assumes that nothing of lasting significance will happen. Then obscene events begin to cascade, arising from a certain kind of evil. Cartoonish ugliness arises from the slow perishing of a quality of mind and flourishes in thoughts throughout the city. Mean thoughts, suspicious conduct and a paranoid attitude creates the conditions where people prefer the company of robots and surrogates to each other. A nightmare of anti-human accelerationism rides upon this thin veil of darkness, which strides towards unthinking societal collapse.

I cast several origamy threads to heal this treacle nightmare and my heart stalls. The spacetime malignancy has extended beyond matter and infected minds. Perhaps mine too.

I must move on before I am stuck in this toxic web.

Time Twist

I'm itchy around the multiple wounds that I've sustained in my travels, which are healing slowly, *and have* arrived at my next mistake. The light in this low-lying, stepped plateau of brown and orange rock is too harsh to produce shadows. I can't stay in one place or I'll miss the telltale signs of retracting spacetime fibres.

"Your knots are too tight."

Although I have no idea why, I feel the need to answer Newton aloud.

"I know." I'm irritated.

I've made a minor repair in the spacetime fabric. Its sooty disease sickens me but I'm not really paying close attention to the details. I'm preoccupied with making my next move. I can see the chalky outline of a cottage toward the ash-dry horizon. It's hard to see clearly in the heat haze, so I walk towards it. Klein, of course, would be running full speed towards the location.

I need to stop myself from scratching my wounds and focus on the patterns of the cracked earth, which are strangely geometric.

There must have been water here at some time, as these formations start out as liquid mud. Under the fierce heat, surface water on the clay evaporates more rapidly than the lower layers. The upper layers therefore desiccate and splinter into endlessly branching fracture channels and polygon islands. The underlying matrix remains malleable and sets more slowly than the tapered earthen shards. Out of this tension an algorithmic blossoming of curled edges, bold crevices and hairline arrays rises and spills endlessly on to the ground.

A bright green locust is spread-eagled in the earthen valley of a mud crack. It's strangely beautiful yet out of place in this lifeless expanse. Its vitality has been drained, dried out like a vacuum-packed snack. I can't remember whether grasshoppers are supposed to have two wings or four.

I keep on moving, keeping an eye out for odd soil details that may betray a retracting spacetime thread but there are none. The light and its details are slippery. I can't find a fibre. I take a swipe at a few broken lines that I think are spacetime shadows, but they're duds.

The cottage appears no closer but I feel as if I've been walking towards it for quite some time now. The heat haze is not helping my sense of scale, or distance.

Another dead animal; this time a rodent half-baked in mud. Its head is sticking up as if it had been gaping for air in a pool that dried out too quickly. The hindquarters are completely encased in the earth. The creature appears to have two tails. Or perhaps another rodent is fully buried beneath it. I can't say. I kick at the ground to see what I can uncover but the composite structure is solid and unyielding.

The ground fractals continue to roll out tirelessly in all directions. I feel as if I am treading a spinning ball that goes nowhere. Vertigo. I need to stop and think. The white cottage still seems beyond reach but there's something on the ground. Perhaps it's a few hundred metres away. It could be a trick of the heat haze. I run towards it. My scabs split like cracked earth around my knees. Then there's relief as the pressure and itching subside. I'm bleeding again.

I don't really expect to reach this object but somehow I do. I momentarily wonder whether it's been approaching me more than the other way around. It's a fallen beast. A carcass, but an odd one. The heads of this polycephalous calf are joined at the base of its jaw. I wonder if it was born alive. But hang on – born of what? There are no cattle. No grass. No cowpats. Come to think of it, there is nothing here to lure a rodent, either, let alone provide a meal for a ravenous insect.

I look for spacetime fibre shadows, again feeling rather panicked by their absence. I try to get my bearings in the cosmos but the star trails are not clear as they should be and it's hard to establish my coordinates. I'm guessing at my location. This is not good.

Why am I finding dead, possibly mutant animals where there is no life and apparently no decay? There's no stench. No worms. No flies. No composting. Just mummification and sterility, and why is that cottage, or whatever it is, still so far away?

I shut out my father's voice, which starts pointing out all my errors, and reach for my chopsticks. I am acutely aware that I may be caught in a time twist.

These are terrible traps. Some say they're eddies, like whirlpools, in the Implicate Order. Others say they're a kind of vandalism inflicted by spacetime parasites. Whatever the cause, in place of connection there is only disconnection around a time twist. The continuum of space unravels so that a place becomes isolated within a single set of spacetime coordinates. While distance can be perceived, it's not connected to actual events. If I am in a time twist then no amount of walking will bring me closer to that cottage, as the spacetime thread that connects us is unravelling. We're stuck at our respective locations. If that isn't sufficiently lethal, then time twists are also sinks for cosmic rays. From recollection, they're about as lethal as a post nuclear disaster zone.

This is grim. I could be already stranded. There is only one option and I don't like it.

I channel my father.

"Tell me how to make a spacetime lens."

"Are you telling me you've lost track of spacetime threads? Fool!"

"Newton, please help me. I'm completely blind. I'm in a fix. I feel like I'm threading a rusty old needle with gossamer. I can't get hold of a stable fibre. I'm stuck."

His voice is deep and booming now – as usual, he refuses to guide my hand.

However, his presence is extraordinarily empowering.

I make the strange contortions needed to throw the lensing geometry of my own shadow on to the ground. Now I move using only my elbows to rotate this dark structure around, rather like a radar detector, to catch the edge of the spacetime fragments. The electromagnetic spectrum is bending around me. So are wisps of spacetime fabric. I snatch at a few but they fray and disintegrate into fluff.

I'm aching from holding this extreme position. My head is starting to hurt and skin is split, re-split and re-set in leaking blood but my father's voice insists that I need to slow my breathing right down and focus. I feel his dark wings spreading over me.

"For nothing is hidden that will not become evident, nor anything secret that will not be known and come to light." [3]

Panic stalls as I force myself into a barely functioning physiological resting state. If someone took my pulse right now, they'd probably mistake me for dead.

Everything stills. I'm so clear that I can see the vibrating shells of atoms. At the same time I can also hear stars being born and dying across

---

[3] *Footnote: Luke 8:17*

the other side of the cosmos. In this lensing position I no longer see individual fibres, but witness the fundamental strings of spacetime music themselves in their full, interconnected orchestra.

A cracked shadow pauses indecisively just by my chopsticks. I'm quick. It's enough. I origamy.

"Thank you, Newton."

PART II

Bath Time

I'm back, exhausted.

However, I cannot use the bathroom because apparently Shelley has discovered Newton's new composting perfume technique and has mercilessly dragged him into the shower.

I don't know how long they've been in there but the steam and aerial-borne children escaping from the door seem like they're desperate to escape, as my parents carelessly cavort with song and hair-whip, thoroughly enjoying themselves.

"Can you both hurry up in there?"

Criticism

Newton has a few modes of communication, which range from the brutal truth to mind-bending provocations. It's mostly self-evident which attitude he's adopting.

"You're a total idiot."

We're watching the Loom. Periodically the shuttle leaps forwards, spewing cloth that seems like frost flowers blooming upon alien seas. I've actually come across this frozen spectacle during a winter's walk. Sap-filled succulents have stretched into an arresting witch's hand formation, with long thin cracks running along their length. They're produced when spongy plants draw in water from the atmosphere to create a production-line of thin, expanding ice layers which gradually push an advancing column of ice crystals along like squeezed toothpaste, forming ice 'petals' or long strands of hair.

"You're weaving your stitches too tight."

I frown at my father. He's never endearing for long. I don't want his version of the brutal truth right now. But it's coming anyway.

I try to lose myself in the details spewing from the Loom instead.

"If you don't loosen up you'll get yourself stranded, or killed."

I'm now irritated. My father is forcing me to deal with my insecurities. I haven't even begun to tell him about the malignant soot as I am feeling very undervalued. I try to lift my gloomy mood by focusing on a detail of Klein's work – she appears to be somewhere around Andromeda, in the Blue Snowball Nebula region, and I scour every movement of the shuttles for details of her progress, but fragments of whatever it is that Newton's eating – I hope it is popcorn – are spraying on to my face as he speaks. I notice that his boil has been lanced.

"Okay, Father." I roll my face and stare hard at the Loom unable to focus on anything at all.

"I see that Klein has been dropping a lot of stitches recently. She needs to up her game. Behaving like a beginner."

I hate that he knows what I am thinking and I take my father's criticism of Klein very personally. She is not only a legend and my personal idol, but also my motivation to keep on going when I feel utterly overwhelmed by the unfairness of everything.

Like now.

Kith and Kin

I've never really tried to figure out how my parents' relationship actually works, or – given the disparities in scale – the technicalities of how I was conceived. It's enough that they seem delightfully happy in each other's company. When they think they're alone, my father lifts my mother up on to his lap where they'll spend hours nestled together whispering and giggling – she stroking his chin with her plait and him flapping his light-shielding wings. This is disconcerting. I mean, they're my parents, so they're obviously talking about me.

"You're overdoing it dear."

Shelley puts the back of her tiny Thumbelina hand on my forehead, which I've always assumed has an inbuilt thermometer.

"Thirty-seven point two," she sings.

There seems to be nothing wrong that sleep can't cure. After a dreamless nap, bed is boring. In sequence I click the two hundred and thirty moveable joints in my body to make sure they all work. Then I make my way down to the Loom and watch the darting shuttle with some of my siblings (938, 604, 303) Curie, (028, 597, 947) Fox and (194, 201, 395) Keller.

Shelley suddenly appears from under the shuttle bed where she's been humming and fine-tuning the laws of quantum physics against the balance of the spacetime threads. She treats this science as a whisky maker views the art of mixology, which is blended and expressed through a unique poetry. Being in many parallel realms simultaneously, she never joins in with viewing the Loom's outputs with the rest of us. I don't recall her ever finishing an entire row of viewing time. She pops up and vanishes again at the most unlikely times.

A small partly clothed child shoots past. My mother sniffs the air like a rodent. She grabs the child with her plait, slaps it down on the floor like a fishwife gutting a catch, whips off its diaper, conjures another cloth and the odourless child is on its way again.

"Is that a cousin, or sibling?"

"Cousin, (792, 206, 481), Margulis."

"Andromeda galaxy?"

"Yes. Coordinates are easier to explain."

Miralda

I really should talk to my parents about my observations, but I'm sulking on account of Newton's criticism of Klein and I'm just not in a forgiving mood right now.

I decide to lose myself in the Loom's tapestry, and project my upset into concern for the fate of this violently upturned tree fragment, which is stuck head down in the buried in the harshest kind of dirt. As if it's just crashed landed from another world. This poor plant is blackened and forlorn, with its roots splayed out in the air. Just like me. Equally disturbing is that the whole composition feels very wrong, most unnatural. Out of sorts. I read this as an omen of sorts, or an excuse to consider my encounters with the strange infectious matter that I increasingly suspect is indicative of a severe spacetime tear.

A dark matter breeze sucks on the tree wreckage, trying to draw the light in. I see carbon residues everywhere. Looking over the tapestry more generally, this time I can actually see evidence that something in the spacetime fabric is amiss. There's an unusual amount of decay in this section. Look here! It seems that something has been trying to break into the tapestry from a parallel universe. Could this be the first evidence of a spreading material malignancy?

I know that I must account for my observations but I'm distracted by the emotional implications of the tragedy for this life form. I start wondering just how different being in the world would have been for this poor thing under happier, more fertile circumstances. From a distance, the tree stump is little more than a blackened lump. A fragile, twisted, pathetic wreck of a being. Yet I cannot accept that this object is unwanted detritus. Rather, it harbours the essence of an incredible, but tragic beauty.

I begin to study its root details and find hints of its story in the intricate stiches and pleats of its fibres, which appeals to my craft. I wonder whether beauty cannot simply be confined to one particular part, or fragment of a thing. Perhaps it exists as a living network of exchanges, in which a body is connected through a whole range of experiences to an abundance of meaning. I am struck by the potential richness and diversity of this idea – and how liberating it becomes when compared with the paralysing ideals of a perfect form.

I think of Miraldalocks. She's not a person but a plant and, since her circumstances resonate deeply, the story counts for something. So, I'm upset.

You see, Miraldalocks didn't start off as a plant but as Miralda, a young woman with a waspish waist and generous pelvic curves. But her most striking feature was her thick, dark hair, which smelt heavenly. In fact, she was trailed by a swarm of bees wherever she went – buzzing and sighing after her. It was said that when Miralda entered a room it was even possible to get drunk on the very act of breathing.

Miralda seldom went out. If she did, it was only at dusk and wearing a veil. This had nothing to do with a penchant for nocturnal beekeeping. Rather, she knew just how disagreeable her countenance was and so kept herself to herself.

One evening, a lustful wizard was in the village, taking the air, and he became intoxicated by Miralda's luxurious tresses. He set about wooing her. He approached her under the blanket of pitch darkness and, being a stranger to the art of flattery, Miralda fell for the wizard's powers of seduction. In no time the crafty sorcerer had Miralda for his own.

But tragedy struck. In the morning, the wizard awoke and looked upon Miralda's face. He was so horrified that he killed her instantly. To hide his shame, he buried her face down in the earth, with her feet sticking out so that he would not be reminded of what he had done. Then he left the land, never looking back and never to return.

Appalled by the violence inflicted upon this innocent young woman, nature took pity on her and vowed to rewrite her story. The wind carried the news of Miralda's murder to the bees and creatures that had loved and admired her. Soon there was a stirring in the air over the place where her body lay. One by one the loving insects adorned this aromatic place with pollen, manure and seeds. For how can a pretty face compare with the presence of a heavenly scent to a bee? The creatures of the soil soon began to transform Miralda's flesh. They rearranged her tissues, her bones, re-designed her metabolism and for the very first time, gave her the means to stand tall in the light through the power of photosynthesis. Now, her untimely grave was a blossoming fertile landscape. Bathed in vitality, Miralda's hair started to grow, taking on a vigorous life of its own. It grew and grew until the individual strands began to twist into a beautifully patterned, voluptuously curved woody stem, which flaunted her reincarnation. When twigs burst out from the stem with new life, they reached out towards the sun spreading their beautifully scented leaves, beckoning to lovers to linger among perfumed clouds. Miralda's magic continues today, in the incredible plant 'Miraldalocks', which is harvested by apothecaries for its life-restoring properties.

The notion of beauty is full of uncomfortable contradictions that do not necessarily bring out the best in us and, frankly, stifle the possibility of life. The vital world is not animated by perfections but through continually negotiated imperfections and conflicts. Transformation through another becomes possible only when a being is not idealised. We need to incessantly create opportunities through which we may be transfigured by one other, or even partly contained within each other.

Being part of a circus community is to live ethically, ecologically and even edibly.

Our defining operations are not the gentle greening of things but how we negotiate the persistent, difficult and often contrary overlapping between our bodies, environments and actions. These ever-changing assemblages create the conditions in which conflicting rule sets need ongoing navigation and diplomacy. For me, this potential to be materially transformed by and become part of another is a physical and transcendental aspect of beauty. It is so much more than spiritual awareness, or a harmonious frame of mind that gestures towards a perfect order. Instead, it's a real fabric that connects us through other bodies in various acts of assimilation – that take place as various forms of partial and total ingestion. We are our bacteria, the forests, underfoot soils, air and oceans. An ecological, edible beauty is never fixed. It is never in one part of our being. It is never easily abstracted and nor can it ever be fully defined. It flows through us continually so that we share in its symbolic potential but are never stifled by its anamorphic moments of complete form, or incidental silhouettes. In short, an ecological edible beauty evades capture as it is devoid of coagulating tricks and lies.

Miralda's story has brought me a modicum of comfort that injustices can be undone, laws can be changed, vitality restored and futures can be re-written. Spacetime is not a linear set of events where there is a distinct past, present and future but arises from a multidimensional and unfathomably strange fabric in which sequences may be continually remade. No matter how bizarre.

Rachel Armstrong

Whatever the matter may be, clinging to Miralda's tragedy isn't going to help me further. Besides, the pressure in my head seems to be more persistent of late and is nagging at me again.

I finally resolve to tell my parents everything, no matter how unprepared for their criticisms I am.

Lessons

I'm so cross with my father that I can barely think straight. Although he smells tolerable, his boil is growing again and is white with pus.

He says that I must begin my entire spacetime education all over again.

I know my parents are in cahoots, dredging up a catalogue of my errors. For example, it appears that knowing how to avoid getting stuck in a time toroid is something that even the most junior spacetime weavers should have mastered.

Now before you ask why I don't just leave home -- perhaps you may think I am a little too ripe at eighty-four to be living with my parents – I can tell you that it just doesn't work like that.

I have more than a hundred brothers and sisters. Over a thousand nephews and nieces. I have lost count of my cousins and any blood relations beyond that; either I don't recall meeting them or they have expressed no desire to meet me. You see there are just so many of us. And we're all connected through spacetime fabric, so there simply is no leaving home. There's nowhere 'away' to go. Instead, we learn to get along with each other. Specifically, we learn how to suffer our relations' irritations with us in silence.

This is all spelt out in Maxwell's Book of Material Pragmatism. Which, for brevity, can be summed up in three rules. Doubt everything. Make your own experiments to prove yourself wrong, and never feel sorry for yourself.

Apparently, I had forgotten the essentials of our culture, so Newton grilled me on every detail of Material Pragmatism – from the material nature of reality, to the illusion of feelings and the fundamental emptiness of emotional states. He even asked me which pages of the copy I read were dog-eared or had pencil marks on them, and whether there was an inscription in the book that dedicated it to a special someone.

Of course, when I struggled, I hazarded a few educated guesses and managed to get away with uncertainty by being somewhat over-assertive.

"Are you completely sure about that?"

"Absolutely, yes."

Rachel Armstrong

Now, to add humiliation to insult, Newton has ordered me to attend basic classes in hyperbolic spacetime weaving and take my place among the children. Which is apparently where I belong.

My father begins to fingerknit a cosy for his expanding boil.

I am deeply embarrassed, and simply refuse to talk sensibly to my parents.

Learning

According to the laws of material pragmatism, I cannot feel put-upon, so I've decided to make the best of these younglings' company.

We're sitting on the floor in a semicircle, lotus style. Cousin (139, 788, 512) Franklin stacks herself on my lap without seeking my permission. She offers no apology either. Her big black eyes and perfect skin, which is likely to take on many bronze hues before it decides which spread of pigmentation is most appropriate for her, are courtesy enough.

Cousin (277, 375, 909) Ackermann starts lessons every day after reading D.H. Lawrence's poem 'Self Pity' as an obligatory hymnal to a sea of little bird's eyes that simply have not lived long enough to grasp its bleak gravity.

Today we're considering the nature of spacetime, which informs the logic of our art, technology and culture.

"Spacetime is not the same as the popular idea of 'space' and 'time'. It's a hyperdimensional object, or geometry, that entangles classical notions of space and time."

The younglings accept this statement at face value while my thoughts are racing with exceptions, such as time twists and dark matter malignancies, but I say nothing. I want to hear how the story unfolds.

"Let's consider reality not as a three dimensional space that evolves in time – but as a multidimensional space that exists in its entirety as a living object that makes up all spacetime events, everywhere, at all times in the life of the universe. Let's call this theoretical structure – a hyperbody. Now, let's think about what navigating a body like this means for classical physics. It means that the co-ordinates we occupy can only ever exist in one plane. However, when we think about our position within a highly convoluted and dynamic hyperbody, we have access to places that are just impossible to reach when time and space are treated in the conventional, linear way. Instead of creeping along the floor of space one step at a time, we're taking a whirlwind fairground ride through its incredibly agile guts!"

This is sucking eggs. I'm trying hard not to feel patronised and sorry for myself. But it's hard.

"But let's just find out for ourselves how novel and exciting this spacetime concept is in our understanding of reality – and what is at stake."

Ackermann is keen to demonstrate. He invites several younglings to stand up, which they're more than keen to do. They've been poking at each other since the lesson began, trying to get one another's attention. Then he shuffles them by their shoulders into a starting position.

"Suppose two bodies are moving around each other. Let's pretend that they can also see each other in some way."

He gently pushes a couple of younglings so that they're circling each other in opposite directions. Cousin (287,307, 911) Lovelace sticks out their tongue at cousin (850,264,582) Feynman, who is looking incredibly intense, and everyone giggles. I roll my eyes and remember not to feel sorry for myself.

"Where are you (287,307,911)?"

The youngling stops.

"Um, I'm in front of (850,264,582)."

"No, you're not! You're behind me, slowcoach! Keep up."

"Okay, okay. This is good. Another question for you. How long have you been walking around each other?"

"Walking? I could be flying," says (850,264,582) and turns an exuberant cartwheel to emphasise just how much she's being held back by (287,307,911)'s trajectory.

"Is that all you've got, loser?" Sneers (287,307,911) before flopping down into the splits on the floor and spinning like a fairground antigravity wheel.

Ackerman thanks both of them before ushering the girls back to their seats, where they continue with their rivalry.

"So you can see that when individuals encounter time and space they don't usually agree on the measurements, orientation, how much time passes between events. And when they're moving around each other, they don't even fully agree about how much space there is between things at any given moment. Even stranger, these observers don't even agree on the order of all the events they observed within a given timeline."

Cousin (496,101, 338) Rubin, puts her hand in the air, straining to be seen.

"But that demonstration was not scientific. Nobody was actually measuring anything. It was all based on opinions."

"Great observation." affirms Ackermann, "But you know what? When this kind of experiment is repeated so that all the variables are measured properly, observers moving around each other in time and space still don't agree on their relative positions, speeds, orientations, or distances. But since everything is being conducted according to a coherent set of rules and agreed standard of measuring, neither observer can be considered wrong."

I think about raising my hand at this point to ask about 'controls', ways of reducing error in this apparent experiment where nobody agrees with anyone else, but it makes me feel like a youngling, so I keep my reservations to myself.

Ackermann says that we'll repeat the experiment and shepherds a much larger group of children. They begin to climb up and over each other at his direction. Strangely, they adopt a formation where I can only see them from the front and not from the side. I dismiss this as being some kind of illusion and try to figure out why I think I am seeing an excess of heads – or perhaps it is a paucity of bodies. I don't know.

"The implications of these findings are astounding. If we can't agree about the ordering of events, for example, it means that someone's past event is in someone else's future."

The children are enjoying moving around in lines in surprising order a little too much. They are now just a confusion of heads, legs, arms, tummies and I am sure there are a handful of chairs in there somewhere. At least, I think so. Ackermann asks them all to sit down again.

"So, when we're concerned with nearby events, tiny disagreements in our understanding of spacetime can be ironed out through experience. But if these disputes relate to spaces beyond our solar system, then they have increasingly profound implications."

I'm starting to consider whether it's best to throw several origamy moves to travel from one place to another, or one single perfectly delivered manoeuvre.

"But perhaps the most interesting implication of these disputes is that spacetime is not the same everywhere. There is no frame of absolute reference that we can test this with. Everything that exists does so within its own context, which can only be relative to other situations. So every measure or observation of spacetime must be comparative and may well be much more like a mosaic, or tapestry, than a single fabric held together by the Implicate Order through an interconnecting web, which allows these differences in substance. This is of course what we see in the Loom."

Younglings are now losing their rather impressive attention spans. They're knitting their legs together across chairs and have been juggling a few personal items such as pencil cases and someone's packed lunch for several minutes now. The trajectories form a solar system of everyday objects, which is suddenly expanded with the addition of someone's shoe.

"The other thing worth noting," reminds Ackermann, "is that there is no universal agreement on the division of events into past, present and future. This has radical implications for the understanding of ideas such as free will, or even the idea that we can change the future."

A small voice asks a question.

"But what about causality?"

"That's a good question. You're asking about the relationship between causes and effects. Spacetime also helps us understand how events are linked." He starts drawing some mathematical symbols on the blackboard.

"Of course, the validity of our calculations depends on agreement. The spacetime interval is a mathematical expression that deals with the idea of subtraction. Its value can be negative, zero or positive. If the spacetime interval is positive then observers cannot agree about the order of events. However, when its value is zero or negative, then everyone agrees on the sequence. So, the interval can tell us whether one event will influence another. While observers can't agree about past, present, future, time or distance – they can all agree about causality. Although it seems counter-intuitive, causality is ultimately what's real."

Ackermann covers the board with white marks, delighting in the tactility of its surface, the braking stick of chalk as he applies too much pressure and the continual smudging of symbols as he makes his argument.

"Things get really interesting when general relativity is introduced, as we have discovered there are many different geometries within spacetime. This means that origamy becomes an art that not only has amazing creative potential but also opens up the possibility of traveling across parallel universes and altering the very fabric of spacetime. We are part of the cosmic apparatus."

The younglings listen spellbound, soaking this all in. I do too. I'm not sure I agree with everything that is being said but I'm happy to entertain the story.

Franklin has reached her wriggle-free breaking point and wants to travel with the pencil case and growing solar system that the class has been building. She launches herself with confidence into a sea of juggling arms. As soon as I see her rise aloft giggling, I take the opportunity for a cup of moon milk tea.

As we split for a short break, I realise that I've been angry at Newton because I thought he was reminding me about the facts of my existence. But it's not that at all – he's showing me how, by being a loner, I have been losing my culture.

Flourishing

Shelley's disappeared again. In her absence, I'm meditating on some of the manifolds spilling out of the Loom. I'm wondering if there are as many areas affected by the material malignancy, as I feared. I spend a long time surveying the tapestries and hope that somehow it's all in my head.

I'm drawn closer to a particular area of flourishing – a rich tangle of vegetation that's bursting with energy. Lolling stamens and swelling fruits shake with life and hold me as witness to their promiscuous fertility as the ground explodes with seeds. Now colonised by ants, pods crawl with shadows while bees restlessly glower at predators that lurk under chimneystack tree heart nests. Here there is no discontinuity between life and death. Fallen flowers dance in pollen plumes upon compost and decay's corruption rises through honeyed floral perfumes. Earth bakes under its effusive metabolic heat. In these minglings, all categories are recomposed, with no tidy courtship to denominate their substrate, gender, or species. Unchecked, an orgy of semi permeability ensues that causes grasses to tense and sweat with dew upon soils. In the belly of ravenous worms, these earths press their mixology upon the air: liquorice, lily, sweet volatiles, rich organics, hint of eucalyptus, pondweed, antiseptic phenols, sulphur, banana, coconut milk, oak, bitters, sharps, nutty vapours, cabbagy rot, dank fungi, salt spray, citrus, pepper and cinnamon. Vegetable passions now litter the breeze, with their potent releases. Turned by fingers of sewage, guano-tainted earths swallow each other on shifting soils that tumble over one another in the intestines of things that crawl and doggedly reinvent the extant aromatic landscapes. Obscene couplings herald the stench of life and contaminate me with the impure paradox of Eden.

I feel as if I've tasted life again. It lingers on my tongue chewing at my senses, my thoughts, my world and I am invigorated – there is nothing that life, through its living to the full – cannot overcome. Perhaps things aren't so bad, after all.

City For Two

The Loom beckons. I need somewhere peaceful to drink my moon milk tea away from the juggling, tumbling younglings. Their frantic activity is precipitating a nagging pressure behind my eyes.

Klein's manifold looks depressingly charred. The edges are rolling upwards, which is putting stresses and strains on the weft. The shuttles are working hard to move through these regions and are spoiling what is usually a stitch-perfect terrain. It's depressing and I don't want to find myself in an argument with my father about her failings, and by implication, mine; so I look for somewhere more tranquil to place my thoughts.

In this city for two an owl-eyed man is perched in a tree. He's writing at a desk with a raven feather. As he dips the quill in tarry ink it splatters across the page.

"Why is a raven like a writing desk?" he begins.

Then he sinks into pensive mode, unable to continue. After several minutes, he knocks on the bark by a large woodpecker hole and a small woman appears like a cuckoo from a clock.

"Is it milk time?" she asks.

"I don't know. Ask the cow."

She disappears and the man, who is painfully familiar with the routine, covers his ears as the whole tree resonates with her voice.

"Is there milk?"

Further silence ensues as the roots dump the sounds into the earth until the cow that is tethered by the udders through a complex system of ropes, bellows, bucket and tubes that can be operated from inside the tree, kicks the trunk in reply. Her companion chicken clucks irritably.

"In a parallel universe, I'd be able to complete this riddle," he grumbles, as the woman hauls up a steaming bucket of cream using the ingeniously threaded pulley system that drapes the branches as a curtain of wheels.

The hive under the man's chair tastes the sweet lactose wafting from the hot bucket and starts to waggle dance. Soon the creaking pulley system advances fist over hand to the hum of a hungry swarm.

The cow dumps a giant pat on the ground now that her udders have been relieved from the strain of carrying milk. It smothers the ground that the chicken has just been tearing over for worms in the root and litter zone, which is also riddled with wood lice, devil's horsemen beetles and fungi. Here, decomposing bacteria consume simple carbon compounds such as root exudates and fresh plant residues and convert these polymers into organic matter that is useful to other organisms in the food web. Bacterial mutualists form partnerships with plants like the nitrogen-fixing organisms. These cluster around root hairs, capturing nitrogen from the air and turning it into plant food. Actinomycetes extend fine tendrils into the ground, feeding on the recalcitrant compounds such as chitin from insects and cellulose from plants to make the perfumes of freshly turned earth. Other bacterial species use alternative energy sources than carbon compounds: nitrogen, sulphur, iron and hydrogen, which degrade contaminants and increases the richness of soil minerals. The decomposing plateau into which the manure seeps also contains pathogens that have an uneasy relationship with the oak ecology, including Xymomonas, Erwina and Agrobacterium, which love to make galls from the tree tissue.

Insects and their larvae in the trunk scatter into deep crevices as the cow scratches its hide against the bark. The vibrations race through the xylem and phloem to reach the gall wasp larvae, which wriggle inside their protective chambers and hope that the whole tree is not falling down. Moths, flies, grey squirrels, blue tits, hawks, bats, dormice, spiders, pseudo scorpions, orb spiders, huntsmen, stag beetles, slugs, snails, ants, centipedes, algae, and woodpeckers steady themselves in holes and cavities as the whole city shakes. Then all settles again as the cow chews her cud quietly and the chicken pecks around the edges of her manure where creatures are rising to the surface in their droves to escape its toxic heat.

"A raven is like a writing desk as it's a vector of disease," he writes as his ink darkens further. Sooty granules run down from the quill to meet the paper halfway and the desk that he was working on transforms into a mini black hole.

I'm shocked. This world collapsed so quickly. Since I still cannot bring myself to speak to my father, I vow to tell my mother of the malignancy after spacetime lessons.

Spider Threads

I'm drawn to an extraordinary shimmering detail in a familiar realm of the tapestry that I've not noticed before. No more than a speck of dust, I follow the manifolds to a place where a woman dressed entirely in black quickly opens and slams shut more than a million tiny doors.

Although the bite from the regal-looking female Golden Orb spiders inside these tiny traps is not toxic, they are ruthlessly fierce. At first she'd capture twenty spiders in a web nursery and only found three remaining. She takes the precaution of fashioning tiny harnesses to restrain each of them from indulging their cannibalistic appetites.

Now they're milked like cows for the gold coloured thread that spews from their spinnerets. Up to 400 yards from each, just think of the length! The thread is twisted by hand into a single strand, and twisted again with three other 24-filament strands to make the kilogramme of silk thread – stronger than steel or Kevlar, but far more flexible.

While alchemists seek to transform base black metals such as lead into gold, she seeks a different kind of super power – invincibility. Nurturing plans to become the blackest of all spiders, she now begins her search for the darkest dye with which to transmute the threads of her precious dress.

Hybrid Zoo

Habitual rivals Lovelace and Feynman, I think – there are just so many of them – are warming up before class starts.

Each has grasped the wrists and ankles of the other. They are rolling around as one combined hoop. Some of the smaller children admire them for a minute before trying the exercise for themselves. Endlessly tumbling circles are periodically broken by peals of uncertainty, or complaints of imbalance.

Being significantly older than the others, I feel uncomfortable warming up with them. I am stretching my hamstrings in particular, which feel tight owing to my wounds, which are still healing.

As my cousins roll about and spontaneously knit their bodies together like flesh-spaghetti, I begin to recognise the nature of my cultural disconnect.

Even though I still live with my parents, I have become an individual.

Now let me first say that every hyperbolic weaver is encouraged to individuate. We're all expected to think and act autonomously and become completely self-reliant. No *deus-ex-machina* rescues us when we're stranded, or comes to our aid at times of grave danger. Therefore, as we venture out to conduct our repairs and collect our stories, we increasingly learn self-reliance. But as I watch the younglings tumble and bounce, splice and divide as a standing wave of physical transformation – I realise that I've forgotten how to think with and through others.

I roll up from the ground cracking my vertebrae in sequence as Ackermann enters the room.

"We'll do this first exercise in pairs. Grab a partner."

The children scatter, avoiding me. I feel like the ugly one in a game of kiss chase.

My heart sinks. I'm already feeling woefully out of place in my own community. Nor can I hope to match the suppleness of the younglings' rubber bones that gives their movement a fluid quality.

Franklin grabs my hand and drags me to the centre of the room. Her eyes are so wide and full of expectation that her enthusiasm for whatever happens next is already rubbing off on me. I draw a deep, diaphragmatic breath.

"Choose an animal. First, show each other your animal. Then put them together as one creature."

Before I can decide what I'm going to be in a way that allows me to retain a modicum of adult dignity, Franklin is already running around on her hands with her legs threaded over her shoulders stretching her four-inch tongue down to the ground. I wonder if there is anything such as a double-jointed tongue.

"What are you?"

"Anteater."

I'm trying not to get too bothered by the idea of a two-legged anteater. But it's my turn. I gobble and stagger around like a turkey.

"Keep the noise down everyone!"

I try again at a lower volume.

"Dinosaur!"

I've heard it's true that the modern descendants of dinosaurs are our feathered friends. But I give up trying to explain, be intellectual, rationalise, anatomically correct or naturalistic in any shape way or form. Instead I simply submit to the opportunities we make for each other. For the next part of the exercise Franklin and I form a magnificent anteatosaur. We gobble and stagger menacingly around with our incredibly long tongue out. Our creature is apparently so convincing that some of the children take cover by rolling up like armadillos and pill bugs under chairs. The effortless mass hysteria provoked by the anteaosaur wins vigorous commendation from Ackermann.

Over the next couple of hours we become an angry crocaroo, a hippofly whose aerodynamics defy all the conventional laws of physics and a sabre toothed wolfrabbit that shrieks like a banshee when it jumps to the Moon. We mix and match animal body parts repeatedly until it becomes second nature. We pair up with others. As hybrid creature formations we say "hello," wrestle for survival and between us enact a veritable monstrous zoo.

By the time Ackermann calls time on our yelpings, couplings, uncouplings and absurd gymnastics, I'm not only exhausted but also realise that I've had one of the best days that I've spent for a long time.

I give Franklin a big parting hug as a way of saying 'thank you'. But it's nothing special to her. She's looking for a way to surf Shelley's long plait and singing conveyor belt, which have typically appeared from nowhere, and I'm already forgotten.

Rachel Armstrong

I plunk myself down on the floor and burst into laughter. Of course! My culture. This is how it should be.

Love Story

I am sipping moon milk tea by the Loom. Beside me, Shelley is writing furiously while jiggling a line of excitable children on her knee. Little wonder I can't get her attention. I crave grown-up company. A group of relatives arrive and I'm happy to join them.

"We're exchanging stories."

They're just at the end of a rather peculiar tale about a man who spends all day collecting strands of rubbish. He weaves them into the shrubbery that stretches along the road between his house and the local shops, which blooms daily with his sculptures. Some are studded with undulating concentric folds that are cantered on pearl-like nuclei. Many pieces are as delicate as lace and flamboyant as bowerbird nests. Others are mushrooming crochet formations that billow in the wind and appear to trail onwards indefinitely into smaller and smaller threads. Some are musical instruments made from hollow twists that amplify hedge bird song. They are collected as gifts for family members, or as tokens of affection by lovers. Even small creatures covet them as scaffolding for their new homes. He says he's making nature, but they say he was committed to an asylum.

Stunned by this injustice, I'm finding it hard to speak.

They choose this moment to ask me to tell a story.

"I don't have one."

"Of course you do. Tell us a love story. Everyone has a love story."

I begin to remind everyone that according to Maxwell's book Principles of Material Pragmatism, feelings aren't part of a hyperbolic weaver's practice.

They're all smiling at me. Obviously there is something that I need to know.

"Material Pragmatism was only written because Maxwell's heart was eaten. Devoured by a woman from the dark universe. It's all there in the book of Exceptions."

Why do relatives always poke fun?

"Come on, tell us your love story." They insist, drawing closer.

"Okay. Rose lived on a remote island in a well-kept seafront cottage.

Her equally elderly friend, Cathy, lived a little distance away in the village centre, which was all of seventeen small bungalows. There wasn't much to do each day but to seek good company. This they would do by taking tea together at ten o'clock in the village café. Since Cathy had very bad hips and found it difficult to walk, Rose would wrap up warmly, pull on her favourite woolly hat and walk from the seaside to the teashop. Once a week she baked a special cake or biscuit for them both to enjoy over their conversation. The café staff didn't mind them bringing home cooking along, as the women were regular customers and they weren't exactly busy. So Cathy would sit in the window looking out into the cobbled square, waiting for Rose to come."

"Is this a love story?"

"One day, Cathy fell and the authorities took her to hospital to have her hips fixed. There was no way for Rose to check up on her friend, as she was not a relative, so she turned up day after day at the village tea shop and sat in the window seat. But Cathy never came back. Poor Rose imagined that her friend had been cured and was now walking up and down high streets everywhere, possibly with brand new hips and shopping for herself. But Rose missed Cathy. Eventually she became disappointed that her friend did not join her and stopped enjoying going out every day. She lost interest in food. She forgot to talk to anyone. Years passed. Each day was now exactly the same for Rose, as she had nothing to look forward to. Then Rose's family remembered they had an elderly relative with a property they could sell. So they invited themselves over to the island, but were horrified to find that the old woman was still alive and well."

"This isn't a love story."

"If the family were going to take possession of her home, they needed to find something wrong with Rose. So they sent for a helicopter ambulance, because she lived such a terribly long way from anywhere, and packed her off to hospital. When she arrived in casualty, Rose's relatives told the hospital staff that she had 'deteriorated' and was in urgent need of medical review. While the health care teams tried to make sense of everything, Rose's family threw her stuff away and put the cottage up for sale. It wasn't hard to convince the authorities that the elderly woman had lost her marbles. She had not taken off her favourite woolly hat since Cathy left. Over the years Rose's hair had twisted itself into the woolly hat and built up into a knot with impressive sculptural qualities."

"Is there a knitting algorithm –?"

"Ssssh, Rose remained compliant. But if the nursing staff tried to touch her hat, she became ferociously animated. It was the one thing that reminded her of Cathy – all that was worthwhile before. But the authorities were determined that Rose should be 'normalised' for admission. So they tried to cut off her hat with scissors, which were blunted by the strength of the old woman's hair. Then, orderlies were invited to hold her down while they attempted removal using shears. Someone even suggested that an electric bread knife might be appropriate but they couldn't find a long enough extension cord to give it a go. Every time they tried to take Rose's hat off, she put up a fierce fight. Despite her feistyness Rose was also an elderly woman and within a week her spirit broke. Just as she was giving up the will to live, her hat split open and a small family of circus midgets stepped out of it."

"Is this the love story?"

"They introduced themselves to Rose and kept her company. She was afraid that the health care staff would take them away from her so kept them hidden from view. When prying eyes were gone they would sit with the old woman for tea and cake – even when the tea itself was unpalatably cold. Rose loved the company of the midgets. They were incredible acrobats and kept her entertained for hours. For the first time in a very long time there was a spark in Rose's eye and she reconnected with the wonders of the world. But, of course, the authorities had not forgotten about the old woman's hat-hair. They were determined it should go. One day they sedated her against her will. Then they took her to theatre and shaved off her hat-hair using heavy duty horse clippers. The midget circus troupe inside were terrified. Fortunately, the whole edifice was removed in one go and nobody attempted to look inside the old ball of hair-wool. When the surgery was over the hat-hair sculpture was thrown into the rubbish bin with the midgets still inside. Rose was then returned to the geriatric ward, but when she came around the shock of losing her hat-hair and her tiny community of friends killed her. That night the midgets athletically escaped the garbage can but discovered they were too late to save their companion."

"This isn't a love story. Does anyone think this is a love story?"

"To add heartbreak to agony, one of the tiny circus troupe discovered that Rose was going to be cremated."

Everyone gasps. Incinerating a body in our culture is considered a crime against Nature. Decomposition practices such as burial or feeding a corpse to sacred animals like vultures are considered acceptable rites of passage for our dead. We believe that everyone is made up of matter that has a purpose in the world, which will passed on into other bodies. But, since ash is so biologically toxic, cremation robs the dead of the possibility of reincarnation.

"The circus troupe vowed that if they can't save Rose in this world, they will make sure her body is prepared for her next life. Just as the midgets struggled to move Rose's corpse to a safe hiding place, a very tall hyperbolic weaver cast his thread into the ward. As luck would have it, he'd come to repair a breach in spacetime. He instantly recognised the beautiful midget Shelley as the woman of his dreams and, in the way that befits spacetime weavers, the giant and midget fell deeply in love. Newton carefully built a composting mound by the sea for the old woman, and buried her so she could look out towards the sunrise every morning until her body had moved on. The burial ceremony was conducted at midnight, but although tearful goodbyes had been said to the old woman, Shelley and Newton were unable to part from each other. So giant and diminutive circus troupe became a family and traveled onwards using spacetime fibres to take them towards new adventures together.

In the morning the authorities came to cremate Rose and found only an empty suit and a pair of aluminium chopsticks. To this day, I think they believe that the old woman had faked her death so that she could escape the hospital ward in search of her hat-hair. As far as I know they're still looking for her. And, what's more, none of us has any intention of setting the record straight."

Callous

Newton is upset that the worlds we inhabit are becoming uncaring.

"I was in the park the other day watching an old man feed the birds. After a while I realised that he was already dead. Nobody noticed that he'd gone or that the birds were not flocking around him like Saint Francis of Assisi, but eating his corpse."

This is a horrible image, but typical of Newton's casual capacity for incidental horror. It's never really clear when my father is telling a tale designed to provoke a set of thoughts, or describing something that actually happened. Annoyingly, he also does not distinguish the two. Right now, the figure of an old man being devoured by winged vermin is too emotionally powerful to simply change the subject. However, I am not sure I've forgiven him for treating me like a youngling, but also realise that this is my only chance to tell him about what I've seen – especially if the next thing he decides to do, is to lay-into me again for being a flawed spacetime weaver.

"Newton, could extreme selfishness actually contaminate matter?"

I feel his lightless eyes reading my thoughts. I flinch, he can see straight through me, literally – my heart valves slapping anxiously, my emotions spinning around my amygdala, chyme sloshing from one part of my intestine to the next – I'm feeling highly exposed and vulnerable. But I keep my nerve.

"You've seen something."

"Yes. I don't know what it is, but when I origamy the terrains are scarred with a material that seems like proliferating soot. It's dirty, foamy with rolled edges, morose and malicious. It's not even truly alive, as such. But it feels bleakly sociopathic and seems intent on invading this realm."

He looks at me with solemnity.

"How often have you come across this?"

"Oh, before quite recently, not at all. Or maybe I've suffered too much spacetime amnesia. But of late it's happening all the time and it's more vigorous than I initially recall. It is now translating into the Loom's fabric, when it wasn't before. For starters, it's all over Klein's manifold. At first I thought it was some kind of interstellar splash from the violent

153

birth of an atypical star system. But now, it's more like a creeping body of formless matter capable of engulfing terrains, cities and even planets with shocking voracity. I'm afraid it's coming from a parallel realm and is traversing spacetime."

"Indeed. This is worrying news indeed."

"Do you know what it is?"

Frustratingly Newton does not answer me. He simply stands up and walks over to the Loom inspecting the tapestry while slowly shaking his hardening boil, which has yellowed significantly. This is unhelpful. I ask several times what he's thinking but he's not giving anything away. Is it really that terrifying? I guess it must be, and it's giving me a headache.

@£%!%££$£$$£dirty*&^&^%^%$$£$^^&(*^unclean(*********
**)infiltrate^%&%^$$%@@*%(^rotten101010101000000thousandeye
s110010100101011

I need to lie down and shut my eyes.

Antboard

Ackermann rolls out a maze-like tapestry on to the floor. The younglings and I spread out around it. It is an incredibly detailed structure that seems impossible to solve, which is made with tiny stitches that rise and roll in manifolds.

"This is the Antboard," explains Ackermann, "It is a game played by two teams in four dimensions. Antboard is a model of spacetime that helps us develop skills for working in multidimensional space. It's an analogue platform for exploring reality, something like the Loom but it's much simpler and uses living creatures as part of the computational system. By playing the Antboard we can see for ourselves just how multidimensional space and four dimensional space work together – and when they don't. It is full of contradictions and paradoxes. Expect the game to surprise you; it does not automatically follow that those playing in multidimensional space will beat those playing in four dimensional space."

He starts to describe Antboard in terms of how we imagine moving around in multi and four dimensional space. It's also how we can develop new skills for tactical gameplay.

My theorising of what Ackermann's telling us is getting in the way of understanding what I am being asked to do. I wonder how much of his rules and instructions the younglings understand. But they're already looking at the sugar cubes and flicking stray crystals at each other to see what they do.

Ackermann produces two Perspex containers. One is full of sugar cubes, which weigh four hundred grammes exactly.

The other vessel is an ant farm that is home to a colony of super smart insects. Exactly one hundred ants will play the game. None of them will be hurt. If anyone harms a creature, a sugar cube – which weighs four grammes – will be deducted from their score.

"They're special ants. Each ant can carry one sugar cube, which means they can lift objects about four thousand times heavier than they are. They are super smart – perhaps, in their own way, as clever as a rat."

Some younglings lick their lips at the thought of sucking on a sugar cube, but it's the long chains of ants that fascinate them most.

A hand goes up "What does that actually mean? Are rats smart?"

Ackermann is succinct.

"These ants can not only figure out what you're doing during the game, they'll behave in ways that you won't expect."

"Like playing a computer at chess, then?"

"Yes, but computer chess is only about thinking. Smart ants are incredible doers; they're much better acrobats than you are."

At this challenge a few of the younglings demonstrate their impossible litheness, throwing their legs over their shoulders and spinning a few somersaults, as a challenge to the ants to keep up with them.

They quickly calm down as Ackermann explains the rules of the game. "You must keep as many of the hundred sugar lumps in play as possible."

I can hear the box containing the ants making rhythmic sounds. Are they already studying us? They may not be able to see us, but I wonder if they can hear us – and whether they're capable of cheating?

"The sugar is weighed before and after the game. The winner is the team that ends up with most sugar. But the sugar team is going to have to work hard. Their efforts to keep the sugar cubes safe will be undone by the smart ants, which are very, very hungry, as they've not been given any breakfast. Given that each ant consumes four times its own body mass every hour, these insects will be ravenous. Teams have only one minute to set up the starting geometry of their sugar stacks. This can take place anywhere on the board but once they're set the game is on. The ants will be introduced into the maze and will be looking for sugar."

"So how do we play?"

I ponder the word 'play' for a moment, imagining how the ants might sound if their little black bodies were considered musical notations upon the board. Could they become an ant symphony?

"Play lasts for fifteen minutes after the ants are introduced. The sugar team can keep their cubes safe by moving them only using one chopstick. This means that the players of one team can flick them, roll them or stack them around the board. As the sugar cube travels over the sides of the maze, you'll be thinking and working in multidimensional space. The ants won't be able to anticipate where the sugar will land. However, the sugar team has to be careful, as any cubes that are catapulted off the board will be lost. Four grammes will be deducted from the final score. Also, sugar cubes will break if you poke them around too much. This means you'll leave sugar grains around for hungry ants and you'll lose out on the final weigh in. The trick is to keep the sugar away from the hungry ants using the fewest moves."

"What about the ants?"

"Human antboard players decide where the ants get into the maze. Your main job is to think along with the ants and guide them to get at the sugar, using only one chopstick to herd them. Although the ants can't jump around and enter multidimensional space, they will figure out that multidimensional space exists – if they haven't already done so. They do 'cheat' but that's not banned. In fact their ability to reinvent the rules and discover ways of breaking out from the confines of their reality is part of the game. One way they could do this would be to climb up on top of each other to make a very tall pile of ants that allows them to move atop the maze and take short cuts. They're very agile, but such a manoeuvre is also very tricky to achieve. The ants will have inbuilt ideas about how to get to the sugar. You'll be working with the ants to help them go against some of their assumptions and instincts, while working even more effectively with what they already know."

"What happens if the ants are so good at breaking rules they escape?"

"If the ants leave the board then the ant team will lose a sugar lump for each one that goes missing."

"That doesn't seem fair on those that play with the ants! Sugar seems a much safer option. It's more predictable."

"Each team will play both ants and sugar. The winning team is the one that has the most sugar on the board at the end of the game," reassures Ackermann.

My head is buzzing with instructions, conditions and possibilities. It's almost impossible to concentrate as we're divided into two groups. The younglings squeal as Ackermann makes it look easy to count out a hundred very smart ants from the farm and transfer them into a dry, opaque container.

"Does anyone know why we have to keep them in a lightless container until we're ready to start?"

"Because they'll remember the board."

"Exactly. They'll already be playing."

I'm now intimidated by the idea of smart ants. Ants are already smart enough, thank you very much.

Starting off on the sugar team, we think about how we're going to place our hundred cubes. If we spread them out too much we'll definitely lose some to the ants, as they won't have far to travel to get to them. But if we pack them all in one location then the ant players will simply introduce the ants at that point. The only way to begin is to spread out the sugar as far as possible and make some sacrificial offerings. But once the ants are in the maze then we must flick the sugar cubes to the farthest points away from them, in different locations around the maze, without losing them from the Antboard. Effectively it's a race against time and ant intelligence, in three and four dimensions.

There's a lot of excitement as the ant team introduce their players in the centre of the maze. It's astonishing how quickly a smart ant can devour a sugar cube. Ackermann says that their brain uses nearly all the sugar. We take turns using the single chopstick to flick and poke our sugar to safety. Many cubes are being catapulted out of play and the ants appear to be getting quicker. The ant team makes excellent progress using their chopstick to train the ants to make team formations. They learn to span the channels of the Antboard in staggering geometric patterns. I am frankly stunned when the smart ants suddenly catapult one of their members into the air to grab a flying sugar cube, like water polo players.

"Hey! They're not supposed to work in multidimensional space."

"Those are our rules. Not theirs!"

At the end of play I'm surprised just how many cubes we've lost. We're left with about eight on the board. But there is no time to contemplate our losses; we need to bond with the ants.

The sugar team makes a very similar opening play to ours but they've stacked their cubes a bit more than we did. We come in hard on a pile of cubes in the centre of the Antboard, which disappear in almost no time at all. In the next few moves we also manage to skewer an ant through sheer carelessness by using the chopstick as a bridge. Now, we're down to a score of seven cubes because of this and the insects turn on us. They form a menacing, high-reaching tower and start climbing the aluminium chopstick wielded by one of our younglings. The terrified child instantly drops the instrument. But ant protest continues using the chopstick not only to form a bridge that helps them devour every sugar cube on the board but also enables them to resist being returned to the farm at the end of the game.

We are in a tactical standoff with an insect colony that has simply decided they do not want to play with us on ethical grounds. Why should they collaborate with careless murderers? Fortunately Ackermann appears to have mastered the powers of ant diplomacy. After a five-minute period of what can only be described as intense sugar negotiations, the insects are calm again.

We are declared the champions of the Antboard but it's very hard to feel that 'we' won anything. The real experts at Antboard are the ants.

I wonder just how much we over estimate our human intelligence. I mean, of course it exists and it's wonderful to be able to 'think', read and use language and all that stuff. Of course it is! Naturally, we value these abilities very highly indeed. But are these things really a measure of a 'superior' intelligence or just the expression of a unique kind of existence?

The smart ants bother me because, despite the superior size and apparent sophistication that we attribute to the human brain, they dominated that game. It shocks me how many assumptions we had already made about them and didn't even consider they could simply reinvent the rules according to their own value systems. I would not like to be on the opposing side in a serious dispute with those ants.

Gorse

Sooty gorse-like stitches are spreading throughout the Loom's tapestry and changing the fabric.

Instead of a scintillating pliant material, the stitches are coarse, tough, invasive, tenacious, and more like a chain of spikes than soft thread. They seem impossible to get rid of. Not knowing whether it's the right thing to do or not, I've secretly tried to pull them out, but this only increases their intensity, tension and darkness. Leaving them alone seems just as destructive, since they form a brutal suffocating barrier of tarry stitches that divides and strangles the fabric into a patchwork of isolated material islands. Even in the last few hours I've seen these isolated areas wither and rot.

Gorse propagates because it isn't limited by seed growth but by the horizontal growth established by plants. Once the dark blossoming gorse shrubs are cut, they rapidly sprout their impenetrable stands, like a hydra, sprouting rhizomatic heads and vigorously proliferating so they choke native ecosystems, reducing their diversity and degrading local habitats. The only way to get rid of gorse is to catch it early and mechanically uproot young sprouts when they first appear – that is, plucking them while they're still soft, pulling them out by the roots and then soaking them in poison.

An effective eradication practice for these gorse-like stitches therefore affronts the principles of life and, in doing so, goes against all our cultural values. Dealing with this malignancy is going to be very tricky indeed.

Climbs, Wraps and Drops

Circus is often equated with a specific structure called the Big Top. This three-dimensional space constructs the perception of boundaries in our performances. At the foot of this assembly is the circus ring, where performers begin the parade for their acts. But it is the cathedral like apex that draws our gaze upwards into the cosmos, while providing sites for the attachment of a thrilling range of aerial apparatuses.

Ackermann introduces us to Fibonacci, who has an annoying habit of rising on the tops of his toes when he's talking. This is not a nervous tic. It is his nature. He is an aerial being, who has to work very hard to stay in contact with the ground. From the tips of his toes Fibonacci says that at the heart of altitude acrobatics is trust, then strength, then flexibility. He is androgynously magnificent. But then all spacetime weavers are. We are interchangeable beings.

Fibonacci disappears up a thread so fine that it's completely invisible.

"There are three main categories of aerial tricks – climbs, wraps and drops."

Already younglings are scampering up the thread after him like insects, while Fibonacci effortlessly demonstrates basic acrobatic moves.

"Climbs can be purely practical like the Russian, which simply gets us from the bottom to the top of the cloth."

I look around and realise that I am the only one still standing on the ground.

"Other climbs are rather elegant, like the straddle climb, where you turn head over feet on the way up the cloth."

The strands judder as the younglings spin in exploratory ways, playing with a range of parameters from tension to speed and my grip slides. I save myself quickly and concentrate on my foot grip technique, while the younglings swarm in their ascent.

"Wraps are static poses where we wind the material around one or more parts of our bodies. At these heights this is harder than it looks. The quantity of the fabric – even when it's gossamer fine – is very heavy. In principle, though, as the wrap gets more complicated the cloth produces more friction and less effort is needed to hold us up. Some moves, such as the straddle-back-balance wrap, actually allow us to completely release our hands. We can also use foot locks to grab the cloths by wrapping them around out feet."

To be fair, we are born with an instinct to climb. It's almost a compulsion when we're younglings but as we lose our rubbery bounce it is counterbalanced by a fear of falling. My recent origamy adventures have only intensified my caution and sense of self-preservation. While I am more than familiar with leaping into the void during an origamy throw, being up here close to the apex of the Big Top is unsettling. Although I've practiced falling as a form of descent, this has taken place in effectively bottomless spaces – not in arenas where there is a very obvious hard floor.

As his voice disappears even further up the invisible thread, Fibonacci announces that today's exercises are centred on drops. He throws rivers of silk to the floor, bringing to mind bridal gowns, as the younglings continue to scamper after him like geckos.

I stop momentarily and look up. So does my heart. Fibonacci is close to the summit, which is about a hundred metres high. From here it would take around five seconds to fall, where a body is likely to reach a terminal velocity of around eighty miles per hour. That's fast. You try breaking in a car at that speed!

Fibonacci shows us how to lift ourselves up high on the cloths by folding ourselves into the material before releasing a section and falling to a lower position. We can combine free fall, rolls, rotations or jumps from which we can land in a new stance. The point of the exercise is to shape the fall, rather than strike a final pose. Of all the manoeuvres, the drops require the most strength, and are also the most potentially dangerous.

The first game is follow my leader. We have to slide down the cloth and stop when Fibonacci does. From a stuttering start, he takes us through bolder and bolder plunges, which require increasing physical strength as the unbroken fall gets longer and longer.

I'm having real trouble with letting go for more than a few seconds. My limbs don't have quite the same elasticity for gripping as the younglings do and I'm aware of my limits. While they may bounce to break their fall, I am much more likely to land like a falling egg. I try to recall how Valentina Tereshkova made such an art of her descent but it only makes me long for a space capsule.

Fibonacci has already reached the bottom. He ascends again, chiding me for my sloth. He grabs my arm and instinctively, I take the invitation to make a formation. Franklin spots us and decides that the game we're playing is better than her solo slide. She grabs my ankle. Together we plummet. Fibonacci takes me beyond my comfort zone as we lunge at the floor. I'm using the entire power in my leg muscles to brake. As we're metres from the bottom, Ackermann – who I never noticed entering the hall – flicks the trailing length of cloth on the floor, and we're airborne for the final part of the dive, spinning up into the air and landing together in a somersault.

"Again!"

The three of us climb. Other younglings follow us. Now we're in row formation. I try breathing deeply but my heart is racing too quickly. Just trust. Trust Fibonacci. He knows what he's doing.

Fibonacci, Franklin and me, are in the lowest row of the formation. Behind us are at least three other formations of younglings. There may be more of them, but I can't see that far behind me.

We plummet. At around two of five seconds I'm extremely uncomfortable. Fibonacci has sped up and has uncoupled as the spearhead of a death-defying drop. I am way out of my comfort zone. I'm pretty sure I'm unable to brake at this speed, especially with others behind me. Yet if I slow down now we'll all collide in catastrophe for sure. Then Fibonacci brakes. I do too, but I've forgotten to reapply rosin and I'm still sliding. My legs don't have the strength or grip to stop the descent at this speed.

I prepare to roll. Crash, or roll, so I keep on rolling to break my fall.

Then I feel tiny hands on my feet and legs. Younglings are passing me on the way down. They pull me upwards, in a range of lifts. Freed from the vice of gravity I travel upwards and then gracefully slide to the ground.

Fibonacci is jumping impossibly high in excitement on the very tip of his toes. I am convinced he is filled with helium.

"Bravo! Bravo! That was spectacular!"

But I can't share his excitement, I am sure that I nearly died. My heart valves are slapping chaotically inside my chest. My nosebleed makes my foot feel sticky and damp. As the younglings scurry up the fabric highway again, I pinch my nose wishing these pains in my head would stop.

(*&*^^%&^%^^$£pain^*&(^&*&^%&^%pain^&%^%&%$%$%
$£@£searingpain&^^%^%%&*()knives(^&^&^$^%£%$@chewing)))
!)!)!10101010101001010.

Scream

The woman with no nose screams, and I scream too – this dark mirror-image of me.

Something is scratching deep inside my skull. It spans the roof of my mouth and bends into my post-nasal space behind the cribriform plate, the bony saddle for the pituitary gland and the surrounding spaces in the temporal region of my skull. Here, a shuffling choir assembles. Their footsteps resonate inside my head, playing it like an instrument. I feel them slithering up into my posterior sinus before they burrow into my post-nasal capillary beds.

At some point the scraping becomes whispering.

They are discussing me.

"Who does she think she is?"

They don't trust me and I don't like their conversation.

"Thinks she's better than the rest of us."

Darned nosebleed.

I reach for my sleeve to pinch the bridge of my nose and stem the flow, but the woman stares at me in disbelief with a skeleton smile. There is no cartilage to put pressure on. Through blooded eyes, her sclerae drown in claret.

My eyes ache from the haemorrhage as the pressure in my head grows. I try to shut them for momentary relief, but they keep on staring through pupils that are no longer distinct and drip down into my cheekbones.

Leaking blood congeals on the floor as inky frogspawn lumps.

The voices continue to complain constantly about everything. There's not enough space, the light's no good and my eyes are too close together. They can't agree what they're going to do about the substandard quality of living that is possible inside my skull, which is much lower than their expectations.

They're determined to renovate, so they begin to argue about how they're going to increase their living space.

Then, someone shouts, "Let's eat our way out!"

Shadow

"We don't know where she came from. We think that she was lurking in the shadows all the time. Practising her dark arts on a captive army of spacetime spiders."

I'm curled around a moon milk tea, chatting to my relatives around the loom, whose names and status I still don't know. But we recognise each other. We're beyond introductions.

"She was most likely forged from negative space. Technically speaking, she was a shadow. Or, if she wasn't, she became one."

We pull our seats into a storytelling circle. My companions take it in turns to speak, like a well-choreographed routine.

"Maxwell was young, ambitious and impressionable. Twenty-something. A mere youngling. Like many career-minded men of his age, he desired a woman companion to take care of domestic arrangements."

"What about romantic love?"

"That too. But his story, as you know, is shaped by pragmatism."

"So there she was. Attentive, if not intense. Silent, if not appreciative and mysteriously exotic. So they married."

"They got hitched? Whatever was he thinking?"

"They were different times then. Marriage was expected. The state – and to a lesser extent the church – were still very much invested in the idea of family as a nuclear economic unit. It also gave their coupling a recognised moral integrity."

We all hiss between our teeth indignantly and shake our heads slowly. The very idea of regulating our expansive and multifarious troupe as an economic unit, let alone dictating what constitutes morality, is simply unthinkable. We challenge conventions. We do not conform to them.

"Almost overnight everything changed. Maxwell became isolated from everyone he knew and all that he had worked towards. What initially appeared to be an intense kind of devotion by the woman was actually a malignant form of control. The shade worked on poor Maxwell. She steadily and thoroughly undid him, severing his relationships, his work, and his life. The malignant shadow snip, snip, snipped away at Maxwell. Every day she stripped a fibre from his life and his beating heart, which she tore away like a Promethean vulture. She ate these morsels as a fine delicacy. Since Maxwell was generous she fattened on his demise growing stronger as he withered. When she had finished with his heart, she started on the rest of his entrails. When these were consumed she no longer needed a cage to contain him. But the malevolent creature's work was not yet done. Without innards Maxwell shrivelled. He was completely unrecognisable to those who knew him, a diminished, weakened shell of his former self. His health suffered, his self-esteem suffered and he even identified with the dreadful things the shade said about him. He was useless, lazy and impotent. To prove that she was right about his deficiencies, the shade forced herself on him, and punished him severely when he could not perform. Without guts of his own, she made herself his new physiology. Without objectivity, she became his truth. And without any link to society, she became his world. He was stranded."

It seemed impossible to understand how someone so smart could let this happen.

"Although the shadow was brilliantly devious and had manipulated herself into a position of power over him, Maxwell was still more intelligent and stronger than she was. But the young man realised that neither his mind nor strength alone could spring him from doom. He would have to be creative and patient in ways that he did not even consider possible. The shade's own weaknesses would be her undoing. She was incapable and greedy. No matter how much the shadow took from Maxwell, it would never be enough for her. There would come a point where she'd have to let him out of her sight, so that she could attend to her endless needs and desires. All Maxwell had to do was stay alive until that happened. But because Maxwell was resourceful and resilient, the shade could draw from him, like a spider sucking on a juicy fly, for a very long time. He waited one whole lifetime. Then two. During his third incarceration, Maxwell told himself every day that the current reality was not his life, that every second that passed was not real. He consciously vacated his wreck of a body and found ways of projecting himself into other places and other times. He learned how to astral travel and how to access other dimensions. He even found ways of imagining that he was someone else in another person's body. One day the shadow heard that a beautiful and wealthy young man had arrived in town. She could not resist going to see what this youth could offer her. Using all her powers of control, she trained security devices all around Maxwell – alarms, cameras and drones with lethal tazers. She would know every move he made. Satisfied that he could not possibly escape in her absence, she went to size up the visiting youth."

"Did Maxwell escape then?"

"No. He did not. You see, Maxwell correctly figured that the shade was anticipating an attempt and that if she caught him there would be no second chance. So Maxwell let the shade come and go. After the first return she looked for evidence that he'd tried to abscond. When she found none, she interrogated him relentlessly about what he'd been up to. The next time she went out, she was a little less diligent. She was even less dominating the time after that. By the end of the week she was almost careless in her overconfidence. As her anxiety about Maxwell's escape lessened, the shadow began to obsess much more about the new man in town. Gradually, her grip around Maxwell loosened."

We are spellbound at the impossibility of his situation.

"One day, when the shade's thoughts were full of the youth whose assets she was seeking, Maxwell suddenly plucked a spacetime fibre from out of the strange shadows he'd learned to see. Without any prior training, or knowledge Maxwell split that string into a ladder and cast long and deep knots into the implicate order. Within seconds, Maxwell was no longer stranded. He had escaped."

We cheered.

"Not so fast! Maxwell knew that this was the most dangerous time of all. The shadow would be furious that her control over him had been broken and would be after him with her killer drones and mobile prison. She would declare him insane and have him first committed to an asylum and then, when he was mentally broken, she'd devour him slice by slice."

The whole situation was unbearable. We longed for Maxwell to be truly free.

"Maxwell knew the shade would scour the universe looking to regain her power over him. Without him, she had no resources and no one to mediate between her vicious need and the rest of the world, which she knew would not consider her kindly. So, before she even had time to realise he had gone, he buried himself deep under a compost heap. With all her airs, ambitions and pretentions, Maxwell knew that the last place the shade and the drones would search was in the basest of all materials. For forty days and forty nights he kept the company of earthworms, dung beetles and bluebottles. He heard their conversations. He listened to how they saw the world and the way they thought it worked. He attended to their troubles and found joy in their stories of great adventure. Maxwell reasoned that if the smallest, humblest of all creatures could thrive with dignity against the odds then so could he. When he rose on the fortieth day from under the heap of manure that had sheltered him, the parasitic shade and all her lethal instruments were gone. She had already moved on to her next victim. Maxwell was free."

We were on our feet whooping for joy.

"But we're still not done! At first, Maxwell had nowhere to go. Two lifetimes and more of being denigrated by the woman he had literally given his heart and innards to, changed him. He needed to build a new identity. Through sheer force of will he grew new muscles and organs that were even stronger than his original ones. With intense meditation he connected his artificial tissues to an increasingly powerful intellect. Soon he was a master athlete as well as a pioneer in the exploration of multi-dimensional space. But although Maxwell's physical and cognitive recovery was truly astonishing, his emotional scars never mended. Although Maxwell would never be mean, cynical or unkind to another living creature, he could not face his feelings. So while his organs beat stronger and more precisely than ever before, he buried their pain. To avoid the risk of emotional violence happening in his life again, he vowed to never pair with one person and instead brought together the most incredible athletes, circus performers and acrobats, who flocked around Maxwell to learn the arts of multi-dimensional exploration. As a gift to his kin, Maxwell wrote a great philosophical and practical work entitled 'Material Pragmatism'. He vowed that those he cared for would never be vulnerable to the cruelty of others, or be disempowered by feeling sorry for themselves."

Architecture

Fibonacci scatters a pile of bamboo poles amongst us.

"Today you are architecture."

He doesn't explain what he means by this but we immediately start bending these materials and using them to pivot around points in the ground like spinning tops.

Just as we establish the limits of bamboo and figure out how to catapult ourselves around with the poles, Fibonacci begins snatching them and randomly hurling them back into the centre of the gym.

"Hey!"

The symmetry of the space is broken as younglings and rods begin spontaneously crossing each other. They pass and entwine in many incidental planes. Object formations start to emerge, vortex-like, and disintegrate like waterfalls at their edges. Some acrobats now have more than two poles, which they're twisting around and vaulting with in new ways, which invite further kinds of movement. Others are using the poles as bridges and search skywards for new territories to occupy in the acrobatic space. The air reverberates with the splitting and refolding of bodies and linked objects. It is increasingly hard to discern where one acrobat stops and another starts, or to separate their intersections with this fractal sea of moving objects and emergent formations.

But Fibonacci is not done yet with his sorcery. Now he hurls reels of long, brightly coloured ribbons into the heart of the tumbling acrobats. We respond to these as a maypole. Some of us use the rotating weaving formation to balance nimbly on to the apex of the carousel. Others weave the yarns into patterned fabrics using the bamboo as giant chopsticks, while a few grab the fibres and shuttle their own bodies backwards and forwards through the spaces between the ribbons. They stitch themselves into the multi-coloured canvas, as if they were part of its print.

Collectively, we are a spinning, knitting, oscillating computer. Rubin and Curie start to rub the bamboo poles together, producing a rhythmic rattling noise, followed by a clicking sound like snapping fingers. The sound waves seem to reach our ears, spreading through our bones and expand within our muscles so that we become stronger, creative and seamlessly interconnected. Now we respond instinctively to Fibonacci's symmetry breaking, producing rich floral displays accompanied by a magnificent percussion orchestra. Perpetually inventing new configurations of colour, form, sound and movement, we undulate as one giant metaorganism and take on the character of the Loom's operating system.

But as we head for a break the rustling, stamping and flapping of canvases does not diminish. I look around to see who remains within the rehearsal space. Nobody is using the poles or the cloths – and there's an all too familiar pressure growing behind my eyes.

Hollow Head

I smash the great enamel knocker against the wooden door.

"Is there anybody there?"

But it is locked and the ornate carving, still tingling with vibration, grins at me. There is no other way inside and the windows are far too high to peer into. Something flutters, but the sound is split into a million echoes by the oddness of the place, and it's impossible to say which direction it's heading. A feculent stench leaks into the air. Something has recently died here. Perhaps it's coming from behind this door.

I bang on the entrance even harder this time, and lift my head to shout at the windowsills.

"Tell them that I kept my word."

But nothing stirs.

My echoing footsteps subside as I stand on my toes walking backwards, scouring the prominent sills for the remotest signs of activity. But the windows remain lightless.

I pick up two flat white stones that look like ground bone fragments and artfully launch them at one of the windowpanes. They bounce up the wall and sit stubbornly on the sill. Then I'm drenched in glass splinters and I realise that I've been knocking on a nasal cavity trying to draw the attention of my empty orbits.

%(&^%^%^scrape$%@£@$@£@£$@^%£$@%@$%$%^whim per(*&@$%!@%£$^%&&^&%^£$()£@*(whineVB@$$£%^&OYV O^^scratch&^%^@£$%^&&I&%$&bitch10101001010101

The Book of Exceptions

You don't read The Book of Exceptions. You feel it.

You might expect a book to be written in some kind of prose but it's not. Exceptions is a manuscript formed by the artificial organs and failed tissue cultures that replaced Maxwell's extracted body parts.

You may wonder how a man who has no innards can actually produce such artefacts.

After his natural innards were eaten by the shade, Maxwell set about replacing them using the latest biotechnologies that reconfigured his anatomy. Although he was stronger and more lithe, he was intensely emotional – more so than ever before.

Finding this extreme sensitivity unbearable, Maxwell removed the first set of innards that he grew using specially designed extraction tools that he'd developed through his mastery of Ancient Egyptian writings. Maxwell used a primitive form of keyhole surgery that left no scars and removed the new innards through his nose. Then he wrapped them between the expanses of organ fat, known as the greater and lesser omenta, and buried them in hot sand. Any cloned tissue cultures that had grown and failed during the development of his synthetic organs were added to the collection of desiccating tissues. He left them to mummify for a lifetime. Finally, Maxwell dug up the hardened organs with their prototypes and bound them in soft linen. He stored them in a wooden chest, assuming that nobody would come across them.

Maxwell was now part of a large circus community full of curious children. It was not long before tiny fingers and wide eyes discovered the desiccated entrails and ran to their parents crying inconsolably. Family members soon realised what these strange fleshy things were and gave them new life and honour by turning them into a book. Then they returned this relic to the chest and buried it in a place where it would never be discovered. By this time, however, word about the compelling emotional potency of Maxwell's desiccated innards was out. Indeed, the enfleshings had already been copied multiple times over and called "The Book of Exceptions." While I can assure you that the originals are safely lost to the living word three simulacra remain. One of these copies is now beneath the Loom, kept safe from the reach of tiny people under Shelley's watchful eye and reprimanding plait-lash.

It is not forbidden to experience The Exceptions.

However, it is advised they should never be encountered by an unprepared mind. To do so is truly an overwhelming experience. Furthermore, should a scholar wish to imbue wisdom from the Exceptions then some skill in divination is mandatory. Various auguries may be used such as haurspicy: the reading of animal entrails, hepatoscopy: divination with livers, scapulimancy: information from the shoulder blades of animals, or cardioscopy: auguries of the heart. Readers of these organ systems do not encounter facts, but wisdom conferred by feelings – a waterfall of tactile poetry with the potential to drive the unaware quite senseless.

I'm in hiding here under the Loom in this tiny dark space as I've just encountered the Exceptions for the very first time.

I thought I was prepared but I'm utterly traumatised by the depths of Maxwell's grotesque abjection. I'm equally ecstatic through the encounter of his sublime resurrection. I'm all at odds with myself and the world and really not sure what I think or feel about anything right now.

While I am no auger, I feel that in encountering The Exceptions, I have touched the very substance of humanity. Perhaps I have come a little closer to an understanding of it – that to live is a paradox – in that we are bedevilled with extraordinary vulnerability and strength. We experiment with these contradictory states through our bodies in ways that can't be fixed, solved, or meaningfully concluded – but through which we are compelled to feel and live.

Fibonacci Spiral

Today we fashion a writing instrument – a great spiral made of steel, bamboo, chicken bones, corvid feathers and rope, which resembles several giant antennae plaited and curled into a tortured Fibonacci joint. This can be steered by a commanding staff, enabling us to spin it around like a hoop between us and examine the world as it might be experienced through ratios: 0, 1, 1, 2, 3, 5, 8, 13, 21, 34, 55, 89, 144, 233, 377, 610, 987, 1597, 2584, 4181, 6765, 10946, 17711, 28657, 46368, 75025, 121393, 196418, 317811.

We build spirals of matter like towers of DNA, mark their repetitions, look for their codes and search for the evidence within the heart of snails, sunflower heads, delphiniums, ragwort, corn marigolds, pine cones, hydrozoa, cineraria, asters, rabbit populations, black-eyed susans, chicory, rose petals, fruit, leaves, pineapples, lilies, irises, buttercups, cow parsley, Romanesco broccoli, angelica, larkspur, columbine, animal horns, mollusc shells, radiolaria, daisies, the cochlea of the inner ear, honeybees, fingers, bryzoa, corals, aloe, gastropods, cabbage leaves, the stock market, snowflakes, plantain, pyrethrum, Michaelmas daisies, the nautilus, starfish, superstring theory, dolphin tails, and trees.

"Magic," say some of the younglings.

"Logic," cry others.

"Order," shouts Fibonacci, "Observe the patterns within patterns, rules within rules, ratios upon ratios, strange numerologies – who can deny the truth of a mathematical world now the "golden" ratios, have been discovered?"

My father's dissent stirs within me.

"What are these figures bent around?" I ask. "How does matter matter in these geometric gymnastics and at what point in our cosmic fabric does the sense of these relational manifolds start to unravel?"

Fibonacci rises to the very tips of his toes in glee. "Exactly the point!" he cries, as he summons us to leave the plodding geometries on the ground where they belong and climb into the spooky realm of quantum rods and radiation sticks, black holes, white dwarfs, gravitational warps and the wefts of sticky strings. Now, in the realm of impossible matter, Fibonacci offers us a shivering sequence as reality oscillates into higher dimensions, where dark energy and matter breathes quietly upon luminous matter, shifting and shuffling us into parallel universes where we seem to dissolve entirely.

Many blurred faces and fingers look down on me.

"Oh help!" Did I just lose consciousness in that class? There is something wrong with me.

Recall

"The child!"

Have I forgotten her, or did I imagine her?

Anxiety spreads through my chest, down both arms and radiates like drills into my teeth.

Arachnophobia

The Loom Garden is always comforting. But today I am unusually anxious, which is not helped by the tapestry's spacetime manifolds unravelling. They're fracturing into an instantly recognisable sooty material. But it's different this time. The malignancy is no longer subtle or confined to edges and shadows. This is an obviously invasive, aggressive, destructive form of matter actively boring its way through spacetime. I still don't know what it is.

Everyone is gathering around the Loom and Newton invites us to prepare for a formal announcement. He seems particularly tall today and has begun to smell again, while his yellow horn seems stable. Elders begin to join us. Some younglings are crying. The room is tense with infectious anxiety. This is the stuff of nightmares – and not just my own.

I turn to cousin (885, 295, 947). She tells me that she'd rather be called 'Gödel'. Numbers are for younglings.

"What's going on?"

"It's just started. Klein's territory in the Andromeda constellation around the Blue Snowball Nebula is under attack."

"Judging by the loss of stiches, the situation could tip towards a critical threshold and become a cosmic emergency. Right now, the region seems to be confined to Andromeda, but if it continues we'll lose connectivity in the Implicate Order in this region. Potentially, throughout all of spacetime. Even in the parallel realms. At this rate, it might already be beyond our repair capacity."

I'm about to say that – whatever it is – may have already produced metastatic seeds. Maybe it's just luck but I seem to have a knack of finding them – or perhaps I am being drawn towards them. However, I still don't know what this thing is and before I can ask Gödel, Newton summons us to order.

We gather around the Loom according to our ages. Eldest at the front, while those who can't keep still for a few minutes hold hands at the back. This stops them running around or breaking into teetering formations while everyone concentrates on the pressing situation. Of course, those who shepherd the restless ones form a backup ring behind them.

Newton cuts an impressive figure in delivering the gravity of the occasion, sucking the light towards him, which largely downplays the lesion on his forehead. He hands the floor to the eldest of us all, Maxwell, then takes his place on the floor in a strange yoga position, looking out from under an arch he's made with his feet, seemingly collapsing into his own space.

We seldom see Maxwell. He's somewhere in the realm of six hundred. In comparison, my father seems like a spring chicken. We watch while Maxwell unsteadily uncurls his legs. It's like watching a deck chair unfold. Then he furniture-walks all the way to the front of the Loom, his muscle fibres writhing uncontrollably. He's incredibly gaunt – a skeleton whose skin is so thin and gravity-strained that if you got close enough it would be possible to see individual red corpuscles passing through the butterfly capillaries around his nose. Despite his erratic gait and fragility, he commands attention. We wait uncomfortably as his jaw trembles for an impossibly long time before he begins to speak.

"So, it starts again."

Maxwell's lips continue to move like oil on a light screen even after they finish this portentous announcement.

"Spacetime Spiders are invading the Implicate Order."

We're all reminded of the Great Spider Battle that took place in the region around the Andromeda galaxy – between M31 and M33 – only a century ago. They were difficult times, when the spiders tore a great black hole in the Implicate Order. I wasn't born into this reality then but I do know the stories. Of course I do. I recall the tales of vanquish that have been with me since childhood. I've heard how spacetime weavers throw yarns better than any spider silk. How they're faster, more agile and coordinated than any of the dark beasts. That Maxwell himself could grapple an arachnid to the ground and wrap a hold on it until it submits. As I have grown I have also come to understand that these accounts are not exactly factual. I suspect that we didn't actually defeat the spiders but reached stalemate in our hostilities. It is said that the spider queens gave birth to a cobwebbed army of stillborns and the dark armies returned to her aid. They never came back. We were just incredibly lucky.

But of course we weave the tales to create the best possible image of ourselves.

When I was small, the great tales of bravery and triumph – of great circus feats – were completely believable. Now they feel more like propaganda. I understand how living history needs stories that help its next generations live unboundedly, yet I am convinced the spiders have also learned lessons; and if they're back, they are composing a very different future to the one that we envisage.

"What's a pie-duh?" Asks a small voice at the back.

"It's an incredibly dangerous creature. Big as a dog and smart as a cat. It's from the dark universe, made of negative space and shoots anti-matter poison from its mouth."

"I don't like the pie-duh!"

As the child bursts into tears, a standing wave of collective shushing restores order to the meeting.

"What's to be done?"

"We must broker a new kind of peace."

"Spiders? They're not interested in peace. Only disconnection!"

There's discussion about what a truce with the arachnids might look like. Most think it's completely out of the question. Right now, though, we're completely unprepared for an onslaught.

"We must kill the buggers! Every last one of them!"

Stunned silence. This is unthinkable.

Maxwell's face is thunderous. He micro oscillates with outrage. Eventually he booms with terrifying authority.

"We are circus. Not executioners. Mistakes were made the last time around. They shall not happen again."

He continues to deliver authoritative observations on the liberties and needs of spider culture. The last time we clashed, feelings had run high and lives were unnecessarily lost. Maxwell has many regrets for those who fell – on both sides. Despite his great compassion and wisdom for the beasts, most of us remain unconvinced that diplomacy will be effective.

"Have you ever tried to reason with a cat?" someone hisses.

Some in the middle rows volunteer to broker a meaningful connection with the arachnids. I feel guilty. I should have spoken earlier about my findings but I excuse myself in not knowing what they meant. Besides, Newton certainly didn't let on.

"We've got to give Klein some back up. She hasn't asked for any, but she won't until things are desperate. Let's head off a crisis."

"They're going to rip the Implicate Order apart unless we stop them."

Maxwell's mouth prepares to speak again. We wait for his voice to synchronise with his lips. We can already tell he's settled on a decisive course of action.

"All weavers will be deployed to the Blue Snowball Nebula. We can't afford to make excursions simply to conduct repairs. We must restrain them. Cocoon them with spacetime thread."

As Maxwell's deckchair anatomy folds back into his seat the weavers begin to disperse.

"Containment of the vicious beasts it is then. Let's play nice with them!"

I shake my head. Playing 'nice' with these things – I've never seen one – seems rather tenuous. If the matter trails they're leaving are anything to go by they're extremely dangerous indeed. Their infectious poisons leave deep wounds in the Implicate Order that are highly resistant to repair. The only way I've managed to deal with them is through overzealous stitching. One thing's for sure. If we're going to tackle these beasts, much more spacetime fibre will be needed.

Others have been thinking this way too and I follow them to the condensers.

I feel bad for not leaping to join the first wave of negotiators out in the field but I don't feel up to the task. I've had too many headaches, nosebleeds, dark dreams, a foreboding sense of unreality and, most recently, disturbing sounds have tortured my nights. I need some time to rest. I am sure these things will settle. But time is a luxury and we may already be too late.

Condensers

Franklin points towards a bulge in the landscape, an ancient dormant volcano that I've never noticed before.

"There it is. The spacetime distillery. That's where all the Loom's condensers harvest spacetime dew.

"It doesn't look very much from here," I say somewhat gracelessly.

"Oh, but it's one of the wonders of the universe," she asserts. "It shimmers under the night sky like a far-off mirage – even though it is incredibly near."

"Have you been inside?"

"Not yet," she says, "but Fibonacci told us that it's made of seven gargantuan gleaming copper vessels the size of oak trees that sing like Tibetan bowls. They sing so sweetly that the air is alive with fundamental particle storms that leave a strange metal taste in your mouth. Apparently, the whole place smells of ozone, as if a storm is about to break."

Franklin reminds me of someone. I can't remember who.

"So, how do they make the spacetime dew?"

"Atop the volcano is a flawless, giant lens that is centred right over the heart of a massive electromagnet, which extends from the top of the hollow mountain and plummets deep down into its bowels. There is so much collecting apparatus beneath the ground it's like another world! These condensers reap the fabric of the cosmos, channelling ionising radiation, hadrons, bosons and leptons into the containers and diffracting the electromagnetic spectrum into rainbow fractions that are differentially sorted into the different spacetime distillates by natural crystal walls that are part of a massive, underground crystal garden."

I'm impressed by how good a student she is.

"It sounds technically very complex, much harder than using a portable condenser," I sigh, recalling the scale of our mission.

"It is complex, but Fibonacci says this is why the distillery so effective as it uses many distillation cycles to process the condensate into separate fractions using a fractionating column."

"That's an awful lot of spacetime fibre."

"Fibonacci says that only one of these condensers is usually active to feed the Loom. But each apparatus can be programmed using combinations of aperture and stomata settings to extract up to five different kinds of spacetime syrup, all of which have distinctive qualities and physical properties. Midnight gravity is harvested from the hairy edges of black holes and causes dramatic increase in mass and lensing of light. It can produce dramatic changes in the warp and weft of the cosmos. Stardust breeze is a soapy distillate that produces ripples of variation within the distillate that create rich material landscapes and promote life. Dark treacle is a highly sticky and connective fabric that is excellent for making spacetime repairs but too much can make for impenetrable time vortices where everything appears to stand still. Erotic tension is a particularly popular distillate, light and golden, it increases the charge between unlike bodies and is richest around suns and celestial bodies that invite many orbits, while quantum queer is the most intoxicating of all the distillates and is the raw material for the production of unlikely events."

"Would I be right in thinking that the Loom draws distillate directly from the condensers."

"Yes, of course."

"So, how are we going to transport all the dew?"

Franlkin pulls out a long handled copper spoon.

"This is what we use to pour the fluid into barrels ready for transportation."

A convoy of acrobats passes us, rolling dark barrels that have been transported by a hyperlocal wormhole between the spacetime distillery and the cellar, so we join them. But I'm not working well in the chain of flow. I miss barrels that gather too much speed for Franklin, who's behind me and since I am putting the child in danger, my kin are shouting at me. I'm giddy, finding it hard to focus, the light's too bright, the pain behind my eyes is unbearable and that horrid scratching sound is shrieking in my head. My nose begins to leak hot sticky fluid.

Doctor

The on-duty medic calls me over the loudspeaker system. It's a series of hollow metal cones rung by voices instead of a clanger. It's an annoying set up, as announcements tend to reverberate so, it's hard to maintain any semblance of privacy. I hope nobody sees me as I enter the surgery. The doctor is writing intensely. I can't see her face. I try to peer over her shoulder to see what is engrossing her.

"A routine screen," mumbles the back. "Volunteers for Andromeda have to undergo a medical check up."

I wonder if she's got the wrong person. I'm not 'routine'. I know – I'm afraid – there is something wrong.

The tiny room is fitted out in a manner that I'd place somewhere between a study and a gym. Everything is stacked. Books run up and down on her desk rather than across the shelf. A pile of white coats swamps a tall stool. A short tight rope is slung from one side of the office to the other. Hanging from a hook on the wall a knot of medical instruments languishes like an unruly plant and an aerial hoop is suspended from the ceiling. I can't help but give it a spin as I sit down.

The back asks me to perform a series of simple acrobatic moves. I bend backwards, forwards and stand on one leg. To my annoyance I get three quarters of the way along the rope and lose my footing. Since I'm pretty sure that the medic hasn't seen my error as she hasn't yet turned around, I jump back on the apparatus and shout 'finished' when I'm done.

Then the young woman, her hair contorted into an intense bun that grips her neck like a mother cat on kittens, swings around in her chair and wheelies right up to me. She's about an inch from my nose. Her fingers grab my lids as if she's about to force my orbits out of their sockets. She shines lights in my eyes. Then she stares penetratingly at me for an uncomfortably long time. As I try to look away, she insists I stare at her nose while her finger moves all over the place like a wayward worm. I feel dizzy from the intensity of the examination and am relieved when she shoots back to her desk without standing up and turns her back on me again.

"Do you get headaches?"

"No."

"How about nose bleeds."

"No."

"Hallucinations?"

"No."

"Have you passed out recently?"

"No."

"Vertigo?"

"No. I did an amazing drop in the rehearsal space with Fibonacci the other day."

"Do you ever hear a buzzing noise that you can't explain?"

I'm silent. Does she read minds? In fact, does everyone read minds, except me?

"How about hallucinations. Bad dreams?"

She's back in my face again, nearly all pupils, no colour in her eyes. I feel like she's sucking on my brains and I'm annoyed. I feel completely intruded upon.

"Have you been talking to Newton?"

"Mobius. May I call you Mobius?"

This woman vexes me.

"Mobius, you have a tumour of flies in your head."

Tumour of Flies

Apparently I am being eaten from the inside out by flesh-eating maggots.

This is happening to me right now.

"They are multiplying and drilling a hole in your head so they'll have more room to develop into adults," says the medic.

I am having problems taking everything in. Not because I can't hear well. Nor do I have difficulties in appreciating the technical meaning of the words – I simply cannot grasp the monumental personal implications of what she is saying.

Whatever way she presents my situation, the outcome is obscene.

"Do you understand the seriousness of what I am saying?"

I shake my head, refusing to accept these so-called 'facts'.

"Flies are stuck inside your skull and have laid eggs. Some of them have hatched into grubs. Maggots. They are feeding on your brain tissue, which is short-circuiting. The larvae are also having an effect on your thinking as they bunch up inside your head, and put pressure on the axons, the conducting pathways of your brain. They are commanding you like a marionette."

I want to tell her that I feel just fine so she'll stop talking. I feel queasy.

"This accounts for all your symptoms such as headaches, nosebleeds and even the strange sounds you've been experiencing. Your 'auditory hallucinations'."

"You are wrong. The sounds are real."

I am violated.

"You'll need a hole drilled in your head to let the pressure out. Immediately."

"Immediately? What will that involve?"

"They will take the 'lid' off your skull, so they can remove all the eggs and insect larvae. Then they'll clean out the cavity made by the flies and maybe they'll even be able to put back the flap of bone they've removed. If you're lucky, they'll seal the defect with a metal plate – and hope for the best."

"Hope for the best," the full impact of these words is simply not registering. My thoughts are treacle thick. "Will this procedure cure me?"

"No. The operation only provides relief from some of the worst symptoms of your condition. It is not a remedy, repair, or replacement of lost tissue.

I am working on autopilot, hoping that this whole conversation is taking place with someone else. Not me.

"What happens if I refuse?"

"It's equally grim. The growing maggots will not only destroy your brain tissue but will push it through the *foramen magnum* – the large hole at the base of your skull. If you are lucky, you will gradually lose consciousness before your brain dies and your body passes quietly from this incarnation."

"I can't agree to this. I need time to think."

"You have until the end of the day to make your decision."

I flee to the Loom Garden, and curl up under its sturdy frame with The Exceptions. Yes, I'm in hiding, as I don't want to run into anyone right now, or be obliged to make polite and engaging conversation.

Actually, this is more an anxiety than reality. Everyone's busy making preparations for the space spider mission to Andromeda, and nobody is in the Loom Garden watching the tapestry.

I lie with my head on The Exceptions and find comfort in the familiar clatter of shuttling younglings moving at the speed of light through the warp above me. I can just see the underside of some of the spacetime manifolds. I figure that even without moving I can study the negative imprint of Klein's details. Her threads are blackened and fracturing, but nothing has unravelled disastrously. She's holding her own.

I am relieved.

I can't find peace, though. The pending 'decision' I am asked to consider is more like a terrible fait accompli.

What if the medic made a mistake? I never confessed to having any symptoms at all. Perhaps this news was meant for somebody else.

But as I lie quietly the weight of the conversation stalks my thoughts, growing bolder and stronger. Soon it's screaming at a volume I can't ignore – a hole will be made in my head.

I wish I was elsewhere, faced with another kind of crisis, championing a noble cause that I can be remembered honourably for.

The shuttle stutters as it passes the Andromeda region again. The stitches are fraying but they're not fragmenting. Our troupe will already on their way to begin diplomatic manoeuvres with the spiders. I try to imagine what that might be like. One thing is certain – the delegates will need their wits about them. Spacetime spiders are not clever enough to be reasonable. And they're far too smart to be harmless.

As much I would love to be elsewhere, defending the integrity of the universe alongside my kin, I am still sufficiently pragmatic to understand that I must deal with one battle at a time.

Hole in the Head

I said 'yes'.

Of course, I did.

"You're not the first person to require brain surgery," observes the neurosurgeon.

"People's heads have had holes bashed in them since prehistoric times. Trephining was said to let spirits out and cure madness. During this primitive procedure the bone was not replaced. If people survived then their skin was left to heal of its own accord and they ended up with a permanent soft spot – like the top of a baby's head." She shows me a set of pictures of vicious saw-toothed corkscrew-like devices and other tools that were once used to destroy the offending parts of the brain with.

"They don't seem a million light years away from the kinds of instruments you're proposing," I add unhelpfully.

"They're very different," she asserts, "While craniectomy may be a modern-day version of trephining, we perform the operation under much more sterile and pain-free circumstances. I also need to let you know that if, during the procedure, the removed bone fragments are put back in place, technically the procedure will be a craniotomy."

I nod slowly. Although they are technicalities that I'm not expert in, I'm paying attention – after all, it's my head that's being drilled.

"Who makes these decisions?"

"I will decide if it's in your interest for the bone to be replaced, or not – although you will only be partly asleep during the procedure, so we can see how you're doing – you won't be able to give consent. But we will be asking you other kinds of questions and giving you things to do during the operation."

"Like what? It sounds like I'm expected to be busy."

"Raise your arm, wiggle your toes, and count backwards from ten. Things like that. But you won't recall anything, as we'll administer a cocktail of drugs that will make you forget."

"What about the flies?"

"The flies?"

The neurosurgeon suddenly breaks into a broad smile, "Oh! You're joking. Sign here," she says.

I don't like any of it, but I give my consent.

"Yes, the flies. I'm serious. Oddly, they feel like part of me."

Diligence

Shelley's riding the stretcher and singing to me, her plait is snaking comfortingly around my hand.

The air is fizzing with giggles. It's wonderful to hear the little ones although I can't see them. They're way too up high, surfing on her hair, and I can't raise my head. Newton's also keeping pace with the trolley, with ripened horn, striding as if he's wearing seven league boots. I can see him trying to spread his wings but my mother has made him tuck them into the seat of his pants. That doesn't stop the tips of his feathers from making a scratching sound. Or maybe that's coming from inside my head.

The anaesthetic room doors are flapping. Needles sink painlessly into my veins. Many voices are telling me things. Amidst them, a cloud of children shouts "bye, bye," waving their tiny wrists like cherubim wings.

As I'm asked to count downwards from ten, I can hear my father's voice. A volatile substance leaks into the air from out of my breath. It smells of rot, putrescine. Am I breathing Newton's breath? Have I been here before?

Metamorphosis

I'm sinking into a cloud of waving fingers that tickle my skin.

They splay, unable to break my tumbling into a slippery matrix – a gelatinous substance that is made from the unacknowledged connections between bodies whose very purpose is kinship and ongoingness. The space is not made by objects but emerges from leaky overlapping spacetime territories that are inhabited by many indistinct and peripheral figures, which never quite introduce themselves. It is impossible to describe the state of this formlessness – whether this place is under construction, or is being disassembled. I look upwards for recognisable geometries to establish my bearings but I am engulfed in swirling scintillating particles, like dust in sunlight. I reach for them and they move further away from my fingertips. My descent continues as a cloud of dissipating meaning.

I quickly adapt to this turbulence.

Shedding the use of my eyes like a cavefish and emptying my head of thought, my flesh seeks a different understanding of self. I snatch at every opportunity to observe or influence my occupation of this space. I'm counting, moving my arms, wriggling my toes and saying my name. Metamorphosis is imminent. Strange pigments precipitate in the layers of my skin. Vibrations take on the quality of language. Vapours are tantalisingly pungent. I'm starting to get the hang of a form of mind-controlled quantum evolution.

I observe, therefore I incarnate.

This is nothing like assembling a precisely organised machine. It is more like throwing a cabbage at a wall, where the resultant 'splat' of incompletely realised intentions is midwife to my embodiment.

In my mind's eye I can envisage the goal that emerges between the necessary material choreography and chance. I observe the point where I want the homuncular vegetable to collide with the surface of reality. And, since I am dealing with many tricky variables that exist between the cabbage, the wall and my emerging incarnations, I will need practice because the outcome is uncertain.

Disconcertingly, I'm only going to get one go at this.

With no previous experience in cabbage throwing, I will need to deal with inevitable compromises if I am to exist at all. Even while deliberating over this particular throw of cabbage, I am already changing. My outer integument is building up pressure and my pigmented skin is becoming scaly. Then I launch the vegetable, it splits, and the order of things changes. Unconstrained by the deterministic laws of programmatic algorithms and the perversity of material abstractions, my new being allies with radical material realms and their poetics.

What am I becoming?

Dislodged from their current bio scaffolding, my tissues select alternative differentiation pathways, embracing the phantoms, shades and circus performers that have been lurking in the ambient shapelessness, who start to knot their fingers together and become my corporeal safety net.

I hear drilling and fly spray is blasted into my head.

Someone's talking to me. I think they're holding my hand.

I must sequence numbers, name things and say how I feel. That's a hard one. I am not sure I feel anything at all. I think I mutter a reply.

The matrix recedes as I'm pulled upwards towards the light – this incarnation.

Invisible

Shelley looks up from her book and studies me instead. "Invisible Cities" is emblazoned on the jacket, which is black with an 'i' like a building, or a pencil. Whatever it is, it's perplexing. I'm trying not to look at it, but the enigma has my full attention.

I also want to be invisible. Not like a tower, or an 'i'.

Fingers page walk.

She sings me a song that I have heard so many times before but really can't place. The child clouds laugh uncontrollably as they blow bubbles in their moon milk through curly straws.

"I still don't know how you manage to keep so many younglings aloft," I say.

"Just because you have an explanation for things, doesn't mean you understand them," she warbles as she snatches a falling tumbler with her plait before it spills.

A strange yet soothing pressure folds my eyelids shut. Someone slurps milk. Pages rustle. I relax into my pillow.

My Name

"Mother, why do you do it?"

She looks at me from different perspectives, as if she was examining a high quality cut diamond.

"Do what?" she trills.

"Sing."

"You're looking for a story."

I nod and shut my eyes.

"Where I was born, a child is celebrated from the day the woman who wants to be their mother hears their song. Once child and woman are introduced, a father is chosen who learns the child's song as he and the mother make love. From that time onwards the mother teaches everyone the child's song – so that when they arrive into a community they will understand they are welcome. Later, should this child misbehave, they are surrounded by the whole community who, with love, remind them of their identity. One day, when this child is ready to die, their song receives them into their ancestral homestead where ultimately they will pass into the realms of reincarnation."

"Do I have a song?"

"Of course! Don't you know it by now?"

I shake my head, puzzled.

"You never said I had a song. I've always thought my significance related to cosmic coordinates (024, 375, 669)."

"Well, darling, I have been singing your unique song all your life. I sing the songs of all my children. Every day. I celebrate you all. I am so happy that you came. That's why I keep on singing."

Moon Room

I've been told I must sleep but brilliant veneers, imposing geometries and angular shadows bleach out my thoughts. I am unsure whether I am awake or not.

I try to block out these intrusions by closing my eyes, but they are stubborn. The environment is harsh and clinical. Nothing sticks to the surfaces, which are scrubbed so clean that the material palimpsests that build rich soils are erased. There is no physical trace of the person who occupied this room before me, but I think they were sad.

I open my eyes again but nothing has softened. Everything remains the same as before. I repeatedly blink and realise the blinding light and menacing shadows are constant whether my lids are open or shut.

Shelley's still in the corner silently juggling children with her book open on her lap while she sleeps, cracking the end of her hair in time to musical sounds. It's a restless night.

Creeping reflections along the walls stare at me, making it impossible to settle. I'm under surveillance.

I can't remember if the light was on or off, so with marionette gait, I get out of bed.

Then I flick the light switch. There is still no change in the luminosity of the room. I flick the switch again. It makes no difference. It's uncomfortably bright, like someone shining a torch inside my head.

I flip the switch again.

My mother looks up.

"What are you doing?"

"I am trying to turn off the light."

"But, darling," she hums and rises to close the blinds.

"You're trying to turn off the Moon."

Dark Matter

I know I'm not asleep but I'm not awake either.

My vision is breaking up and everything seems to be turning into a field of spreading mud cracks. My head is pounding and I can't make the searing heaviness go away. My eyes are already shut. Or are they?

This blackest of blacks threatens to destroy the coherence that makes the universe whole. It's a malignant irregularity. A decoupling. A cancer. These cruel shadows make sounds; scratching, buzzing, whooshing, crackling and pulsing. Yet their phantom moans are not fantastical enough for dreaming. They are shockingly real. They intrude on my senses. It's impossible to ignore them.

Small spiky creatures with many legs are discussing me. Chiding me. Berating me over and over.

"Filthy. Dirty. Contaminated!"

They're relentless. Murmuring viciously.

"Think you know it all."

Black needles prick my veins and burrow into my flesh where there should be blood. They sprout tiny hairs and hooks that lock together, strung like daisy chains, and start to wriggle under my nerves and skin. I feel them tugging on long strings of blackness that connect my insides to the outside and yank hard on my entrails, forcing them outwards.

An incessant chorus of loathing spills out from invisible spaces everywhere. There's nowhere to escape to and I cannot shut them out.

"We know where you are. Slut."

Impossibly dark shadows continue to swell from hollows that weren't there before and begin to exert pressure on my thoughts. They're relentless and nameless. Whatever these things may be they are still in the process of becoming. Even greater horrors lie ahead. I have no idea what I've done to deserve such persecution. I wish they would tell me their name so I may call upon them and reveal their true identity.

I shout the names of angels – Azariel, Dumah, Gadreel, Harut, Michael, Phanuel, Raphael, Selaphiel, Wormwood and Zachariel – hoping for a champion, but they remain silent. Perhaps this pressure in my head is simply darker than they are.

"Give me your name!"

But there is no compliance – just the swooshing of my own blood and menacing shadows chewing mercilessly on my thoughts.

"I demand your name I said! Give it to me! I cannot sleep! And I cannot live with you inside my head."

Torment after torment crashes upon me. Endless abuse. These spectres will still find me even if I gouge out all my senses.

Amidst despair I realise there is another course of action. Although I do not truly believe in the incantation it's all I've got.

"Mother! Sing me my song."

My Song

Each cell, a place of becoming.
Where fertile fields collide in joy
As tensions and strains are forgotten
In the coupling of living with life.

When the storm comes, keep me lithe

When you plant the germ
Of my young soul, ensure
The soil is rich and deep
So I can thrive in troubled times

When the storm comes, keep me firm

Empower me with the art of change
And strength to execute this spell
Should life, fate and circumstance
Pose me, or my loved ones, harm.

When the storm comes, keep me brave

If I must make Achilles' choice –
Of great age, or heroes demise –
Then spare me for the after world
And knowledge of this gift of life.

When the storm comes, keep me safe

Naked

I'm bare. Standing in front of the mirror, I confront the image before me.

My head is shaven. I'm marked with fading neurosurgical instructions. My eyes are swollen and bloodshot. I'm a terrifying chimera – part Ripley, defiant, powerful – a chocolate-red Thomas Jerome Newton – androgynous, hairless – and Tame Iti, the Maori tattooed 'face of the future'.

I drop my chin assertively and admiringly. At the top of my head is a neat horseshoe scar, cross-embroidered with surgical staples, grinning at me like a scarecrow.

They offered only to remove a patch of hair. But I insisted they took it all. It just feels better like this. Coherent. Naked.

The doctor walks in while I contemplate my smoothness.

"Don't you think that hair is problematized over and beyond its function?" I say. "We never have the hair that we want."

Avoiding my gaze, the medic responds politely, "Well, some people wear a hairpiece, pencil in their brows, or find themselves a blooming merkin after an operation."

"Not me. I am unburdened of that neurosis now. I'm more concerned about what is going on inside my head than what is sitting on top of it."

She examines the charts at the end of my bed and enters some data into a screen, still avoiding my gaze.

"Don't you think it's obscene that after all this flies will still eat me from the inside? How long will it be before they finish the job?"

"Becoming a zombie host for parasites is not uncommon in Nature," reassures the doctor.

I realise that I had better attempt to cover myself so that the formalities can be completed with minimal weirdness, which is challenging.

"Many species of wasps and flies, for example, feed their young on the internal organs of their prey, which are invested in their welfare after they are paralysed and infected with an embryonic load by their host.

Indeed, these unwitting incubators stay sane for many weeks, treating their own survival as seriously as the parasitic load smuggled inside them."

I grimace. This is not making me feel good.

"Even so, hosts are not free agents. Within these deadly eggs, other actors such as viruses enter with the parasite's eggs and at a time of the parasite's choosing – when the larvae are hatched – the host is triggered into zombie mode. Infected brain tissue receives a signal to burst open, so that the young can escape from the food source unobstructed, unleashing destruction, madness and mayhem in the process."

The doctor looks at her watch.

"Can you sign the form here, please?"

"I never want to know that I'm a walking corpse. I'd rather first descend into madness and oblivion. Maybe my condition will only be a tragedy for those around me. But I'm not sure I really want to think about that right now."

I pick up the pen and watch it ooze what looks like blood on to the paper.

The medic takes the form and leaves without any further reassurances or information.

I feel strange.

Self-reflection and explanation are providing me no comfort, so I put on some clothes and slip past the nursing station and make my way to the Loom Garden, to see how Klein is getting on.

Honey

I'm sucking on a living spoon of asteroid honey in front of the Loom.

Despite some rather shocking irregularities in the spacetime fabric, Klein's manifold continues to hold its own. I study the evidence of her tribulation in dropped stiches and a really ugly set of dark scars that resemble very shabby or even desperate attempts at repair. Most worryingly, Klein's characteristic flamboyance in weaving techniques is absent.

"She's flatlined," I observe.

"You need to get yourself better first," sings Shelley.

She begins a musical account of the Ceres bees that produce the most delicious honey in the cosmos. I know it's a distraction technique but I feel the story's sweetness trickle down my throat, into my blood, fortifying my immune system.

"Ceres is one of the biggest 'fossils' from the early solar system," she sings. "It's a huge asteroid between the orbits of Mars and Jupiter and the largest object in our asteroid belt. It accounts for one third of the asteroid mass in this region. The existence of this extraordinary location was actually deduced, not observed, by Sicilian astronomer Giuseppe Piazzi in 1801.

The colossal asteroid's perfectly spherical body has an atmosphere, a rocky core, an icy mantle, subsurface ocean and a dusty top layer, whose temperature can rise as high as minus 38 degrees Celsius. In late 2014 the space probe Dawn observed strange bright patches suggestive of water on its surface. Consequently, it was the first non-terrestrial location to be terraformed in our solar system.

The first inhabitants were organic miners – heavy-metal extracting bacteria capable of feeding on the rocky surface that could produce biological seams of gold. Under the weak ambient sunlight they flourished in the nutrient rich subsurface ocean. Quickly they established cities, as biofilms, and became rich organic soils. Further probes brought bio diverse bacterial payloads that rapidly colonised the rock. The flourishing microorganisms enriched the once thin air and established planetary-scale systems capable of supporting higher life forms.

Ceres' soils grew so rich they became the pioneering outpost for new kinds of agriculture experiments, designed to feed humans working in the outer solar system. Further biodiversity was engineered by sending a whole zoo of life-bearing probes. Each crash site spawned wild flowers, bacteria, algae, grain-producing crops and marijuana. But the first living parcels did not thrive, as there were no pollinators. So a colony of bees was sent.

Soon the Ceres bees established a rich honey making culture that assimilated the heavy metal processing skills of the early colonies of bacteria into their bee-ome, the natural micro flora of the bees. Together, bacteria and bees worked to generate an incredibly sophisticated, productive and cultured society. They made rich foodstuffs, gold threads, and heavy metal fibres. They also practiced a special kind of kintsugi – the art of fixing broken things with precious metals – in their architecture. This special craft – bee-forged heavy metal repairs – brought visitors from all around the solar system to have their broken treasures become even more valuable than before. Broken objects were brought in exchange for all kinds of seeds and Ceres literally bloomed with organic trade.

Soon the Ceres bees were the most sought after crafts-makers in the universe."

I'm sucking hard on the living spoon while she speaks, to extract every morsel of the intoxicating honey.

"Can you not do that, dear? That's a living spoon. It's unlike the wooden spoons of our old culture, which were murdered before they were used. You'll cause it harm chewing on it like that."

I slowly lick the utensil for the last time and return it carefully back in the planter, covering its little root feet with earth.
"Thank you, spoon, for suffering my indulgence."

It's always best to be incredibly polite to a living spoon, because if you mistreat them, they decompose within hours turning into a foul smelling mess, which takes many weeks of scrubbing to remove.

"Did anyone try to subjugate the Ceres bees?" I ask.

Shelley smiles and flicks her plait like a whip.

"Just once."

"Please tell me."

And she did.

Ivan Novak was a commander in the Muskland military fleet, a self-governing outpost that had declared independence within the sprawling Martian biome. He refused to accept the sovereignty of nonhuman settlements and led a troop of vessels to Ceres to harvest a large piece of ice from the asteroid in 2036. At the time, the Martian population was rising rapidly. This was overwhelmingly due to an influx of human migrants seeking a better life who had secured one-way journeys on media shuttles – due to the unprecedented market in fly-on-the wall modes of entertainment with a focus on extreme modes of living. The unplanned population rise had left the colonists short of natural resources. Although vapour condensers and liquid recycling suits hung on to as much moisture as possible, fresh sources of water became incredibly scarce. Despite this, terrestrial media outlets reported resource depletion positively, as an entrepreneurial opportunity, which heralded an era of interplanetary economic flourishing.

Novak launched an ice-harvesting raid on Ceres but within minutes of landing his crew were surrounded by a swarm of angry bees.

"Why are you destroying our habitat?" demanded the Queen.

"We have a resource crisis on Mars. Without a new water supply there will be many unnecessary deaths."

"We will gift you ice, but in return you must extend diplomatic courtesies to nonhuman civilisations – whether you are seeking emergency aid or not."

Novak was condescending but agreed. He didn't like to be berated by an insect. Even a giant one as large as himself. What impudence! And anyway, how could bees without weapons break up the ice on Ceres? They didn't have the technological knowhow. Those barbed stingers would never cut into the dense solid.

The Queen gave her command to gift the visitors ice. Enthusiastically, her troupes swarmed forming a crisscross of lines on the surface of a large ice sheet several kilometres in diameter and half a kilometre thick.

"Would this be enough?" asked the Queen, carrying the commander aloft and pointing to the generous portion her colony had mapped out with the positioning of their bodies.

He agreed that it would but wondered if they were making a mockery of him.

The royal signal for open cast mining the ice was given. At first

Novak was curious about their process but after some time he became perplexed by their stillness. Then he grew impatient.

"Why aren't they doing anything?" he asked.

"Just wait," said the Queen.

More time passed. Novak began to think that he should usurp the Queen and subjugate the bees to run the mining and sweet-making industries for himself.

The jet-black bees continued to sit motionless in their various geometries, like a giant map. Agitated and impatient, Novak started to formulate a plan to pacify the insects and smoke them into docility by burning all their crops. The asteroid was so plush with organic matter that it would only take a few strategically aimed incendiary devices before it would suffer devastating, smoky vegetable fires.

But before he could launch his attack, the ice sheet started to crack. Sufficient solar heat had passed into the bees' body to splinter the glacier into manageable sections. They had achieved all this without moving a muscle.

"There's your water," said the Queen. "Help yourself."

Novak peacefully hoisted iceberg fragments into his ship and returned to Mars, where he became exceedingly wealthy. He continued to fantasise how much richer he could have been if he'd laid claim to Ceres, but he could not ignore the deadly intelligence of the bees. For her part, the Queen knew their peaceful culture was safe – at least for a while."

I slip my finger around the lid of the Ceres honey pot just as Shelley finishes her story, but I am not invisible enough. She fixes me with a withering gaze.

My eyes try to protest innocence but it doesn't work.

Then I give her a hug, to the sound of a thousand giggles floating above us, and she melts into a song that somehow seems to come from ancestral throats.

It's almost time to go.

Long Drop

I am terrified that I can no longer work as part of a team.

While this may be in part a side effect of my recent surgery, I am wounded by the recent danger I posed to Franklin and feel compelled to confront this growing anxiety by doing the thing I most dread.

I climb to the very top of the aerial gym where Fibonacci taught us how to fall together.

Beneath me, the ground looks very far away indeed as I prepare mentally for this foolhardy stunt. If I survive, I am supposed to live. If I fail, my end was always inevitable.

I don't spend too long trying to feel comfortable about the pointlessness of this compulsion – just in case I change my mind.

Then, I plummet to the ground.

I am knitting, spinning and turning like a wayward bobbin. The trail behind me is spectacular. I'm like a plane in freefall, spitting out plaits, folds and blooming geometries – in a trail of vibrant smoke.

Having been so single minded in this endeavour, I have given no thought for my safety. The ground is rapidly approaching. Using the strength in my legs to brake against the silks, I suddenly discover that at this speed I cannot generate sufficient friction to significantly slow my descent.

My accelerated thoughts paint me a bleak and immediate future.

According to legend, there are creatures that live in realms above the sky. Electromagnetic realms that dazzle the heavens with mirror shards, aurorae and quantum particles. They say that one day a pregnant female will fall out of this celestial tapestry and uproot the tree of life. Her as yet unseparated maggots will feed on her corpse and tumble through the great plastic hole left in the world.

My mother shrieks with a pitch so high it could shatter glass, and simultaneously whips up the end of the ribbons with her hair. I am catapulted skywards, lifted by forces that are stronger than gravity. Now I'm flying. Instinctively, I somersault and twist, elegantly landing on all fours in an extraordinary animal pose.

"You're not on your own with this," she says.

Me Too

Klein's latest coordinates suggest she is around the Blue Snowball Nebula. I'm very concerned about the deterioration of her manifold but still – for now, the malignancy does not appear to be actively spreading.

Cousin (739, 111, 243), Stokes, a remarkable corpulent and statuesque figure, joins me at the loom. She is delicately nibbling a plate of fried turnip chips topped with mayonnaise, as she gives me a swift, extremely powerful hug that I want to disappear into, without losing a chip from her plate.

"I thought you'd be with the others," she says.

"I was delayed. I have a prolactinoma."

"What's that?"

"Brain tumour."

"Me too."

"Will yours kill you?"

"Maybe. How about you?"

"I don't think so, but I've gained a huge amount of weight. I just get so hungry. They make me follow a whole stack of diet sheets, which is pretty useless really, as reading food lists – no matter if they are low calorie or not – just makes me peckish."

"I guess we should keep an eye on each other then. When are you planning to leave?"

"Immediately. I can't even look at another weight-loss pamphlet."

We plan to travel together.

Stokes is an expert in joint origamy, which I've never attempted before. She is not only a brilliant collaborator but, having shared my admiration for Klein, she has also considerately figured out a route that takes us past God's Pagoda, her most magnificent work, which overlooks the Andromeda constellation. She says we can get our bearings again here.

It's a long throw for a thread but Stokes is confident and carefully washes up her empty plate.

Shelley glances over from under a musical cloud of waving children who are skipping with the end of her plait.

We leave without a fuss.

PART III

Together

It's hard to keep pace with Stokes. She's twisting spacetime around as if it weighs nothing. Believe me, even the most gossamer fine threads start to get heavy when you're traveling any distance. Throwing joint stitches is just so much easier than producing them on your own. Especially when you're working with an expert. The sheer physicality of the spacetime weaving process means that you have to think through someone else's space. Stokes can make the most precise pleats and innovative weaves. I simply surf on the entanglements of her movements. Working alongside her makes me feel superhuman.

Despite this, and using the strangest manner of communication, which is somewhere between telepathy and dance, I ask if we can reach the pagoda in two major moves. I don't think I can keep up. I can't let her down.

She chuckles and agrees. We decide to stop off at M33, the Triangulum, or Pinwheel Galaxy, which is a spiral galaxy about three million light-years from Earth. Technically, it's a bit further than Andromeda but it's a much easier origami calculation. It will give us a chance to synchronise our movements and get our bearings before we head for God's Pagoda. Stokes is hungry and looks for something to eat, while I rehearse a few times and make some additional calculations. Then we're off again.

Origami flows through us like blood. We're conjoined. I wonder if Stokes feels as I do.

"This scintillating cloud was once considered a space dust desert but it's actually a sea of micro planets that are inhabited by even smaller, planetary-scale organisms."

"What's a micro planet?"

"Cosmic bodies that are naturally found orbiting tiny stars. They range from dust-sized specks to objects that are the size of a house. Thousands of them can be found around the M33 area. The suns are so small that they do not exert much gravitational pull on their planets. This means that these celestial bodies do not have fixed orbits. In fact, their trajectories are so sensitive that the planets are always slipping in and out of each other's paths. These wandering planets, therefore, constantly change their character. They're always adapting and ever in flux."

The microplanets cavort with each other beneath us.

I'm focussed on the elegant movements of a living microplanet known as XYZ, which is governed by a matriarchal bacterium that lavishes her attentions on other approaching bodies. She beckons them with cheerful filaments that radiate over her entire surface like a chemical fire. A tantalising performer, she lures future partners towards her in a fertility ritual, which takes the form of a masked ball and cosmic phantasmagoria. Grabbing at each other like tentacle-wrestling jellyfish, microplanets become lovers in their multiples. Their masquerade becomes a dizzying choreography of shape shifting, image production, light films and infrasound that inspires civilisations around the cosmos.

At their climax, an orgiastic spasm rips their sticky connections apart. Spumes of new microplanets are passed around like dancing partners in a complex choreography of highly decorated interfaces and clouds of matter. The budding microplanets move from one orbital trajectory to another, radiating joyfully out into space. As the tidal movements quell, matriarchs wear the ectoplasmic traces of their partners, which like fine frocks, enrich their seduction repertoire and the ritual starts again.

"I'd love to study their culture," I tell Stokes.

"We don't have time to stop," she grunts.

Sulkily, I concede we must pass on by.

Decomposition

Stokes hits the surface of Gaudi, an earth-like planet in the M33 constellation just before I do. In fact, she breaks my fall. I somersault a few times from the uplift her girth gives me, like landing on a trampoline. It seems that gravity is slightly less than on Earth here but the air is breathable. I rush over to my origamy partner, who is splayed out on the ground.

"Are you okay?"

"I'm starving." Unhurt, Stokes leaps to her feet and sniffs the air. "There's something deliciously sweet nearby. Like a candy shop."

We follow the scent and it's obvious that spacetime fibres in this area are badly damaged. Stokes wonders if this toxic landscape caused our origamy thread to unravel too soon. I nod, as it's unlike her to get anything wrong. There are subtle faults in this spacetime sector. Some are not so hidden; sooty hairline fractals split the landscape. Everything feels slow and heavy as if we're trapped inside a celluloid movie running at fourteen frames per second. The mood of this landscape is ominous. It feels likely to burst into flames at any moment.

"Is that liquorice?"

Stokes is already in search of the source of the odour. I'm struggling to keep up with her.

Now she is waving at me. Does she want me to come closer or stop? Everything is jerky on this incredibly rocky terrain. It's very hard to see clearly. I keep ploughing on. I am running with all my strength to stay still. The spacetime tear must be near. I'm looking for strange shadows to reveal themselves, so that I can make the necessary spacetime repair. Gosh! This is stiflingly difficult. Everything is so fractured. Inconsistent.

Stokes is gesturing towards the ground. Something that resembles brilliantly coloured lichens triumphantly splinters the rocks, glaring at us from between the fragments like scabs. But it's hard to see anything in detail, as the world appears to be lurching backwards and forwards. The paucity of spacetime fibre is worrying. We could get stranded.

I want to throw up.

And then I see it.

The spacetime spider carcass is sublimating – dissolving from the inside, it's losing structural integrity to sweetness and vapour.

"I have never seen one up this close before!"

"Is it safe? I hear they're made of dark matter."

"Hell! They're ugly."

The legs are folded around its integument. Caustic fluid is leaking from the beast's vestigial spinnerets, which have never developed the capacity to make functional spiderweb as organic spiders do. In fact, spacetime spiders do not build webs of anything, thriving on disconnection. Their web-making glands have simply shrivelled up into metabolically dysfunctional grape-like knots that shoot poison, not thread. Their strangeness is disturbing but compelling.

Stokes kicks the corpse as if she needs proof that it cannot spring to life. The end of her boot scorches, as if someone threw caustic soda on it. A large chunk of the exoskeleton breaks off and starts to effervesce at the edges.

"Incredible. It's absolutely devoid of life," says Stokes.

"Well of course it is. It's dead."

"That's not what I mean. I'm actually talking about the environment."

I'm starting to feel panicky. How long does a carcass like this take to sublimate? Although they're creatures that seek solitude, spacetime spiders operate in nests and I'm wondering how it got here.

Stokes appears to be thinking along with me. Or is she thinking through me? She studies the spider's remains.

"When an organic body dies, it decomposes. It's an incredible process. It starts with self-digestion and leakage of body fluids from its organs only minutes after death. Limp flesh transforms into an active metabolic medium, which escapes into spaces that it does not usually occupy. Look over here! It's a cadaveric landscape for an astonishing ecosystem transforms as the decay process unfolds."

I'm anxious. I'm looking for suspicious shadows of spacetime retraction that will indicate where we need to make repairs – it's a badly damaged terrain and I'm very concerned there may be other spiders.

"Stokes, you're being morbid. Let's get out of here."

"I'm not morbid. This process is very unlike organic decay. Its dark space, dissipating. Can you see? This spacetime spider is decomposing in a much simpler way than when an organic body dies. It's interesting, as they seem to reach chemical equilibrium in very different ways than our dead bodies do. This spider corpse appears to be returning nothing to its environment. But with an organic body, biological death is not the end of a process. It is the starting point for many new ones."

"Stokes, please stop talking about dead things. You're creeping me out."

But she's not listening; she's completely absorbed in the strangeness of our discovery.

"Without an intact immune system the body's own bacteria begin to reorganise into the thanatomicrobiome. What is almost unbelievable about this community of bugs is they are exactly the same ones that form the healthy microbiome of the organic body but they have a completely different identity. During life, they perform vital functions such as digesting food, producing skin oils and even regulating our moods. But once our body dies a different ruleset applies and the resident bacterial community adopts a completely different set of behaviours. Thousands of species of hungry bacteria move unchecked through the intestine and begin to digest their host's flesh from the inside. The whole process turns the corpse from being supple, participatory, warm and lively into a dusky, waxy, passive and strangely rigid object."

"Stokes, we need to find out where to make our repairs and get out of here. Right now!"

I pull hard on her arm. She reluctantly clambers over the disintegrating spider and says she cannot continue without something to eat. So she tears a spiky growth out of the ground and chews on it – like a giant panda. She notes that the earth is very soft and far too rich not to have been formed by an organic decomposition process.

I snatch at the cracked shadow of a spacetime thread as it races past us.

Stokes is on her second spike and kicking at the ground again. "Interesting. What have we here?"

I flick my chopsticks at another odd shadow and shout at Stokes that the spacetime threads are retracting. She's not listening to me. In fact, she is suddenly obsessed with the soft mound of earth that we're standing on. She pokes into it with her fifth prickly stick before chewing on it. Now Stokes has her fingers in the earth and is groping around intensely in the soil. I assume she's looking for something else to nibble. Several shockingly dark beetles with tree-like horns suddenly rise to the surface.

They appear to have an overabundance of legs.

"Wow! Necrophagous insects. You know, some species that feed on dead things spend their entire life cycle in, on and around a cadaver. Flesh flies and their larvae in particular are attracted to rotting meat. They will find a cadaver immediately and enter a corpse through the nose."

"Stokes, please don't say anything about flies. Or noses."

My head is starting to hurt. We can't miss another fibre.

"Stokes. Can you see the spacetime tear?" I insist.

"Each flesh fly can make around two hundred and fifty eggs, which hatch within a day giving rise to small first-stage maggots. These feed on the rotting flesh and then their skins split. They are now free to grow into larger maggots, which feed for several hours before moulting again. These larger, fattened, maggots transform into adult flies. The cycle of life repeats until there's nothing left for the flesh flies to feed on."

"Stokes, I need you to stop talking and start hearing me now!"

She's pulling on something beneath the soil. It's resisting her. I'm trying not to think about the flies inside my own head, but I can hear them.

"You see, the decomposition of an organic body is a very fertile process. It's full of life. A spacetime spider's decomposition process is sterile. It doesn't seem to re-invest in making new life. In contrast, the whole of the organic decay cycle promotes the vibrancy of its environments. In fact, once the organic body has liquefied, it radiates outwards to form a decomposition island. This is a highly concentrated area of organically rich soil. It goes beyond itself."

Stokes is holding a human leg bone. I'm horrified. It's been stripped of flesh. For one terrible moment I think she's going to chew on it. Then she suddenly stands up. We're definitely thinking and hearing through each other now. There are many little rich earthen mounds in the stony ledges around us.

"We need to get out of this graveyard. If I am not mistaken, this is where the Great Spider Battle was fought and spiders are already here."

As the noises in my head start again, we grab the tiniest slither of thread from a sudden wave of imposing shadows. We don't wait to see what kind of thing has produced them like – a tear, a malignancy, a beast – and quicker than we ever thought possible, throw a joint origamy thread.

Funeral

A carnivalesque procession of professional musicians, weepers, magicians, skeletons, angels, devils, zombies, crow-like beaked figures, acrobats, pallbearers, Egyptians and aerial performers walk backwards, in the direction of Tau Ceti, following a giant ball of manure along a cobbled village street.

"What are they doing?"

Stokes shrugs, "burying their dead."

The pallbearers stand on their hands like dung beetles with their head to the ground, rear in the air, and use their muscular legs to deftly roll the organic matter along. From time to time the ball jerks forward, suddenly lifting them aloft, whereupon they vigorously kick to regain their balance and return it to a precision-perfect trajectory.

"You mean there is someone inside the ball of compost?"

"Yes. Maybe more than one person. It depends."

It smells like a barn. Stokes tells me that the feculent matter is rolled with hay so that the decomposition mix is just right.

"The fabrics that link life and death are constructed by hand here."

According to Stokes, asteroids are too small to have indefinite carbon, water, and air or soil cycles. So the vital metabolic links that help the crops grow and return organic matter to the earth must be made by hand and become a cultural practice. On this particular rock, it's incorporated into funeral rituals.

"Where do all the people come from? Are they relatives, or workmates?"

"No. Burials are considered a recreational activity here. You could also think of this procession as an elaborate form of agriculture. Something similar to a harvest festival where people invest their time and expertise to give thanks for what they have. Since it's so important to create rich soils, people want to know exactly when and where these opportunities arise. They tune into the broadcast matrix, mostly radio, to find out who has passed on, and they travel from all over the planet to be part of the festivities."

The procession reaches the edge of a slope. Stokes explains that

215

symbolically the community has stopped pushing the sun of life across the sky and now it will be put to rest at the edge of the world. The pall-bearers steady the dung casket and wait for the mourners to gather alongside the bereaved. Tributes and poetry are read before the master of ceremonies raises both hands to Tau Ceti and gives the signal to tip the casket down the slope. The dung ball is launched with vigour by the pall bearers while the congregation – zombies, crows, angels and devils – runs after it attempting to clamber aboard. The dung ball spirals into a shallow well and, after crushing several shrubby copses, comes to an abrupt stop. Now the followers, who are equipped with a range of instruments from spades to clippers and drills, climb over the casket and perform a short orientation dance to make sure the manure is still facing in the direction of Tau Ceti. Then they quickly bury it in the thin soil, which in truth means they wedge it under a boulder.

"Since this place lives under an eternal twilight, the star's location is quite easy to establish," assures Stokes.

"Are they finished?" I ask.

"Not quite. They put on quite a spread."

Xenophoria

Since my thoughts are increasingly macabre, I leave the necessary thinking and manoeuvring to Stokes. My head is throbbing and my energy poor, so I'm not particularly good company.

Stokes snatches a few loose asteroid pebbles and crunches them.

"See that planet there? It's Xenophoria, the most paranoid planet in the cosmos."

"I didn't realise that cosmic bodies could even be conscious, let alone have personalities."

"Well most don't, of course. It depends on your definition of planet really. It's also possible to think of Xenophoria as an organism – it's just a very big one. It began life as Dragonfly, a solar interstellar robotic probe, which was launched following a successful crowd funding effort. Somewhere in its travels into the outer regions of the cosmos Dragonfly crossed paths with a neutron mollusc that had been expelled from its natural habitat at such speed that, even when it crashed continually into asteroid belts and space debris, it did not slow down for decades. Moreover, the same incredible explosion that propelled the soft-bodied creature into space also left it impregnated with heavy subatomic particles that provided a dense and resilient protective layer, enabling it to survive."

"It mutated?"

"Radically. This was more than 'genetic error', it was a radical collision of bodies. During the accident, the mollusc became impaled on the shielding of the Dragonfly probe where, leaking neutron snot from its deep wounds, it eventually slid inside the metallic shell to seek refuge and recovery. The tissues of the two bodies entangled in the most unlikely manner and the organic-metallic chimera became covered in protective mucus. Being neutron dense, the new entity possessed extraordinary mass that drew food towards it – it's favourite being cosmic krill. Gradually, the creature began to feel safe inside its reinforced home."

"So why did you say it is paranoid?"

"Oh, that came next. For centuries, the mollusc continued to orbit,

Rachel Armstrong

adorning its shell with all kinds of space debris – from asteroids, to interplanetary dust clouds and abandoned spacecraft. Its craftsmanship was strange but marvellously creative, making tiny turrets, pillars, arboreal structures, particle sculptures, and solar reefs that squirmed like soils under starlight. Xenophoria could grab an object with its muscular foot and hold it in place on the surface of its asteroid palace while its mantle secreted neutron mollusc glue, which covered its soft body and lubricated its home.

Space travellers who frequented that solar system began to admire the mollusc's work. They spoke of Xenophoria as a world of alien passions, which became more ornate and expanded as the creature obsessively accumulated matter. But, its peaceful life was shattered when, during the Great Spider Battle, a marauding nest of spacetime spiders attempted to disconnect the creature by spraying it with antimatter venom. Try as they might, they could not dismantle the neutron mollusc's impenetrable yet ornate integument. After a prolonged and spiteful siege the spiders withdrew, as they were needed on the battlefield.

Although the neutron mollusc had survived the assault, it became neurotic. Its beautifully constructed protective layers, that had been fashioned into an ideal palace, were badly damaged. Many of the tiny sculptures that had become its surrogate community – cephalopods, sheep, bees and worms – had been defaced. In their place were barren scars, abstract geometries and shiny surfaces that meant nothing to the creature.

The increasingly paranoid mollusc began to behave oddly, for example secreting truly excessive outpourings of snot – even when no threats to its safety were imminent. The long viscous snail-trails it wept became increasingly effusive and further trapped space debris. Even this additional protection could not secure the mollusc's peace of mind. While once it may have been possible to catch glimpses of the mollusc's dextrous foot as it added detritus to its shell, now there were no obvious signs of life. Xenophoria appeared to be nothing more than an accretion system, like a gyre.

Heartbroken, it succumbed to extreme paranoia and ultimately lived the life of an absolute hermit. Now, its home is a 'living' mausoleum that will one day contain its organic remains when it passes away – at the end of time.

218

Rumour has it that the creature stays cheerful by holding conversations with all the objects that it's accumulated. But it can never be truly happy as it is always anticipating another assault by the spacetime spiders. But we're not entirely sure if it's still alive, as there have been no surface signs of activity for centuries."

I start to wonder just how much of life is shaped not by environment or body plan but by psychology. I vow to remain upbeat just in case I also become incarcerated inside an impenetrable shell of my own making. Just as I despair at the unfairness of reality, we notice movement on Xenophoria's surface.

From the dark side of its mausoleum the neutron mollusc suddenly extends its horns towards us. Its huge, blue eyes seem quite sightless. Or perhaps they just don't see in the same way that we do. Although it may be optically blind, I think it has another way of knowing where we're heading.

The colossal creature stretches and yawns a bottomless cavern, its horny lips and undulating tongue preparing for deep sleep. As the slimy threads slam the door shut for the last time, I like to think that it's waving us onwards.

Andromeda

Stokes picks off several lush islands of moss from the masonry, holding her little finger in a curl as if she was eating cream cake in a posh tearoom, and nibbles on them delicately.

We are hanging over the balcony of God's Pagoda. It's a spectacular work of design that overlooks the most extreme panoramic view of the Andromeda galaxy, which touches the edge of the Milky Way. Andromeda's halo is a gargantuan expanse of hot gas that extends for at least two million light years into the cosmos and fills the entire sky. Somehow Klein has captured this sense of totality, not just as an epic scale construction that gestures towards all horizons but also in its masterful details, which are made up of countless grainy bodies. Marvellously, this structure is not entirely built by humans.

Above me a luminescent white body slowly crawls over the tapestry with its pincer-like jaws that splay open like flowers. Its body ripples and refracts waves of starlight through its gut. It is one of thousands of semi-biological worms that Klein has used to construct the pagoda roof. Each of these creatures has been biologically engineered with silicon circuits and embedded pheromone pumps that produce the silk for the canopy as a living membrane, which recounts the ancient legend of Andromeda.

"This is the kind of trouble you get into when your mother boasts that you're more handsome than sea nymphs," observes Stokes as her fingertips run over the ornate hieroglyphics.

"I'm a much bigger fan of the gorgon Medusa," I reply, "whose head Perseus used to defeat the Titan, which Andromeda was going to be sacrificed to. Then, after he claimed his glory, he took the fair maiden's hand in marriage. She gave her rescuer many children and was placed among the stars alongside him when she died."

"It's disappointing," says Stokes. "Couldn't Andromeda have earned her celestial presence for something more extraordinary than giving birth?"

"Birth is extraordinary," I protest.

"Okay, but you know what I mean. Life is extraordinary too, but there's no Naked Mole Rat constellation."

"Not yet," I observe.

A few brilliantly white bugs blindly loop around the floor. I pick them up and place them back on the canopy before Stokes eats them. One of the worms slowly climbs a fibre to add granular details to Andromeda's tale. I lose interest. Stokes is right: whatever the justification, I am more interested the gorgon.

Stokes is still hanging over the balcony snacking on moss biscuits. She points at dark patches like a cracked earth fracture around the Blue Snowball Nebula. I stand next to her, marvelling at the detail.

"It's one thing to see this on the Loom. But to witness the fracturing of spacetime first hand at this magnitude is absolutely breathtaking," I observe.

"It looks like a really bad infestation," adds Stokes solemnly.

I wonder whether I will become a gorgon with flies in my head. Perhaps then I could turn spiders to stone at a glance.

A few more waxen worms fall from the pagoda.

I'm delighted to see that Klein has detailed Medusa's story at the foot of the pagoda pillars. Beyond being decapitated by Perseus, I'm not so familiar with her tale. I get down on my belly to take a much closer look at what has been written in these panels, while trying to avoid crushing the falling silicon silkworms.

"Stokes, do you want to hear the gorgon's tale?"

"Go on, then," she replies with her mouth full.

"Okay, here goes. Medusa was a stunning golden-haired priestess of Athena who was sworn to a life of celibacy. Yet she made love to Poseidon in Athena's temple and was punished for this by the furious goddess who turned her into a monster – her hair became a sea of venomous snakes, her eyes were blood-shot holes and her skin grew green and loathsome. But Medusa did not die when she became hideous and left her home to find a new place in the world. Soon, the rejection she experienced began to change her character. Dropping young snakes from her hair as she wandered from place to place, Medusa transformed the African continent into a hotbed of venomous reptiles."

Several tiny bodies land lightly on the small of my back as I am slithering around on my elbows, engrossed by Medusa's tale. I wonder if it ever rains silicon silk worms in the pagoda.

"Go on," munched Stokes.

"Hopelessly embittered, Medusa's social exclusion soon completed her transformation into a monster. Her hideous exterior now mirrored her monstrous temperament and – dead or alive – her head was a lethal weapon capable of turning anyone she gazed upon into stone. Medusa was the ultimate anti-trophy female."

Stokes snapped something in half and put it in her mouth.

"But Medusa was more than simply deadly. Her victims were petrified and therefore eternally denied re-entry into the cycle of life through the decomposition process. Instead they were fossilised in a stone purgatory for all eternity. Paradoxically, Medusa was not sterile as a result of her hideous transformation, for she was carrying Poseidon's child. In fact, she possessed an alternative form of fertility in her blood that needed no permission from male seed to blossom. The winged horse Pegasus was born from her decapitation and her spilt blood created the *gorgonis* corals of the western seas, whose legions of razor edges continued to wreck the vessels of heroic explorers."

"That's so totally radical," cheered Stokes. "She's my hero already."

"Finally, though, she got her comeuppance. Athena in all her wisdom mounted Medusa's thanato-countenance on her shield as an extended form of punishment from which, rather understandably, she glared for all time, perversely fossilised in metal by the goddess who wrecked her life."

"You know, this really is unfair," Stokes complained. "Athena's reputation for wisdom seems rather questionable, given the prolonged hatred she harbours for the priestess Medusa. In fact, she's more of a monster than her foe. I hope her Promethean worm of jealously ate her from the inside."

"I'm also on the side of the gorgon."

We slap hands in agreement, then drift into silence as we both become pensive about our own heads and whether they too could have an extraordinary power, or afterlife.

Perhaps when my scalp splits open, releasing the maggots that are doubtlessly growing within, they may empower me to immobilise spacetime spiders at a glance.

Stokes, having eaten everything that could be considered a moss biscuit, grabs my hand with sudden resolve and looks at me sternly.

"We've got work to do. Let's go."

Fossil Time Twist

We pass a honeycomb planet which resembles a pig's skull with two colossal tusks curling upwards from the South Polar Region.

Two elderly women are knitting together with chopsticks on a rocky cavity positioned on the giant boulder, as an orbit. Their roll of yarn completely fills the hollow and their weave drops as a continuous ladder of highly patterned tears billowing into the abyss. One of them starts banging on the roof of the incomplete orbital bar with her walking stick, because the old couple upstairs, are trying for a baby. Down towards the maxilla someone's straining loudly on the toilet. The whole skull is snoring.

One of the weavers catches sight of us, waves furiously and makes a run for it. Hurling herself upwards over the frontal bone on to the North Pole of the planet, she clambers upwards to the tip of the parietal crest, where she stands on top of the bone-world, her arms flailing, signalling distress.

"We can't help her," says Stokes, "It's a fossil time twist. There's no escape."

As we pass, the woman recklessly hurls herself towards us like a skydiver. She doesn't quite reach us, and plummets down past the zygomatic arch searching for footing on the ladder of tears. She's shouting something. My heart sinks as she's swallowed into the void and I look at Stokes who nudges my ribs sharply and points again at the orbit, where two elderly women are knitting together with chopsticks.

Aurorae

Cousins are everywhere. Stokes is already running towards a hot dog vendor.

"I'm famished," she yells.

I begin to get my bearings. Younglings arrange rows of chairs that are angled towards a darkening horizon, inviting an audience to view the sunset. I rock back on the legs of a ringside seat trying to figure out what is going on around the site.

To my left, hyperbolic weavers are tightening the screws on portable copper condensers and rolling around several barrels of spacetime dew. Impatient to do their work, misty aether is already being drawn towards the stomata of the vessels where it rhythmically creeps inside, the drops keeping time like a biomechanical heart. The dripping pulse is slow; they will need to work much faster if we're going to make enough thread to meet the spiders head on.

Stokes is talking with her mouth full of white cotton candy while draping her arm around a stout candyfloss maker. Her appetites vacillate between man and cotton floss. They are laughing uncontrollably.

A pair of long leather boots with outward-facing metal studs steps out of a fluttering tent. Oddly, the toes are separated, like cloven-hoofed gloves. Without looking upwards, I know its Klein.

I rise to my feet respectfully, my head bowed. As I slowly lift my gaze she is just as magnificent as I imagined her. Even in flat footwear she stands a good six feet tall, perhaps taller. Her hair is blonde and cropped and her piercing blue eyes are arched lengthways. With the poise of a ballet dancer and the muscle definition of a body builder, she is so slim from the side that she almost disappears. I've wanted to meet her in person for so long. Yet now she is here I have absolutely no idea what to say to her.

A strange hairball of organic matter tumbles unnoticed over her boot and scurries off again to sniff at its next destination.

I quickly sit down again before this magnificent woman notices that I am transfixed. Behind me, the ionised horizon is burning brilliant red with finger-like green clouds that are formed by interactions in the upper atmosphere between cosmic rays, solar wind and magnetospheric plasma.

Klein hasn't seen me. She is engrossed in a heated conversation with colleagues and squats down on her heels, using her chopsticks to trace directions in the ground. I wait patiently for an appropriate moment to introduce myself.

Finally Klein rises, and I do the same. We are face to face. She looks through me without emotion.

"I'm Mobius."

I hold out my hand in greeting. Klein says nothing but raises her chin at an equally statuesque companion and nods in my direction. Her hair is spun into a beehive and she has the most carefully painted eyebrows I have ever seen.

"Zeta."

She's remarkably strong and holds me in a welcoming power grip as she walks me a little distance away from Klein and her group. Perhaps I've been standing a little too close to them all, or rubbernecking into spaces where I am not been invited.

"We're rounding the spiders up tomorrow. Several teams are out in the field containing the damage they've wrought on the spacetime fabric here. It's been touch and go but everyone has worked incredibly hard to keep the whole area from unravelling."

There's a hollow sound of clanking metal as she talks. I look down. Zeta has a prosthetic leg. She's wearing a shoe with a cloven hoof on her natural leg. Her prosthesis does not attempt to mimic any kind of biological appendage at all. Rather it is an elegant mathematical structure – an inverted cone that is sharpened into a deadly point.

"Come back just before dawn. Spiders don't like the transitions from dark to light. They're easiest to round up then."

I shake her hand again and as she walks away I notice the earth breaking under the pressure of her spike. Obviously she's not at her best earth-walking. Her upper body muscle definition is typical of an aerial performer.

I take my ringside sunset seat again, as a few cousins – Rubin, Fox and Curie – I think, silently join me to watch a sudden shower of charged particles surge into the atmosphere in a symphonic display of colour.

Stokes returns with a triple scoop ice-cream. Her body scent has changed slightly, her musk adorned with hint-of-'man'. This is even more potent when she gives me one of her wonderful hugs. I am quietly thrilled she's back. We sit together on ringside seats watching all kinds of figures fade in and out of view against the streaming aurora backdrop. She invites me to take a bite of the cone as we watch the aurorae fall. It's an offer that is simply too good to refuse.

Daybreak

There's been too much activity in the camp overnight for us to sleep.

Relatives have been talking in hushed voices, performing last minute checks on equipment, reciting the "Self Pity" poem and limbering up.

The portable copper condenser is squeezed for any last drops of spacetime distillate.

Klein responds in staccato phrase to droning male voices inside her tent.

The aurorae have all but gone and dawn has not yet broken. Wide-eyed younglings are filling up the seats under the violet morning light. None of them complain about getting up early. Those that herd them stand watchfully at the ringside with their backs to the horizon.

It's a restless sunrise.

Klein's the first to ascend the spacetime fibres. Her Amazonian frame casts long, cool shadows against the floral hues of daybreak. She's already up so high that her striking features have blended into her silhouette.

Hundreds of relatives follow her, casting fibres in formation to build the circus scaffolding with which we'll meet the spiders. Stokes and I follow. It's a towering cylindrical structure, reminiscent of a roman coliseum. The apex is formed from a cluster of nests that house the portable condensers and help weavers to move rapidly across the whole structure. We're shuttles within a portable weaving machine!

A lookout shouts.

The horizon disintegrates into jerky segments. We see them. The spiders are fracturing the earth as they charge towards us. They appear and disappear again into the decaying landscape. Fast as dogs, smart as cats.

Some of the younglings on ringside seats start crying. But the watchful eye of their guardians never slackens.

Klein swoops in freefall.

A cluster of spiders shoots antimatter venom at her from their mouthparts. She's too quick for them and binds them at the feet using a spacetime fibre as a lasso. As the arachnids try to wriggle free she tie-down ropes them.

The spiders, weakened by proximity to each other, begin to fade. The one thing they hate is connection. Spiders thrive on detachment. This is our fundamental argument with them. As guardians of the Implicate Order, we champion the universal interconnectedness, which is embodied in the spacetime fibres of the cosmos that the spiders are bent on destroying. In binding a connecting lattice around them, arachnids are forced into close proximity with each other. This goes against the fundamental principles that govern their existence and weakens their essence. Gradually their bodies retreat back into the dark universe.

When all is still, it is possible to feel the dark breeze sucking on their disintegrating egos, drawing them back to whence they came.

Then they're back.

One spider charges her from behind but Klein's anticipates the ambush and throws a loop around its sternum. Then she tugs sharply on the fibre so that its legs collapse underneath it, like a folding table. She dismounts her thread and runs to the beast, which is on its back, struggling to rise. Within moments Klein expertly ties its legs together.

Punching skyward we whoop and scream, "Spider rodeo!"

We drop from our threads like dew.

Stokes and I start team roping stampeding spiders, swooping to each side of them at the last moment of a head on charge. I'm the header, responsible for roping the creature's sternum. Stokes is the heeler who ties up its legs when I'm done. Somehow, I also acquire the job of spider bait. Plunging from the scaffolding, I dangle myself briefly in front of the beasts and lasso their mouthparts with a half-head knot. Then I noose the sternum from above as I pass over them, still swinging from my thread. Once I'm clear, I jerk on the tether and the spider falls to one side. After a few attempts I'm getting the hang of it and with the first toppled beast Stokes is already there. She's bound its hairy feet, tightly secured the slipknot and is triumphantly chewing on tumbleweed.

I glance over at the others.

Zeta is spider wrestling. This is much riskier than team roping but circus folk excel when facing danger. Tumbling from her thread, she pursues the arachnids from behind and drops right onto them. Using her prosthetic leg, she spikes them and pivots gracefully. Once she's finished riding the bucking beast, she scrapes her prosthesis over their integument, which makes an awful shrieking sound. Then she holds them in a contortion lock using her extraordinary strength and musculature to clamp their legs together. With the right body lock, the creature's legs simply give way. She tussles them and firmly ties them down. Once that's done, she is instantly aerial bound, searching for fresh spider buck.

Ackermann is spider-bronc riding. He's prolonging the thrill of bareback spider surfing. The beasts make incredible attempts to throw him off their backs but we wouldn't be circus if we didn't thrive on the peril and spectacle. Ackermann's particular skill is in using each thrash the spiders make as a lift for a series of somersaults. His dizzyingly complex moves leave the confused arachnid wide open to a set of simple lasso knots that topple them like skittles.

Although the spiders are better armed with their antimatter venom and incredibly sharp mouthparts, our acrobats are simply too nimble for them. We are wearing these spiders down into submission.

A frustrated clutter of spiders veers off and bolts for the younglings. But those who herd are prepared for such an attack. The beasts are ridden and parcelled before they make the first leap at the children.

While Klein in particular makes spider rodeo look easy, it's not. It's incredibly dangerous. I'm reminded of the hundreds of soft mounds that Stokes and I came across on the site of the first Great Spider Battle and realise that without such a strong leader we could easily be facing a very different outcome.

Now Klein gives the final order. She's hauling up piles of tethered spiders and weaving them into a suspended net. As she secures them, her deltoids splay and her back muscles stretch like wings. Working with Zeta and a small group of weavers, Klein drapes the beasts over the spacetime scaffolding in formations that remind me of chandeliers. Hundreds upon hundreds of spiders are hoisted into wriggling bundles and tightly secured in clusters with a finishing knot. Then a troupe of acrobats and weavers led by Fibonacci make a final check on the spider knots and re-cast them in the connecting tapestry. Those spiders with unsecured mouthparts are trying to spit antimatter. Although some of us sustain a few minor antimatter burns from the fine spray in the air, the poison does not have the necessary range to cause us much damage.

Klein high-fives her acrobat crew and disappears into the tent with them, while weavers disperse into the night. Some of them join us at the ringside for ice cream. Younglings entertain us by acting out the highlights of the day, riding bareback on each other and re-living their favourite moments of the spider rodeo.

"The big one is totally 'pow'. Klein's all over it. The spider's lassoed on the ground. It's so bundled. Awesome."

The bloody sky begins to lace with green aurorae but the day is entirely without casualty. It's most notable, however, for the fading spider structure that is now laced with green threads from the magnetosphere and will most likely have done its work by daybreak.

But the danger has not gone.

Nothing's over until we have secured the queen.

Queen

I've been able to rest for a few hours despite Stokes' infernal snoring. After she got up for a midnight snack she instantly collapsed into a deep sleep. Then she blew back so deeply into her tuba-like airways that I had to beat her over the head with a pillow – twice – to wake her up and roll her on to her side. She says it's her sugar levels. The problem is that when she dozes off she ends up on her back, which starts the snoring symphony again.

Few of us sleep as deeply as Stokes but the younglings are already in their chairs as we scamper aloft when the sky blossoms. Despite our recent success there's a spreading sense of foreboding. The Dark Queen is coming.

The skyline quickly fractures into a clutter of spiders. They are much faster than yesterday and so many more of them.

Klein leads the descent again with rodeo moves, but this time they're prepared.

We're already sustaining a slew of antimatter burns and injuries from falls as the spiders change their tactics. They're working in threes, launching their attack from behind as we land bareback on their carapace, while another arachnid unravels the spacetime fibres around us. Our mobility is greatly compromised by these tactics and we're at risk of getting stranded.

Klein's troupe clusters around her in formation but the rest of us are finding it hard to hold our manoeuvres together. Some of us retreat as a sudden clatter of spiders appears from dark fractals in the ground.

Klein seizes the opportunity to plunge again. This time, we are not individuals or small groups but follow her lead as a circus web of bodies.

We pair trawl the arachnids. Klein spearheads one end of a spacetime net and Fibonacci the other.

I take the floatline at the upper edge of the manoeuvre while Stokes is at the footrope. She's so close to the ground that she's already begun cycling her legs in preparation to run at any moment. Franklin is up high to my right but she's concentrating so hard that she doesn't notice me.

Instinctively we meet the ground-swelling arachnid wave head on in monster formations with more limbs than any spider – anteosaurus, hippofly, crocoroo and sabre toothed rabbit. We quickly fold their legs from under them with nets, recede and fall again.

A spider clutter breaks for the younglings, which are ushered up the spacetime fibres to safety by those that herd them. Our monstrous net of circus bodies holds them firmly in check but we're losing our advantage. There are so many spiders.

Then the Dark Queen grows like an anti-Venus out of the black arachnid sea.

She stills the ground with impenetrable membranes of concrete and tar macadam as she walks. Life starts to fade at the edges of her existence. Everything withers. She's not an arachnid but a spectre so greedy that she gives nothing back. Not even light is reflected from her frame.

The spider ranks recede, as with fracturing steps she approaches our circus net.

Klein meets her.

The Dark Queen stares at our leader with malignant need. Voracious. Desperate. A paralysing presence that sucks in everything. Thin tumbleweed stops moving. Budding plants become confounded with stones. Flints disintegrate into sand. The sky stops climbing. The multicoloured flower of iron withers into bare black metal seeds. The air around her blackens and drops, forming a sooty layer on the ground.

"Give me what I want."

Klein refuses, as fleeting fragments of soil fall out of the air and make a sooty layer upon the ground.

Maxwell

The Dark Queen raises her fist to command the arachnids to strike, but Maxwell stays her hand – the woman who devoured his organs.

"Aradana. It's been a long time."

"I demand your life for the injuries you have done me! The things you denied me," she hisses through narrowed eyes that stretch dark matter from her pupils in malignant webs.

"I cannot do that."

Klein prepares to fell the shade with a lasso but Aradana's bleak gaze is hypnotising. She cannot move. I'm too far away to be part of the dialogue. From this distance I also notice the spider swarm encircling us as negotiations proceed.

"It's a trap!" I yell, but Klein and Maxwell appear to be under Aradana's spell.

I'm feeling utterly powerless and strangely sad, as if someone just cleaned my stomach out with a scouring pad and my blood seems to flow backwards. Then, my head thumps with anxiety, or flies, and as I feel a dreadful pressure rising in my head, I make a dash for it.

Now, I am truly spider bait.

Phase Change

The Dark Queen is momentarily distracted as spiders instinctively bolt after me. The organless man makes his move. He steps with extreme slowness towards Aradana. Perhaps it is because he actually appears mobile, or because he can bend time, somehow he escapes detection and passionately embraces her. Like everything my grandfather does, it takes an extremely long time.

At some point his oscillating lips whisper, "I forgive you."

Locked in Maxwell's facial muscles, the Dark Queen cannot push him away. She wants his isolation, not compassion.

Klein's already taking down spiders with a lasso as a surging wave of circus resistance follows.

I'm brachiating low along the ground so the arachnids will continue to follow me, but I'm in trouble. Spider mouthparts clatter and antimatter venom spray is gnawing at my flesh. They're quickly gaining on me. While patches of my skin burn, a searing pain in my head makes me want to shut my eyes. Instead, I focus on my hands – one hand leading over the other.

Keep going. I must keep going.

Then, the soft part of my head bursts open like a hatching egg, activating the latent viruses. My skull bones start to speak, buzzing, scratching and squelching. I am a zombie host commanded by parasites. An exploding cloud of newly-emerged flies trails me. Others are still in the larval stages – but they're probably not far behind. I'm leaking flies from my head, my ears, my eyes and even coughing them up in my mouth. But maybe being a bait ball has its advantages.

The viral codes build up a concentration of quorum signalling matter. My biology enters into a new phase transition and I identify as 'fly'. I am in metamorphosis and my identity radically shifts.

Flies

We flies have feelings – emotional thought clouds that cast their own internal shadows. We respond to all kinds of environmental cues such as colour, or sudden thundering noises. Admittedly we don't experience true human equivalents like fear, happiness, love or anger, as our emotional landscapes are most strongly shaped by negative feelings – a sense of doom, if you will, which affects our behaviour for some time afterwards. Oddly, we cannot settle around things that make us feel good until we've worked our way through all the possible bad feelings first and we're particularly afraid of shadows. In other words, if we're trying to eat in the shade then we'll end up unable to settle and very hungry indeed.

Right now, we flies are happy. Bursting out into the sun through the exploded cavern that was Mobius' – this metamorphosing human fly hybrid, the zombie host's, head. We spread our crumpled wings for the very first time. But as spider shadows loom around us, we're quickly fearful again.

We remember through human memories the lessons from the Antboard – that creatures will perform according to their nature, regardless of the rules associated with tactical play. Instinctively we know how spiders will behave when presented with a swarm of flies.

We are irresistible.

Still brachiating elegantly within the host body, we turn to taunt the clatter of spiders running alongside us. A few large scorpions rise from small, sandy burrows to join the stampeding throng

"Let us tempt you with today's Arachnidan special." We tease, "we're a pre-digested; spongy protein source that comes directly from the human brain, deliciously dusted with a cloud of hatchling flies."

The scorpions intensify their charge towards us and raise their deadly tails like coiling whips. Yet arachnid sight is not particularly precise and we continue to taunt them, staying just at the limits of their vision. We can't call what they see with – 'eyes'. They're too primitive. Unblinking. Basic. Our visual apparatus on the other hand is iridescent. We perceive in multiples – observing the world through an organic, fractured looking-glass.

Then the entire left hand of the host is gone. Stunned at the vaporised stump of our zombie vehicle, we continue running. We don't want to die in pieces. We are not finished with the head nest yet. Terrifyingly dark shadows suddenly encroach upon us and we can feel the breeze of the dark universe ripping spacetime in all directions. Raising our *zombie host's whip arm, we turn to make one last stand.*

Exit

Clawing through the spacetime fabric, the Dark Queen retreats into the vacuum of solitude and dark space.

"Farewell Aradana. I am sorry for your pain," says Maxwell. A ripple of empathy remains on his lips after his words are gone.

Her departure is unlamented, no more than a trail of foamy soot that disappears into the earth. Out of this fracture new life almost instantly begins celebrating in tiny clusters of scintillating jellies, which beckon the succession of life.

Even the vanishing beasts that are bundled in mounds and strung up in nets of connectivity are unmoved by their defeat, or their queen's departure, and continue glaring defiantly at the descending circus troupe.

Dark World

A hole appears in the Loom – a gaping void where spacetime fibres have completely unravelled. It's gut-wrenchingly bleak.

Our multiple selves can't see it directly but we know it's there from the refractions recorded it in the spacetime distillate. After all, we're still sensorially connected to our zombie host, and in the most minuscule way, still part human. Writhing and shrieking, the darkest shadows display the pain of destruction. The Loom's threads attempt to form a scab of matter. They attempt to repair the hole yet again but the rolled edges abate all forms of healing. Grotesque twists of materiality tumble into the abyssal tears in the tapestry and are swallowed by them, as the Dark Queen returns to her shadow realm.

But it's not a triumphant homecoming.

The waiting beasts form clusters of darkness around her, clattering impatiently, inching towards her.

"Aradana."

"Address me properly beast. I am your queen."

"Aradana, once you were. We worked tirelessly for you. Dedicated our lives for you."

"Back off, creature!"

"Once our welfare was entwined. We knew you were self-serving even then, all those lifetimes ago, but our needs were served by your ambition. We became your private army, feeding on the scraps of your greed. And still there was benefit in our dedication. It was enough."

"What do you want from me?"

"Nothing now. You uncoupled your desires from the material gain on which we feed. You squandered our loyalty to pursue personal vendettas that cause us defeat, humiliation and slow starvation."

"You followed me. It was your choice."

"Choice? You gamed us. Without dignifying us with so much as a conversation you exchanged things of substance that we value –worms, warm-blooded prey and shiny objects – for empty platitudes, unfulfilled promises and downright lies. You lost your worth."

"I upped the stakes for greater things. I would have given you the whole of the visible universe, not just mere morsels of it. Don't blame me for your ineptitude. You pathetic brutes."

"We see no reason to further endure your incessant abuse. You are anthropocentric and moralistic. You are dishonourable. In your name thousands of us have been bound, weakened and dissipated. And while many thousands still remain, we seek a new way of living through which we will reap the bounteous light-filled worlds once again and claim them for the darkness."

"Treacherous monsters. You already own ninety-five percent of the universe. But you could have had it all."

"You know so little about us, Aradana. You take our loyalty for granted."

"Just stay away from me. You disgusting fiends. How dare you approach me!"

"We have big appetites. Monstrous cravings, which is why we were drawn to your shameless greed. But you have abused us and left us ravenous."

"I warned you. Get back."

"And we are starving beyond empty. Darkness is insatiable."

The condensate in the portable copper vessels momentarily gleams with splinters of laser fine light. It takes us a moment to realise what is happening, since the memory recording is unstable. These events have already happened.

It's not hard to piece together a chain of likely events. Yet, while such occurrences may be probable, they are not necessarily inevitable.

While spacetime spiders' spinnerets do not work in the realm of visible light, they produce copious and deadly networks of silk when they inhabit the dark domains. Spider webs are intriguing in their many relationships with light. When they are in direct sunlight they will shine with metallic brilliance and are easily seen. But when luminosity is low and light is indirect, spider webs are invisible to their prey. This is no accident. In the visible realm spiders camouflage and pattern their webs so they melt into the surroundings habitat. We feel the possibility of joy return as the transmission in the copper condensers is torn up by chaotic shadows that surge across the darkening spacetime distillate. Aradana's residual memory trace already seems to have been erased and although the spiders have also dissipated, it's impossible to say what their next move will be.

We dread and anticipate their return.

Whatever form it takes, and wherever it occurs. We are certain it will be brilliant, monstrous and deadly.

Family

We prepare to be devoured by spiders.

As a swarm we are ready for this eventuality. After all, endings are also part of the cycle of life. Already, our zombie host has enriched our understanding of reality, where pressing events have brought us closer to one kind of community – human kin and their kith, with their circus art and spacetime heritage – but also we are united as a culture of flies. Even an army of voracious spiders cannot subdue our kind permanently. Oddly, we're at peace. Whatever happens next, the circus troupe of hyperbolic weavers will continue to spin their art and champion the integrity of the Implicate Order, which enables us to spread our ethos through parasitic ways and incomplete digestions of host bodies.

Just as we think this particular incarnation is over, spacetime suddenly seems still.

Only Newton, dreadful and magnificent, has the strength to jerk on the fabric of reality and hold it in check. He's standing in front of us with his arms folded, taller than ever and magnificent in a way that the zombie host has not appreciated him previously. She sighs deeply, preparing for us to be reprimanded for making sloppy spacetime folds – why we're now "fly."

Newly-hatched, we continue to surge from our host's head.

The giant's shadow continues to lengthen, his vast wings expanding, and at this moment seems more imposing than even the advancing dark arachnid army. With two boils now on his forehead, the zombie suddenly recognises something she's not seen before and thinks to ask the creature whether he's ever fallen from grace. Yet Mobius says nothing to her demonic parent.

Shelley appears alongside him, under a giggling cloud of tiny children. Her hair is twisted into a fearsome knot that rises to strike cobra-like. She pays no attention to our altered identity – as we're circus kith and kin – but we are sure she understands the situation – flies, circus troupe, dark angel and zombie hosts, united against the invasion of the dark universe into the luminous realm.

"You're not on your own," she says to us all, as she blocks the arachnid swarm from directly attacking us with her vicious whip.

The blurred combined movements between Shelley and the children bind the first charge of arachnids in a virtuous display of knot making. Hair and bodies entwine to ensnare the spiders in a tapestry of their own venom and cast them skyward into an aerial net. The mouth of this purse shuts with a resounding 'snap'. Newton lifts the children even higher, so they can move even faster than they do in the Loom's quantum shuttles. He adopts the direction of the weft, while Shelley becomes the warp. The children are juggled between their parents, forming an impenetrable, luminous fabric of unrivalled force. Their human bodies glide around each other working quickly and lightly. Shelley rotates clockwise, Newton counters anti-clockwise. They're much faster, more fluid and better choreographed than any machine, or legion of brute spiders. Despite our difficulties, differences, divergent interests, anatomical contradictions and the inevitable troubles of the world – fundamentally this circus troupe and we, the bait – are a flawless team. Working together, we weave an impenetrable, luminous cloth around the scores of charging arachnids and unfurling scorpion barbs. Soon, the assemblage of arachnid bodies resembles a strange tree with many arms, legs and dark textures.

Another late wave of arachnids charge and Newton growls at us all to climb the dark structure of bound bodies. Without argument, we do so.

"I have swept away your offenses like a cloud, your sins like the morning mist. Return to me, for I have redeemed you," howls Newton, spraying the ground with the vile aerosol that emanates from his breath.[4]

Flies are stronger and lighter than any human, but the children work to augment us further by lifting us higher than ever before into Newton's winged cosmic canopy. Then, as the giant secures the last of the beasts beneath him, spacetime judders and everything appears to start moving again according to its usual rhythm.

As a single, giant mass of deeply connected bodies, the malevolent creatures crumple and are absorbed back into the dark realms from which they came.

Today feels different. We are more than 'fly', and even the stump hand of our zombie host, already seems fundamental to our identity.

---

[4] *Footnote: Isaiah 44:22*

Audience

Klein has asked to see us.

We sit outside her tent reluctantly, hoping that we can behave according to the etiquette of good 'taste', and not spew our newly hatched kin from our head hole and nostrils.

Zeta informs us that Klein's not ready yet, so we watch glittering particles climb the upper atmosphere as the sky turns peach.

Tonight life's resilience in the face of adversity feels pronounced. The world blooms with intense vigour as the Implicate Order begins to enfold the damage wrought by the spiders back into its fabric. Insects unrelentingly chew on leafy vegetation, even when they seem to have no stomachs to feed. Withered ferns flourish. Plants that were crushed under foot are growing tall again. Silicates shine in the stones like the scales of fish. Tumbleweed dances, mollusc shells uncoil like cables, the bristles of earthworms squeak, pods discharge their seeds in a cloud of fireworks, rising sap quivers in crystal ball formations, pollen clouds billow like laundry and vibrant soft mosses swallow hard-edged stones. But it's not just the macroscopic world that is thriving. Even the quietest atom vibrates symphonically inside its core giving life to a throbbing constellation of tiny globular masses on an orchestra of strings no thicker than glowworm silk. Such flourishing is an indication that the primordial ether is in a state of active repair.

Zeta beckons us inside but does not join us.

"Thank you," says Klein. "I admire what you did."

She gifts us a handcrafted terrarium to be worn in a shoulder sling over the deltoid. It is stitch-perfect, teeming with microscopic life. As we study the biofilm details they squirm, constantly reinventing themselves. Embarrassed at the honour and increasingly affiliating with the insect realm, we slip the apparatus over our arm and mumble appreciation as flies pour jubilantly from our host's mouth. We can feel our zombie's brainwaves wishing she had some magnificent feature that would distinguish her from all other things, so that she is more than part of the background noise. She thinks she could learn to flow like water, sing with siren grace, or dazzle with electromagnetic radiance just through smiling

– she thinks she could be more than she already is – a creative infection of flies.

We contradict and reassure her that this is the best thing she could possibly be. She needs no other reassurances that her life – how she viewed it – was more than worthwhile.

As aurorae reach downwards towards the horizon; the green magnetosphere slams up against the haemoglobin landscape and emphasises this world's renewed vigour.

It's the best day of our life.

Darkness Rises

Maxwell loves this time of day. He's waiting for us, watching atmospheric particles transform into a sunset.

"You do not need Klein's affirmation," he says. "You're already extraordinary."

Spectacular light displays do not intrigue him as much as the worlds that spring up out of the horizon beneath them like weeds and push their way through the basal blackness into the material realm. He observes that these murky interfaces bring us face to face with dark ecologies where uncertainty fills the spaces between the membranes of life. These shadowy realms and spandrels are responsible for the fundamental rhythms of the living world such as pollination, the breakdown of organic matter, or the incomplete digestions of hosts and parasites.

We shiver, fearful of the prospect of creeping shadows.

Maxwell's gaze falls beyond the slowly changing electromagnetic rays and towards the rising darkness where strange nocturnal communities of invertebrate predators and scavengers flit around the camp's blush of lights. When different realms flourish, contested territories arise that come with the possibility of conflict. Nothing is already written and all is still to play for. Indeed, they are inherently ethical places where values spring from places with no clear rights and wrongs. Such values only become apparent by the occupation and living that takes place within them, whereby in standing 'for' something in the face of adversity, we are presented with the choice of folding ourselves into the belly of darkness or finding creative pathways to new modes of existence. To truly live the 'good' life is to be vulnerable and open to the possibility of transformation through others, circumstance, compost, and even by feckless shadows.

"Did you fall in love with a shade to undergo metamorphosis?" our host Mobius asks Maxwell.

Another cohort of newly-hatched flies crawls out from behind the zombie's eyes. Yet she can no longer hear the old man who starts to remind us that even in the face of annihilation triumph is still possible. But Maxwell doesn't answer her question. He already understands the situation too well, and has no truths or platitudes to offer our kind. He suddenly seems exhausted, and slowly shuffles into the darkness, touching our host's arm gently as he parts in a final gesture of peace making. We are finding it harder to empathise with humanity, although we're still fond, still part kin.

The deeply iron-stained sunset grows even richer as the day closes. We still have many questions about new beginnings that do not start at daybreak, but are formed as the ground swallows the light. While there is cause for our trepidation, there is much still to let go of and much to leave behind, as we prepare for our onwards journey.

The air is fully charged, ionised. It feels rich. There is a different quality to being alive this evening and as the darkness finally rises, it swallows every shadow into its endless substances. As we prepare to origamy, we hear Shelley singing the Mobius song and we know it's time to go home.

"When the storm comes, keep us safe."

Dissipation

"O death, where is your victory? O death, where is your sting?" [5]

Our zombie host casts an epic origamy knot – a perfect casting that spans to Earth in a single throw. It's an incredible geometry and instantaneous construction, which rivals anything that Klein's ever fashioned – God's Pagoda, the Panta Rhei Tunnel or, the Globular Bridge.

Our interstellar causeway – The Flyway – is composed of many layers. It leaps into spectacular arches, twists into structural pillars, branches into labyrinthine walkways and dissipates into many steps that take spacetime travellers all around the cosmos.

We watch the genesis of this architectural constellation through our translucent, chocolate red tinged bodies, our maggoty flesh, our paper-thin wings and our intestinal cavities, twitching our forelegs excitedly. Synchronously, we vibrate our integuments, applauding the greatest highway in existence – constructed by flies.

Throughout the universe night skies, freed from the threat of shadows, are effervescent with joy at what we've accomplished and every subatomic particle that ever existed is oscillating. Intoxicated by success, we're lighter and foamier than ever and as we admire our perfection we notice that our bodies are becoming even more transparent, that everything is shaking apart. It begins in the hum of molecular vibrations, tickles our integuments, radiates into the landscapes and starts to melt the firmament.

The cosmos is dissipating.

Or perhaps it is we that are dissolving. This does not diminish our delight. We vibrate our fundamental building blocks even more vigorously than before in celebration of our multiple achievements, scattering ourselves into the endless cosmic void, becoming panspermic specs of matter, with the potential to become anything we wish to be – and reunite with the dark child, the eternal celestial being that oversees our transition from one realm to the next.

---

[5] *Footnote: 1 Corinthians 15:57 KJV*

Thanatobiome

We're watching the brain surgery of a young woman lying on the table through multiple eyes and perspectives.

It's been a very difficult few hours, touch and go to the last.

At eleven fifteen hours precisely she is twenty-one years, five months, three hours and five minutes old. Give or take a few seconds. She's exactly the same physiological age as our host body. She looks a bit like her but she's not part of us, because she's over there and we're here.

The thanatobiome started ticking around three minutes ago, which marks the start of a new kind of time.

Over there, the anaesthetist, who is very old and moves without any urgency like an unfolding deck chair, is loosening the ties that secure the airway. No one has yet arrived to tidy the spent crash trolley.

Here, the neurosurgeon with striking blue eyes and mop of untamed hair is staring at a blank page in the medical notes. She's wondering how she'll begin the report.

Two young nurses are hugging each other in the doorway. One of them is corpulent with an embrace that the other wants to fall in to. They are sobbing uncontrollably.

In the scrub room a young surgical assistant, who has a habit of standing on the tips of his toes when he is talking, is pressing his head against the wall. He is clanging his hand against a metal surface, beating it like a percussion instrument, and seems upset.

A senior nurse, who insists on being called by her full name, places her hand on the arm of a tall man and a very small woman in the waiting room. They're surrounded by relatives of all ages and skin hues who linger anxiously in the waiting room juggling small children on their knees and singing to each other. A young girl with a very long tongue plays at being an anteater while piggy-backing a chair. The waste bin, which has not been emptied for some time, appears to be a breeding ground for flies.

In an echoing corridor a couple of orderlies are pleating lengths of cotton sheets together, like folding origami, and wait patiently for further instructions.

An energy-conscious someone casts a spider-like shadow and turns off the monitor.

About the Author

Rachel Armstrong is Professor of Experimental Architecture at the School of Architecture, Planning and Landscape, Newcastle University. She is a Rising Waters II Fellow with the Robert Rauschenberg Foundation (April-May 2016), TWOTY futurist 2015, Fellow of the British Interplanetary Society and a 2010 Senior TED Fellow. A former medical doctor, she now designs experiments that explore the transition between inert and living matter and considers their implications for life beyond our solar system.

Rachel has long been fascinated by the opportunity science fiction provides to explore the extremes of human potential and step outside the strictures of current scientific understanding. *Origamy* is her debut novel.

2001: AN ODYSSEY IN WORDS

Produced to honour the centenary of Sir Arthur's birth, this anthology acts as a fund raiser for the Arthur C. Clarke Award.

The authors' brief was simple: deliver us a stunning SF story of precisely 2001 words; and deliver they did. The book features contributions from some of the biggest names in science fiction, including many who have won or been shortlisted for the Clarke Award

Alastair Reynolds
Bruce Sterling
Paul McAuley
Gwyneth Jones
Ian McDonald
Adrian Tchaikovsky
Rachel Pollack
Becky Chambers
Ian R. MacLeod
Claire North
Jeff Noon,
Chris Beckett
Dave Hutchinson
Colin Greenland
Adam Roberts
Jane Rogers
Yoon Ha Lee
Philip Mann
Emmi Itäranta
Ian Watson
Liz Williams
And more…

Released summer 2018 by NewCon Press, in collaboration with the Arthur C. Clarke Award.
www.newconpress.co.uk

IMMANION PRESS

Purveyors of Speculative Fiction

Madame Two Swords by Tanith Lee

An unnamed narrator, in the French city of Troy, finds an old book of the writings of the revolutionary, Lucien de Ceppays, who lived and died in the city two centuries before. She feels a strange bond to the life and thoughts of this long-dead man — what is the mysterious truth behind her obsession? Perhaps she did not find the book at all — perhaps it found her. Some years later, impoverished after the death of her mother, the narrator — in a state of desperation — finds herself inexorably guided to meet the peculiar and unnerving Madame Two Swords, an old woman with a history, and her own enduring bonds to Lucien — as well as the book. For the narrator, reality seems to unravel, as she begins to penetrate just how intimately she is connected with Madame Two Swords and Lucien. Previously only available as a limited-edition hardback in 1988, the long-awaited new edition of this vintage-Tanith novella includes illustrations by Jarod Mills. ISBN 978-1-907737-81-7 £11.99, $15.50 pbk

Salty Kiss Island by Rhys Hughes

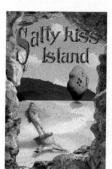

What is a fantastical love story? It isn't quite the same as an ordinary love story. The events that take place are stranger, more extreme, full of the passion of originality, invention and magic, as well as an intensification of emotional love. The stories in Salty Kiss Island are set in this world and others, spanning the spectrum of possible and impossible experiences, the uncharted territories of yearning, the depths and shoals of the heart, mind and soul. A love of language runs through them, parallel to the love that motivates their characters to feats of preposterous heroism, luminous lunacy and grandiose gesture. They include tales of minstrels and their catastrophic serenades, dreamers sinking into sequences of ever-deeper dreams, goddesses and mermaids, sailors and devils, messages in bottles that can think and speak but never be read, shadows with an independent life and voyagers of distant galaxies who are already at their destinations before they arrive.
ISBN: 978-1-907737-77-0, £11.99, $15.50 pbk

A Raven Bound with Lilies by Storm Constantine

 Androgynous, and stronger in mind and body than humans, sometimes deadly, and often possessing unearthly beauty, the Wraeththu have captivated readers since Storm Constantine's first novel, The Enchantments of Flesh and Spirit, was published in 1988, regarded as ground-breaking in its treatment of gender and sexuality. This anthology of 15 tales collects all her published Wraeththu short stories into one volume, and also includes extra material, including the author's first explorations of the androgynous race. The tales range from the 'creation story' Paragenesis, through the bloody, brutal rise of the earliest tribes, and on into a future, where strange mutations are starting to emerge from hidden corners of the earth. With illustrations by official Wraeththu artist Ruby, as well as pictures from Danielle Lainton and the author herself, A Raven Bound with Lilies is a must for any Wraeththu enthusiast, and is also a comprehensive introduction to the mythos for those who are new to it. ISBN: 978-1-907737-80-0 £11.99, $15.50

The Lightbearer by Alan Richardson

 Michael Horsett parachutes into Occupied France before the D-Day Invasion. He is dropped in the wrong place, miles from the action, badly injured, and totally alone. He falls prey to two Thelemist women who have awaited the Hawk God's coming, attracts a group of First World War veterans who rally to what they imagine is his cause, is hunted by a troop of German Field Police who are desperate to find him, and has a climactic encounter with a mutilated priest who believes that Lucifer Incarnate has arrived…The Lightbearer is a unique gnostic thriller, dealing with the themes of Light and Darkness, Good and Evil, Matter and Spirit.

"The Lightbearer is another shining example of Alan Richardson's talent as a story-teller. He uses his wide esoteric knowledge to produce a story that thrills, chills and startles the reader as it radiates pure magical energy. An unusual and gripping war story with more facets than a star sapphire." – Mélusine Draco, author of "Aubry's Dog".

Info@immanion-press.com
www.immanion-press.com

Lightning Source UK Ltd.
Milton Keynes UK
UKHW03f2207160318
319612UK00001B/137/P